PUCK ME SECRETLY

A VANCOUVER WOLVES HOCKEY ROMANCE

ODETTE STONE

Puck Me Secretly

A Vancouver Wolves Hockey Romance

Copyright © October 2018 by Odette Stone

www.odettestone.com

ISBN: 978-0-9950200-6-1

First edition, October 2018

Cover Design: Lori Jackson | Lori Jackson Designs

Grace, you're a force of nature. And the best part about "that" job was meeting you. Thanks for being you. You're one of the most unique human beings I've ever met, and if I had half the talent that you have in one of your pinkie fingers, I'd be set for life.

PROLOGUE
SPORTS WORLD NEWS REPORT

"WELL, Dave, we got breaking news that hockey player, Max Logan, assaulted his own teammate, Joseph Flanynk. We have all seen footage of the fight that spilled out of the Minnesota Marmot's own dressing room. They reported that Flanynk has undergone facial surgery and he will not play for the rest of the season."

"Jim, did you see this fight? It has gone viral across the sport's world and would make Conner McGregor flinch. Never, on or off the ice, have I ever seen a fight that extreme or violent."

"Max Logan has a lot to answer for. Supposedly, the Minnesota coach will bench him for the rest of the season."

"Jim, if he does, that will cost Minnesota their chance at winning the Stanley Cup."

"Dave, I think Logan took it too far this time. I'm not sure if he can ever come back from this. I would bet that Minnesota is actively working to get rid of Max Logan."

"Jim, I agree. But if that happens, the chances of Logan being accepted on a trade is almost minuscule, despite his skills on the ice. A GM can't risk this kind of off-ice antics because it can derail a team. Tonight may have been Max's last professional hockey game."

CHAPTER 1

I STRODE into the airport lounge, stepped up to the bar, and tossed my bag on the chair beside me.

"What will you have?" the bartender set a coaster in front of me.

"A gin and tonic, please," I pulled out my wallet. "Make it a double."

I was heading home. Liquid fortitude was in order.

My phone vibrated.

"Hey, Mom."

"Sweetheart, how are you?"

"I'm fine."

"Your dad and I are excited to see you."

I didn't bother to hide the amusement in my voice, "Mom, only two months ago, you were at my graduation."

It had been no small accomplishment to persuade my parents to let me spend the summer in New York after I graduated from University, but they had caved.

"Rory, you know what I mean. We're happy that you're moving back home. It's been a long four years."

I begged to differ. It had been the greatest four years of my life.

Wanting to be independent, I had picked a university far from home. But now my bid for freedom was ending, and the prodigal daughter was returning home.

I loved my parents. As helicopter as they were, they loved me. Sometimes too much.

"It'll be nice to be back in Vancouver."

"It thrills your father you'll be working with him. He's been talking about it for weeks."

The tension in my stomach grew tighter. My father always wanted a son to follow him into his business. But since I was his only child that lovely honor now fell onto my shoulders.

Crushing me.

I had no intention of joining my father in his business, but we negotiated a deal four years ago. If he let me go to university in New York, I would return to Vancouver and intern with him for one year upon graduation.

"I think they're calling my flight for boarding, Mom," I lied. "I should go check."

"Okay. Your father and I have a charity benefit tonight, so we'll send the car for you."

"Sure, sounds fine." My parents enjoyed significant societal commitments. Warm airport welcomes were not something we did as a family.

"Love you, Rory."

"See you soon, Mom."

I hung up the phone. Not caring that it was only noon, I motioned for the bartender to pour me another gin and tonic. Boarding started in 30 minutes and I needed liquid courage to get on my flight.

A man approached the bar. I studied him from beneath my eyelashes.

Smoking hot.

He stood well over six feet tall and his light brown hair touched his collar. From the silver military style watch on his wide wrist to the navy dress shirt that opened at the collar, he looked expensive. His dark jeans fit over his sculpted ass. Super-hot and so not my type. I didn't go for athletic men, and I didn't go for wealthy ones. He was both.

As if he had a sixth sense, he turned so I could see his face.

Holy fuck.

The breath sucked into my body as I took in his incredible jawline that narrowed towards his chin. His cheekbones were so chiseled they'd make Di Vinci weep. Slanting blue eyes studied something behind me. Pulling my eyes away from him, I tossed back my drink.

A voice crackled over the loudspeakers. "**Attention all flyers, Canada West, flight 335 to Vancouver has been delayed. Your new departure time is 12:50 PM. We apologize for this inconvenience.**"

I refrained from groaning. I hated flying.

"Another one, sweetheart?"

"Yes please, make it another double."

"Sure thing."

The hot guy sat at the bar, a few seats away from me. Out of my peripheral, I noted that he checked his watch when the announcement sounded. Then, he motioned for the bartender to bring him a drink.

During my four years in New York, I preferred to date artists. Most of my ex-boyfriends were brilliant painters with sweet souls. What they lacked in physique they more than made up with their intellect and sensitivity. This guy appeared to be the typical guy who avoided talking about his feelings, preferring to watch sports and drink with his buddies.

He was also built to fuck.

The thought rushed through my brain like a bad buzz. I sat frozen, my drink halfway to my lips. Where had that thought come from? I studied him with discretion. The sports television above the bar held his undivided attention.

The Baby Men, as my father had coined my boyfriends, had one major flaw. They all sucked in the sack. Maybe it was their lanky, thin frames or the fact they were more cerebral than physical, but my sex life, to date, had been lackluster.

Hot guy had massive shoulders, and an athletic body. To be honest, his power scared me. Like a dark angel who could crush a woman's heart without even trying. He'd take charge in and out of the bedroom.

I learned early in life that I don't want to give anyone power or control over me. My entire life I suffered in a power struggle with my dad. Why would I date someone who wanted to dominate? This guy was pure alpha male. An exciting prospect in the sack, but the rest of your life promised to be a living hell.

A voice crackled over the loudspeakers. "**Attention, please. This is the first boarding call for Canada West, flight 335 to Vancouver. Departing passengers should proceed to gate number 23 immediately.**"

I downed my drink so that I felt buzzed enough to manage take off. I headed to the washroom. My long black hair hung straight down to my waist. I could nothing about my bleary blue eyes, but I touched up my lip gloss and squared my shoulders.

Fake it, till you make it.

I walked to the boarding area and sat down on one of the hard, blue seats. Despite the alcohol coursing through my veins, I felt panicky.

I can do this!

The boarding line diminished until only the airline staff remained at the gate. I could not seem to get off my chair. My churning gut told me not to get on that flight.

"**Ladies and gentlemen, Canada West, flight 335 to Vancouver is closing its doors in one minute. Ticketed passengers must board immediately. I repeat, this is**

the final boarding call for Canada West, flight 335 to Vancouver."

Did it matter if I took a later flight? My parents wouldn't care. They were at a function tonight. I could get a hotel, or even better, return to NYC.

Above me, the overhead speaker crackled. "**Rory Ashford, please report to gate 23 immediately. Rory Ashford. Please report to gate 23.**"

With heavy, reluctant limbs, I walked up to the gate. The attendant glared at me as she took my passport and my boarding pass.

"Didn't you hear the announcement?"

I tried to speak, but no words came out.

She snapped my papers back at me. "Have a nice flight."

CHAPTER 2

AS I MEANDERED onto the plane, I couldn't shake the sensation I was walking to my doom. I avoided the glares of annoyed passengers as the flight attendants closed the door behind me.

I checked my ticket. Seat 2A.

I stumbled when I realized that the hot guy from the bar was in seat 2B.

My t-shirt rode up my torso, only inches from his face as I worked to shove my bag in the compartment above his head. He watched me without expression until it jammed in.

"I'm sitting next to you, in 2A." I worked to keep my voice casual.

He stood up, towering over me. With limited room, I brushed across his hard body while I clamored to my seat.

"Thank you," I murmured, feeling tipsier than I wanted to be. That last double gin was hitting me hard. After putting on my seatbelt, I double checked the latch three times before pulling the safety manual out from the seat pocket in front of me. I read it twice, checked where the nearest emergency exit doors were and the secondary exits. I checked under my seat for the inflatable neck cover with the whistle even though I knew we wouldn't be flying over water.

I glanced up into two icy blue eyes.

I talk too much when I'm nervous and right now my anxiety was off the charts. "I hate flying. I avoid it at all costs."

He didn't respond, but he held my gaze.

I tightened my seatbelt. "People say flying is statistically safer than driving in a car, but I know a ton of people who've been in car accidents, and they're fine. No one walks away from a plane crash."

I stopped talking when the flight attendant started the safety demonstration with a bored expression on her face. I gasped as the plane lurched backwards. I peered out the window as our aircraft got pushed out from the airport building.

The plane crawled towards the runway. I listened to the captain drone on about flight time, headwinds and estimated time of arrival. Fear gripped me as the engines fired up, rumbling beneath us. I should have taken the bus. Or the train.

I wish I had taken the train.

The power of the engines vibrated beneath us as the plane raced down the runway with a terrifying speed. I whimpered.

Hot guy unwrapped my ice-cold hand from the armrest and covered it in his massive grip. I shut my eyes and worked to not hyperventilate.

"What's your name?" my voice trembled.

He took his time answering. "Why?"

"If I die holding your hand, I want to know your name."

"Max."

"My name is Rory."

The entire aircraft rumbled around us as it lifted. The powerful force pinned me back against my chair. I squeezed my eyes shut, praying we wouldn't die.

The plane steadied from its intense ascent into nothing but air. It took a few minutes, but I opened my eyes.

When I'm nervous, I talk. And right now, the words poured out of me. "I had such a bad feeling getting on this flight and my gut is never wrong."

He still held my hand, so I tugged against his grip. He took his time releasing it.

I turned to him and once again his near perfect features shocked my senses. More words, without permission, flowed out of my mouth. "I finished school in New York and now I'm heading back home to Vancouver."

He waited but didn't speak.

I tried again. "Are you from Vancouver?"

"No."

"Are you visiting?"

His blue eyes narrowed at my obtrusiveness. "I'm moving there."

"Oh." I glanced down at his left hand. No wedding ring. "By yourself?"

"By myself." His tone was dry.

I re-tightened my seatbelt. "I have a new job there. Which I'm dreading."

Silence fell between us. I snuck a glance at him and his steady gaze met mine. He wasn't speaking, but he was listening.

"I have to intern for my dad's company. My dad thinks his business is my legacy. He wants me to follow him in his footsteps. Either that or give him several grandsons who can take over the minute they're old enough but..."

"But what?"

"But it's not like I'm ready to get married or have kids. So that option is out."

I stole a glance at him. He was still listening.

"I've had boyfriends before, but they were more for fun, you know? It's not like I would marry any of the Baby Men."

"Baby Men?"

"That's what my dad called my boyfriends, because they weren't like you."

A quizzical expression crossed his face. "Like me?"

I cursed my lack of filter.

The booze in my veins was making my tongue slippery. I squinted, as I tried to back out of this conversation. "You know." I waved my hand in his general vicinity. "You're all sporty and bossy looking. I bet you like sports bars. My dad likes sports bars, but the Baby Men preferred chess bars."

"You think I'm bossy looking?"

I turned and took in his chiseled features, big hands, and huge shoulders. He was all alpha and definitely bossy. "Trust me. You're bossy."

"Why do you think I'm bossy?"

Because you seem like a take charge kind of guy. Especially in the bedroom.

"Are you telling me you're not bossy?"

He held my gaze until I squirmed. "No."

"That eye thing you just did. Total bossy move."

Those beautiful lips curled into a smile that would have set Mother Theresa's heart on fire.

"What's a chess bar?"

"A chess bar is a place where you go to play chess and drink. Like a sports bar, but chess is the sport."

That damn smile widened. "Chess is not a sport."

"You sound like my dad."

"Chess is not a sport," he repeated.

"It's an intellectual sport."

"It may be intellectual but it's not a sport."

I flipped my hair over my shoulder. "Fine. The point is, I wasn't ready to marry any of the non-sporty, intellectual Baby Men so that means, I have to intern for my dad for an entire year." I gave a huge sigh. "And I'm dreading it. This business is my dad's passion. Not mine. But he's determined that I take over the reins when he retires."

"And you don't want to."

I gave him a sad smile. "I want to do my thing. My parents have planned my entire life out for me."

"That sounds like a lot of pressure."

"You have no idea."

Blue eyes scrutinized me. "I say go for it."

"What does that mean?"

"Give this intern year everything you've got. Do the best job possible."

I narrowed my eyes at him. "Why would I do that?"

"At the end of the year, if you decide it isn't for you, no one can accuse you of not giving it your best shot."

That was decent advice.

I yawned. "My dad would like you."

"Why?"

"Because you're not a Baby Man." I tucked my feet underneath me. "I think I might pass out now."

CHAPTER 3

BANG.

Disoriented, I woke up with a dry cotton mouth. I reached for my bottle of water and turned on the screen that displayed our location. We were 36,000 feet above North Dakota.

Max's seat was empty. I got up to pull my iPad out of my bag. Once reseated, I craned my head, peering over the seats. I caught sight of Max's navy-blue shirt at the front. He stood a full head above the flight attendant, who seemed to be more than enjoying her conversation with him. Her head tilted back so she could stare at his face. Now her fingers fluttered at her neck. He touched her arm and walked back towards our seats.

I said nothing when he settled down beside me.

"You're awake."

It surprised me he was the one starting the conversation between us. "Yes."

"So, why did you date those guys?"

"Which guys?"

"The chess players. The babies."

"The Baby Men?" I chugged my water. "They're sweet guys. I

had one boyfriend who liked to show up at my apartment with a picnic basket of treats, a bottle of wine and a candle."

Max made a noise that sounded like a derisive snort. "You're kidding."

"What? Chicks dig that kind of thing. Baby Men make great boyfriends. They're sensitive, compassionate souls."

"Stop." Laughter traced his voice.

"What?"

"No one buys that bullshit that chicks want the sensitive man."

"Speak for yourself."

He leaned forward so he could watch my face. "Chicks don't want sensitive guys, they want..."

"Bossy men?"

He shrugged. "If that's what you want to call it."

Alpha. Bossy. Dominating. Hot. Take charge. Man's man.

Yeah, there were a lot of other words for bossy, but I didn't want to flatter his ego. "Unlike other women, I'm not interested in the 'take charge' guy. I want my boyfriends to talk about their feelings."

"Come on."

"You don't believe me?"

"Women think they want men to talk about their feelings, but they don't."

"That's not true and I can prove it to you."

"How?"

"Why don't you tell me how you're feeling right now?"

"You don't want to know." He leaned back in his seat.

"That's not true," I took my turn to lean forward so I could stare up at his face. The idea of this big man sharing his feelings captivated me. "Tell me."

"You can't handle it."

This conversation was intoxicating. "Yes, I can. It's easy. Tell me how you're feeling."

His eyes narrowed on my face. "Okay. I feel horny. Horny enough that I'm debating picking someone up."

My entire face flushed while my traitorous stomach did a slow flop. "You're planning on taking someone home with you?"

He shrugged. "Or take them to a closet to have a quick fuck."

My brain struggled to compute what he was telling me. In animated detail, I pictured him and the flight attendant slipping into some closet. There would be no foreplay. He'd drop trou, and they'd wildly fuck. It pissed me off that jealousy snaked through my stomach.

"This conversation is over." I turned my face away to hide my flushed cheeks.

He laughed. "Told you."

"Told me what!"

"You don't want to talk about a man's feelings."

I turned back to him. "Those aren't feelings. Those are..."

"Are what?" His gaze was on my mouth, distracting me.

"Those are base instincts. Like hunger or fatigue. Those aren't emotions."

"You said nothing about emotions, you asked about my feelings."

"That's the same thing."

"I feel like fucking," he teased, and my stomach clenched hard at those words. I hated that he was turning me on.

"You're the perfect example of why I only date Baby Men."

His face broke into a hot smile. "You only think you want those guys."

"No," I stopped him. "I want them. The more sensitive the better."

A loud bang sounded. I turned to peer out the window. "What was that?"

"Nothing."

Another considerable bang sounded, and the plane lurched to the left. I slid across my seat toward the window. Some passengers cried out, but the aircraft righted itself.

"Are you okay?"

My heart pounded in my chest. "Yes."

We watched as a flight attendant half-walked, half-ran up the aisle.

"Is that normal?"

"It's fine." He spoke a moment before the plane lurched a second time. Hard.

The seat belt lights went on.

Ding. Ding.

Ding. Ding.

"Oh God," I chanted between cold lips.

People around us chattered in an anxious tone.

A female voice spoke over the speaker. "*Ladies and gentlemen. Please fasten your seatbelts now. I repeat, fasten your seatbelts. Do not get out of your seats.*"

I realized that my seatbelt was not on. Worse, I had only one half of my belt.

"My seatbelt," I pawed frantically for the other half. "It's gone. I need it. Where is it!"

A big hand dug under my ass and then he held up the other half of my belt. With shaking hands, I secured it around my waist.

"It's turbulence." Max craned his neck, watching over the seat ahead of him. He seemed alert, not scared.

The plane whined as it tipped forward, so much so that we braced ourselves against the seats in front of us. The faint scent of burning rubber wafted in the air.

A thought pierced through my panic. I needed my life vest. I reached beneath my seat, pulled up the plastic square and ripped it open. I struggled to unfold it and pull it over my head.

Max watched. "We're not over water. You don't need that."

"We could land in a lake or go off course and hit the ocean."

I fumbled with the strings and yanked them hard. A loud hiss deafened me, as the vest billowed with air, imprisoning my head in a rock-hard vise grip. I clawed at the vest, trying to pull it off my head, but it suctioned around my neck like an evil yellow plastic serpent.

"Get it off, get it off me!"

"Rory."

"Please, Max, please," I begged, turning my eyes towards him.

"Hold still," he instructed. His face loomed in front of mine, so close I could smell his minty breath and a hint of orange. He tugged at the vest until he figured out how to deflate it. We didn't speak as he pressed on the plastic while air hissed around my face. Finally, it was deflated enough that I could squeeze it off. I threw it on the floor.

"Better?"

Another bang and the plane pitched nose forward. It reminded me of a rollercoaster.

"I wrecked my vest! Now I'll drown."

He laughed. *No sane person laughs when their plane is crashing!*

"It's not funny." I tasted salty tears on my lips.

"Sorry, you want mine?" His sympathy appeased me.

I turned to him, my eyes wide. "What will you use?"

"I can swim."

I swallowed my guilt. "You sure?"

He reached beneath his seat and I watched as he unwrapped the vest. "Don't inflate it until you get out of the plane."

My frantic fingers touched the flat crunchy plastic that I wore around my neck like an ugly necklace. "This is so bad. I had a terrible premonition getting on this plane. Why don't I ever take my gut serious?"

The plane jostled so hard my teeth rattled. People shrieked when the baggage bins flapped open and bags rained down. A male voice behind us chanted the Lord's prayer.

I pressed back in my chair, my fingers like claws around the armrests. *This was it. I would die.*

"I should've known this would happen. Since I was a kid. I haven't been able to get on a plane. It's like I knew. It was a premonition. And I overrode my fears. Now we will all pay for that!"

"Rory," Max put his face in front of mine. "Calm down!"

"We are going to die!"

"Shhhh," he soothed. "We're not going to die."

A ding sounded and above our heads, oxygen masks dropped from the ceilings. Gasps of horror and cries sounded around us.

Except mine didn't drop. A single mask hung in front of Max's face.

"Where's my mask?" I frantically twisted in my seat. "Help! Help! My mask didn't drop!"

No one paid me any attention. Everyone was putting their masks on.

"What do I do? *What do I do!?*"

"Hang on." Max leaned over towards me, his arms above my head. "It got coiled around something."

My mask dropped in front of my face. Too late. I was already hyperventilating.

Breathe. Breathe. Breathe.

He tilted my head back and something cold covered my mouth.

"Take a deep breath," he instructed. I sucked in air that smelled like plastic.

The whole plane trembled.

A female voice, quaking with fear, instructed us over the loudspeaker.

"Brace, brace, brace. Head down. Stay down."

"Brace, brace, brace. Head down. Stay down."

We were going to die!

Max's large warm hand pushed me forward so my head pressed between my knees. The whine of the plane intensified.

I turned towards Max. Too big to put his head between his legs, he leaned forward and braced his head against the seat in front of him. Our eyes met.

Everything seemed to happen in slow motion.

People screamed and cried.

The flight attendant chanted out the same instructions.

The plane's engines howled outside the window.

"Where are the exits, gorgeous?"

"What?" I cried, my voice muffled by the mask.

"Where are the exits?"

Why was he so composed?

"There's one at the front and two emergency exits in row 11 but I don't want to die. I've never been in love."

"No one's going to die."

I babbled like a mad person. "I wanted to give my art a real chance. I want to have kids one day. And I haven't had a real orgasm with a guy."

His blue eyes widened.

Behind me, a woman sounded like she was being murdered. Her scream chilled my blood.

I craned my head back to see her.

He reached over and pushed my head back down. "Tell me why you've never come during sex."

"What!?"

"Keep talking. Focus on my face."

Fear kept the words flowing. "All my friends talk about these great sexual moments, but something is wrong with me. I had to fake it with all the Baby Men. Every single time. I've never told anyone this, but I think something is wrong with me."

"Nothing is wrong with you. Blame the baby boyfriends."

"You don't know that!"

"I know I could make you come in two minutes flat."

"The point is," I licked my salty lips, "Is that I won't have that chance. Because our plane is crashing. This is it. I missed my chance."

The plane jostled so hard, I feared my seat would rip off the floor.

I whimpered. His big hand returned to the back of my neck. Comforting me.

Our eyes met.

"You're nice."

"Not really.

"I'm glad you're here in my final moments."

"Don't think about that, sweetheart. Think about anything but that."

This was the end of my life. Shouldn't I be experiencing a profound flashback of my life? That movie reel when everything important floats in front of my eyes? Instead, all I could focus on what how dark and long Max's eyelashes were.

We stared at each other. I saw no fear in his eyes, only resignation. Who was he? Why was he so calm? Did he actually think he could make me have an orgasm?

I wanted to know. Stupid really, but who can predict your last thoughts.

"How do you know you could make me orgasm?"

He held my gaze. "I know how to fuck."

"But how do you know women weren't faking it with you?"

His eyes narrowed and his face, from beneath his mask, broke out into a huge smile. "Are you for real?"

"I faked it with my boyfriends."

"Trust me, I could get you off."

The jet engines drone deafened. Around us, people cried, sobbed, screamed.

It might sound stupid, but as long as I never let my eye contact break with Max, I was immune to that horror. We refused to focus on our impending deaths. Instead, we focused on sex. With each other. It reminded me of flirting with a cute guy at the bar and the whole place disappears except him.

Part of my brain understood how stupid this was, but I didn't want to have my final moments cluttered with adrenaline and debilitating fear.

This weird flirting made me feel good. And I wanted my ending to be nice.

"If we survive, I will let you."

His gaze held mine, but he didn't speak.

"Only if you want." My face burned.

Blue eyes crinkled in amusement. "It'd be my honor."

"Really?"

His big hand squeezed my neck.

Except we were lying to ourselves and each other.

Reality has a way of squeezing in. Our plane was crashing, and we were all going to die.

My eyes clung to his gaze. I didn't want my ending to hurt. I preferred for it to be instantaneous. One minute you're alive and then you're not. "Do you think this will hurt?"

The noise around us was so big, so life threatening, I almost couldn't hear his voice. "No. It won't hurt."

I faced death. A calm sadness overwhelmed me as I mourned everything I had missed.

We stared at each other. His face was so beautiful. I wanted to memorize that face. I wanted to live. I wanted to go back in time and not get on this fucking plane.

"This sucks so bad," I spoke as everything faded to black.

CHAPTER 4

I OPENED MY EYES. Cornstalks surrounded me. The sky above me was a clear blue. The sun warmed my face. My head lay in Max's lap.

"Max" I whispered. "Are we dead?"

He glanced down at me. His cheekbone had a small cut.

"We survived." He put his warm and comforting hand onto my forehead.

"I'm alive?"

He considered me with a serious expression. "I told you we'd make it."

I stared up into his blue eyes. I didn't quite believe him. "I think you're lying. This field and you, this is my version of heaven, isn't it?"

"Your version of heaven?"

"I'm glad you made it to heaven with me."

"Don't get ahead of yourself."

"Did we live?"

"See for yourself."

He lifted me up. I gasped. The remnants of our plane indicated it had slid the length of the field, plowing up all the plants in its wake and now lay tilted to the side. People wandered around like zombies with ripped and torn clothing. Passengers cried or hugged.

"Holy fuck," I breathed. "We lived."

"We lived."

"I don't remember the crash."

"You blacked out."

I clawed at my body, making sure I was intact. My yellow life vest hung around my neck like a plastic bib. "How did I get off the plane?"

"I carried you."

"You carried me?" I repeated, distracted by the passengers that moved in front of us. "Did anyone get hurt?"

"Someone has a broken leg. Everyone lived. Everyone got out."

I turned and studied his face. "You're bleeding."

"It's only a scratch."

Emergency vehicles approached from the distance.

Still drunk, I sat in numb shock and watched as the rescue vehicles came bumping through the field, with wailing sirens and flashing lights to announce their arrival.

Rescue workers tended to the injured while firemen sprayed the plane with foam. Max and I sat, side by side, watching the chaos unfold in front of us.

School buses arrived. Someone on a bullhorn gave us instructions. Our two choices of destination were the hospital or the hotel. Max refused medical attention, so I followed him onto the bus that would drive us to the hotel.

At the hotel, they directed us to a boardroom where a woman in a crisp navy suit handed us each hotel room keys.

"On behalf of the airline, I would like to extend a heartfelt apology. I have booked each of you into a hotel room."

She gave us each a bag. My bag was pink and Max's bag was blue.

"You will find in your bag toiletries and clothes. We have also provided complimentary credit cards for $500 for anything you might need to purchase in the next 24 hours. We have included brochures for phone numbers of counselors who are standing by 24/7 in case you need to talk to anyone. Tomorrow customer service representatives will help you make further travel arrangements. All complimentary of our airline. We ask that you please return to the airport by noon."

"Okay." I was in a dream. Or in a movie.

She flashed a strained smile at us. "I have a cellphone right here. Would you like to make a call or have me call someone?"

I nodded, and she handed me her phone. I dialed my mom's cell number, and the call went straight to voicemail. I remember that Mom was at some gala tonight.

"Hey Mom," I glanced at Max, who stared at the floor while he listened. "This is Rory. My flight had some... issues and.... well, now I'm in North Dakota. And the airline is being nice. They're putting me up in a hotel. When I know what time I will arrive, I'll text you so that you can send a car. Love you!"

She held out the phone to Max. "Would you like to call someone?"

He shook his head.

"Please understand that we will be in this boardroom all night. In case you need anything."

Together we walked to the elevator.

"How are you doing?" Max pressed the up button.

I thought about my answer. Flying was one of my greatest fears and I had survived a plane crash. You'd think I'd be in a state of hysteria. But the fact was, I had survived. I had cheated death.

"I feel alive."

We got to my room, and I stalled. I didn't want to be alone. "Where is your room?"

"Right next door."

"Okay."

"Are you okay?"

I spoke without conviction. "Yes."

He towered over me and for one heartfelt second, I thought he might hug me. But he didn't. He stared down at me with that hard-to-read expression.

"Max, are you sick of me?"

"Not even close."

"Well," I paused, trying to find words that had meaning. "Thanks for saving my life."

He gave me a ghost of a smile.

Don't leave me.

I don't know where that thought came from, but I searched his face, wondering if he could sense my anxiety.

He looked resigned again. "Come knock if you need anything."

"Oh," I blinked. *I guess not.* "Okay."

I watched as he moved with athletic grace towards his own room. He unlocked it, gave me one last glance and disappeared into his room.

CHAPTER 5

IN A DAZE, I walked into my hotel room and stopped in front of the big mirror. Dried black streaks of eye makeup stained my cheeks. My hair stuck in a million directions, and I still had the yellow life vest limply hanging around my neck. I looked like a crazy person.

With shaking hands, I pulled the vest off. I didn't know what to do or how to feel. So many thoughts, so many emotions rushed through me.

Was this real?

Had I actually cheated death?

What is Max doing?

Why didn't I die?

Feeling disoriented, I sat on the bed. I needed to zone out. I didn't want to think about what I had just experienced. I clicked on the television. Every channel, including CNN, broadcasted the crash. Announcers stood in the field, with the crash site behind them, and with excitement, explained that this was a miracle crash.

Yeah, so not helping.

I turned off the TV and laid back on the bed.

Despite considerable odds, I had survived my greatest fear. I had survived a life-altering plane crash. Shouldn't I feel different? Shouldn't I have big endorphins pouring through my body, giving me a new perspective on life?

Only, I was *still* me.

Nothing had changed.

I took a hot shower, shrugged on my complimentary robe and sat on the end of the bed. I stared at the wall between Max's room and my own.

What was Max doing?

Did he feel different?

Max had displayed unbelievable courage through that harrowing event. While people around us fell apart, he had held me together. I had lost my shit on that flight and he had cocooned me from the worst.

And we had survived.

Now I was alone and the only person I wanted to be with was him. I didn't understand that, but that is how I felt.

What would happen if I popped over to his room to see how he was doing? He told me that if I needed anything, I only needed to knock. But I didn't want to impose. Hadn't he done enough for me? He had spent the day taking care of me, so I wasn't sure he wanted to continue to deal with me.

I can't be alone right now.

I shoved my feet into my pink converse sneakers which created a ridiculous fashion statement with my robe, but I didn't care. I moved down the hallway, made it as far as his door, but then couldn't bring myself to knock. Turning around to go back to my room, I muffled my gasp when his door opened.

We studied each other. Max's unbuttoned navy dress shirt teased me with a hard expanse of corded muscle. His damp hair indicated he'd recently gotten out of the shower.

Blue eyes took in my runners and housecoat. "I didn't hear you knock."

"I was going back to my room."

"I was coming to check on you."

That made me feel better. Enough so I could speak my truth. "I don't feel like being alone."

Without speaking, he held his door open wide. I inspected his room.

"Nice room."

"Is yours different?"

"No. It's the same."

"I've seen a lot of hotel rooms in my life."

I glanced at him, interested in the small tidbit of himself that he shared. "Do you travel a lot for work?"

"Yes."

What did Max do for a living? I debated asking him, but he wasn't giving me the vibe he wanted to talk about his personal life. I respected that he guarded his personal life, and it's not like I wanted to spill any more of my guts.

He studied me as if he was trying to figure out my train of thought.

"Do you want a drink?"

"Yes please."

I sat on the edge of his bed and watched as he knelt in front of the minibar.

"Gin and tonic?"

"That sounds nice." I watched as he poured my drink.

"I don't have ice."

"That's fine."

He poured himself a scotch, handed me my glass and then sat on the chair by the table, a few feet away from me.

We drank in silence for a few moments. The man before me was a total stranger, but I felt drawn to him.

"How are you doing?" He broke the silence.

"I thought I'd feel different."

"How so?"

"Shouldn't a near death experience change my outlook on life?"

He continued to watch me with that intense blue gaze.

I had to know. "How were you so calm?"

"What do you mean?"

"Everyone was screaming and freaking out and you didn't react. How did you know we'd live?"

"I didn't."

"Excuse me?"

He dumped the rest of his mini bottle of scotch into his glass. "I didn't think we'd live."

Shock rippled through me. "But you told me. You told me it'd be okay."

"I know."

"I believed you."

"That was the point."

I sat back and processed that. Max had believed we would die, but he spent his last moments trying to comfort me and make me believe we'd be okay.

"Why would you do that?"

He shrugged. "Atonement?"

What did that mean? I realized I needed to rethink my stance on bossy men. I had assumed they were all one dimensional, but this man felt like a jigsaw puzzle. "I don't understand you."

He didn't answer, but I didn't expect him to. I looked anywhere but at him. I suppose I should go back to my room, but I dreaded being alone.

"You want to watch a movie?"

I lifted my eyes back at him. "Here?"

He shrugged.

I answered by kicking off my shoes and climbing up the bed. "You pick."

AFTER THE FIRST MOVIE, we ordered room service. I had a burger with fries, he had a steak with salad. We didn't speak other than exchange light banter about the movie. We were two survivors who didn't want to face the aftermath alone. Or maybe it was just me who didn't want to be alone, and he was atoning for more unknown sins. I didn't question it. He kept me company, and I refrained from pumping him with questions.

After our meal, we both resettled back on the bed. Stretched out beside me, assuming I would stay for another movie, he flipped through the movies. I was an independent person, so I couldn't quite reconcile myself to this need to not be alone.

"What do you want to watch?"

"You pick, I'll watch anything."

He picked a popular box office movie I had already seen, but I didn't tell him that. The movie started and failed to hold my attention. The man, that lay beside me with his hand tucked behind his head, was all I could think about. Questions burned my mind. Who was he? What kind of job did he have? If he told me he had an office job, it would surprise me, but he didn't strike me as someone who did manual labor. Maybe he worked as a fireman. But would a fireman transfer to another city to work?

The question came out of me before I could stop it. "Are you American?"

Blue eyes shifted towards me. "Canadian."

"Oh. Were you working in the US?"

His eyes moved back to the television, letting me know he didn't want to talk about himself. "Yes."

"I loved living in New York. Have you ever lived in Vancouver?"

"No."

"I was born and raised there."

"Do you want a different movie?"

I shook my head. "No. It's fine." I forced myself to lie back and remain quiet. I tied my hair in a knot on my head. I scratched my arm. I fluffed my pillow.

He paused the movie and rolled over onto his side, his head propped up by his arm. "What's going on?"

"What!"

"You're restless."

I stared at his gorgeous face. "Don't you want to talk?"

"About?"

"Anything."

"Why don't you talk."

I had nothing to say. I had a million questions but none of them seemed appropriate. "Why are you moving to Canada?"

"For my job."

"Did you get transferred?"

"Something like that."

"Are you excited?

"Not particularly."

"Do you know anyone in Vancouver?"

"Nope."

"You know me."

His blue eyes held mine. "Rory, I don't want to give you the wrong idea here."

My face burned hot. "What do you mean?"

"We can't take this friendship past tonight."

This conversation should be making me indignant, but I only felt disappointment. "Okay."

"Today was a tough day, but when I get to Vancouver, my focus has to be free of distractions."

"I wouldn't distract you."

His eyes dropped to my mouth. "You're already a distraction."

My stomach fluttered, and an energy passed between us. I realized this was the moment I should get off the bed and head back to my room. He all but told me he wouldn't see me after tonight and one-night stands were not my thing. Yet, I seemed stuck on his bed.

"Is this where you try to make me have an orgasm?"

A smile spread across his face as my words set in. "No. Definitely not."

"Why not?"

"Because I'm not the right guy for you."

"Why do you assume that I want something more than tonight?"

"Have you even fooled around with someone you weren't dating?"

No, I hadn't. "What's your point?"

"I don't want you to get hurt."

I had all but offered my body to him and he was refusing. I thought about the blonde flight attendant. He had been considering disappearing into a closet with her for a quickie. So maybe it was me. Maybe he didn't want me. The rejection made me scramble to the end of the bed. I put on my shoes. "I get it."

"What do you get?"

"You're not that into me."

He reached forward and grabbed my hand and tugged me back, so I faced him. His serious expression traced over my face. "What do you want?"

I swallowed, now unsure about everything. The old me would have said goodnight and gone to my room like the good girl I was. The new I-just-survived-a-plane-crash me blurted out, "I want my orgasm."

His kiss caught me off guard. It shouldn't have, considering what we were discussing, but when his mouth moved onto mine, I initially didn't kiss him back. I was too shocked. I couldn't help but compare his kiss to other kisses, but it didn't compare. The Baby Men were impatient and sloppy, but Max kissed me like he had all the time in the world. I lay back and his mouth followed mine.

I sighed again as my eyes drifted shut. His mouth slanted over mine, tasting of scotch and male. When he deepened the kiss, when his tongue played with my mouth, my weightless hands drifted up around his warm, thick neck. I moaned when he exerted more pressure, opening my mouth further to him. Who knew a man's lips could feel so good? Who knew a kiss could feel so magical?

I arched my neck back, my fingers still tangled in his hair, when he trailed his mouth down my neck. I loved getting my neck kissed, and he was fantastic at it. Tingling sensations traced down my spine and I could feel my body respond to the touch of his mouth on my skin, but unlike the Baby Men, he took his time, making me feel like there was no rush.

His hand tugged at the belt of my robe. I stared at the ceiling, with half-shut eyes. Max's warm mouth traced along the tender skin beneath my jawline. I felt his breath, the scrape of his teeth on sensitive skin and I sighed. I felt my robe push open.

My eyes opened wide when he lifted himself over me. I could feel the heavy fabric of his jean-clad legs against the naked skin of my inner thighs. Should it bother me I was naked while he remained dressed?

My eyes opened wide when a big hand moved up to cup my breast. I fought a ridiculous need to giggle, but that feeling died when his mouth captured my nipple and he sucked on my breast with an intensity that made me come off the bed. My fingers dug into his hair while my stomach did cartwheels.

My breathing changed. I could feel my ribcage rise and fall as he rhythmically sucked on my breast causing all sorts of weird sensations to shoot down into the pit of my stomach. He moved to my other breast, and I squirmed as those sensations intensified. Why didn't it feel like this when the Baby Men kissed my breasts? Why was it so different with him?

I covered my face with both of my hands when his mouth moved down. Teeth grazed my rib cage. A tongue teased my belly button.

I felt two strong hands, move down my thighs, teasing the soft skin and pushing my legs open. I cried out, lifting my head, watching as he lifted my calves over his broad shoulders. His face was inches away from my bare apex.

"You smell amazing," his dark eyes lifted to my face. "Do you taste as good as you smell?"

I blinked in disbelief, unsure if he wanted me to answer. "I don't know."

His smile bedazzled me and then, without breaking eye contact, his tongue licked up the length of me.

My hips jerked up, and he wrapped his big forearms around my thighs.

"I don't think I've tasted anything this good."

I moaned and covered my face with my hands. His mouth delved between my folds. Big hands imprisoned my legs, holding me down. Max had complete control over my body. He sucked, feasted, nibbled and lapped at me. He tortured me with his tongue until I panted. He fanned a flame in me that became so big, it threatened to burn me up. Intoxicated, my hips strained against his hold on me, wanting more. Begging with little jerks and thrusts for my release.

Never had my body felt like this. He roused in me a hunger, so intense, I thought I would lose my mind. My head tossed back and forth, and my fingers moved down to dig into his thick hair. Unabashed, I cried out, loud, demanding noises, as my body burned with an ache.

"Please," I cried. "Max, please."

He lifted his head, watching me.

"Yes," I gasped, when he invaded me with his fingers. Without shame, my hips pumped up and down trying to increase the friction.

"You want this so bad, don't you?" his dark eyes watched me. "Such a dirty girl. Look at you. So needy and hungry. So lush and wet for me."

"More," I choked out my demands. "Give me more."

He twisted his fingers and stroked something deep inside me. My head fell back, and I stared unfocused on one spot on the ceiling. Transfixed, only focusing on his fingers, swirling and caressing.

He bent his mouth down and sucked onto my lush nub.

My world exploded. My hips bucked up. My back arched off the bed while my eyes rolled in my head. He kept on sucking and my orgasm never seemed to end. Pleasure rolled on top of pleasure. I hung, suspended in time, unable to do anything but surrender to the intensity of the moment.

His fingers slowed and then stopped, and I became boneless. Slack and wasted while I twitched and quivered.

"You're so fucking beautiful."

A mangled laugh bubbled out of me.

I felt him move back up over me, and then his face was above mine. I opened my eyes to his. He appeared dangerous. Eyes dark. A savage hunger made his jaw tight and his eyes narrow. He seemed to be hanging onto his control by a thread.

"You have no idea how much I want to fuck you."

"I want that too."

And then I ruined it by yawning.

He rested his forehead against mine, his eyes squeezed shut. And then he rolled off me, stood up and pulled me onto shaking legs. I blinked as he pushed the robe off my body. I stood naked, watched as he pulled the bed covers back.

"Come on, get in."

I crawled in. I stared up at him. Exhaustion, from the plane crash and my orgasm, pulled at my eyelids. "Are you going to lie down too?"

He leaned down and gave me a lingering kiss on the lips. "Soon. First, have a little rest."

"Okay." I felt happy.

And then sleep claimed me.

CHAPTER 6

PISSED DIDN'T EVEN DESCRIBE my emotions. My anger overruled my fear as I boarded my flight to Vancouver. Take off? *No issue.* I was too busy stewing over how I had woken up alone in Max's hotel room.

He left a note. A fucking note.

I pulled it out for the tenth time: **Had fun. Hope you get back to Vancouver okay. Max.**

What the actual fuck.

Anger flowed through my veins like molten metal. Raging, glowing, bubbling and boiling. Burning away my hurt and my pain.

How could he?

How could he, after everything we had experienced together, walk away without even saying goodbye? I knew he didn't want to see me in Vancouver, but to not say goodbye?

The most frustrating part was I had no outlet for my fury because he was gone. He had disappeared out of my life.

And for that, I think I hated him.

WHEN I WALKED off the plane, both of my parents waited in the airport lobby with concerned expressions on their faces.

"Hi," I hugged them both. "How are you guys?"

Their eyes met briefly before they focused their attention back to me.

Dad cleared his throat. "How was your flight?"

"Fine."

Mom touched my face. "Darling, are you okay?"

My eyes were clear. And my face was devoid of expression. A mask to cover how I was feeling. "Yes."

I realized Dad was standing in the airport at 2 PM on a workday. Dad never left work in the middle of the day. In fact, this might be the first time.

"Why are you two here?" I asked, glancing between the two.

"Sweetheart," Mom turned to Dad for support. "You survived a plane crash."

"I know." I also had the most life-altering night with a man who blew my mind and then snuck out while I slept. Ask me which event made me more upset.

"We thought you'd need support." Her eyes searched my face.

I shrugged. "I'm fine. They recovered my purse and my phone, but my suitcase is toast."

Mom covered her mouth with her hand, tears filling her eyes. "Oh, my poor baby."

"It's fine, Mom. I'm fine. I'm just tired."

"That's my girl. You're a true Ashford." Dad spoke with pride in his voice. When I did something spectacular, he liked to remind me I was an Ashford.

I decided not to tell him I blacked out before we crashed.

"So, should we go?"

My parents did not know what to make of me. My entire childhood, I could not fly. My parents had sent me to hypnotherapy. They had medicated me and when that failed, canceled their share of overseas family vacations because I became too hysterical to get on any flight. It was only when I left for New York that I had been willing to step on a plane. So, it was understandable that they didn't understand my reaction or lack of reaction to surviving a plane crash.

I didn't understand it either. I guess when you survive your greatest fear and live to tell about it, it becomes a non-issue. Besides, I had more pressing issues to work through.

———

MY PARENTS WANTED to talk about the plane crash, but they didn't understand what I had experienced and I had no desire to explain it to them. The only person I knew who understood what that had felt like was Max. I wished that I could commiserate with him or talk to him. That night I annoyed myself, because instead of sleeping, I spent my time thinking about him.

Did he think about me?

He had warned me he didn't want to take our friendship past last night. I had thought I had understood what that meant, but I hadn't anticipated how bad it'd make me feel.

Worse, I wanted more. More than he wanted to give me. I wanted more of his kisses. I wanted another orgasm. I wanted to go back to lying on the bed and watching a movie with him. I wanted the chance to ask him more questions. Who was he? Where had he gone? What was his story? Did he feel alone arriving in Vancouver by himself?

Max could be anywhere. And I didn't even know his last name.

———

THE NEXT MORNING, bright and early, I showed up at the breakfast table. Dad sat at the end of the dining room table reading the sports section of the newspaper and Mom made notes in her diary.

"You're up," she exclaimed, so happy to see me. I gave her a quick hug.

Dad folded the newspaper down to inspect me. "Good morning."

"Good morning."

"So, I've been thinking about your role this year, Rory," Dad spoke with authority.

"Darling, give the girl a chance to breathe," Mom admonished. "She only arrived home yesterday."

"No," I interrupted. I wanted the distraction. I wanted to stop thinking about Max. I also decided that I wanted to get this year over with. The sooner I started my internship, the sooner I could get on with my life. "I would like to begin as soon as possible. Why not today?"

Even my father, who was the king of maintaining a stone face, couldn't keep the surprise off his face. "That's great."

"I'd like to work in the media department. I would like to use my skills as an artist, maybe work with the graphic designer. I could help with the website, learn the ropes from the bottom up."

My plan was solid. This could set me up with some strong working skills for when I entered the real working world. It would also put relevant work experience on my CV.

"Nonsense," he scoffed. "You're being groomed to take over for me. You'll start as my right hand."

Fuck. Me.

"Dad. Can we talk about this?"

"We just did." His eyes narrowed at my hoodie and jeans. "I'm leaving in 30 minutes, so borrow clothes from your mother. Business professional."

I knew that tone of voice. It was his CEO voice. The do-not-fucking-cross-me voice.

Good thing Mom had two walk-in closets bursting at the seams with designer threads. And lucky for me, we were the same size. I was partial to jeans and t-shirts, but my mom had impeccable taste in clothes.

Mom gave me a worried look.

I responded with a tight smile. "Mind if I go shopping in your closet?"

DAD and I sat in the back of the car while his driver drove the car through the early morning Vancouver traffic. Dad talked on his phone and I stared out of the window. Only 365 more days of this. I could do it. This was payment for my four years in New York. I would be a good employee for the duration of the year, but the moment I finished this internship, I would break out of this cage and be free.

I glanced down at the black, fitted dress I had borrowed. It had capped-sleeves, a round neckline and came to a stop above my knee. Black and white splashed Louboutin spike heels, a slim platinum watch and big diamond stud earrings finished my look. I had pinned my hair to the nape of my neck and my make-up was subtle. I was dressed like a well-heeled businesswoman.

The car pulled up in front of the Aurora Stadium. The huge hockey arena was as familiar as our family home. I had grown up in this stadium. Mom used to brag that before the age of five, I had attended over 200 hockey games. When I was a baby, they had set a crib up in our deluxe family viewing box, because she never wanted to miss a game and she never wanted to miss my bedtime. I grew up in the world of hockey and I knew it like the back of my hand. But that didn't mean I wanted to live and die here. I wanted to explore the world and what it offered me, and it frustrated me that my future was pre-ordained.

Dad was the owner and GM of the Vancouver Wolves NHL hockey team. He also owned the stadium and even named it after me. Aurora was my legal name, but only granny called me Aurora. Dad dabbled in other business ventures, but this team, this franchise, was his baby.

We got out of the car and I worked to keep up with Dad's long strides in my tight skirt. The second we got out of the car, he dumped information on me. Player stats. Contracts. Negotiations. This shit bored me stiff, but I forced myself to listen and take note.

I had made a promise to him. I would make him proud this year. But in a year, I would walk away with a clear conscience. I would give this job my all and then no one could accuse me of not trying. But damn, it would be *one long year*.

We walked through the stadium concord and up to the corporate offices.

"I have a surprise for you." Dad held the door open for me.

Uh oh. "What kind of surprise?"

We walked past a series of desks and offices towards his office. His office had a window view of the world outside and a full glass view of the rink below. He paused at the office next to his and ushered me in. This office faced down onto the stadium. Someone had furnished the office with a gorgeous oak desk, matching bookshelves, a leather couch, and the matching chairs.

I peered at him in question. "Whose office is this?"

"Yours," he grandly gestured with his arm.

Oh shit. Stepping into a position I was under-qualified for, was blatant nepotism. Taking the second-best office in the house would increase the size of the target on my back.

"I don't deserve this office," I protested. "I haven't earned it."

"You were born into this position. You don't have to earn anything."

My father watched my reaction, and I realized that this was my surprise. He thought this would make me happy. I took a deep breath and realized that I could do this job one of two ways. Fight him every step of the way and we'd both be miserable, or I could work with him and make this year a great father-daughter year.

I choose the latter. "I love it, dad. This is amazing."

His smile was huge. "I've been waiting for this day since you were born."

No pressure. I swallowed. "Well, I hope to make you proud this year."

He winked. "I know you will."

CHAPTER 7

I HIT THE GROUND RUNNING. I spent the morning reviewing player contracts, that were so dull, they made my eyes glaze over. Then I watched a meeting between my dad and an agent. The agent was trying to negotiate on behalf of his player. My father bulldozed over him and the agent left with his tail between his legs.

My father's admin, Julie, brought me a salad for lunch, which I ate at my desk while reading more contracts.

Mid-afternoon, my dad showed up at the doorway.

"Come on, grab your coat," he instructed. "First practice for the pre-season is starting."

I got up from behind my desk and hurried after him. Julie dropped a pile of files in my arms as I walked by her desk.

"Today, we'll discuss each player, their weaknesses and strengths. Your main goal for the first three months is to understand each player's ability on the ice, so we can further enhance our recruiting and negotiating tactics."

What the fuck.

"Dad, don't we have scouts and a team of people hired to do this?"

"We do. We have 31 scouts, which is a dozen more than any other team has, but I leave nothing to chance. You need to know who your team is and what it requires before you can recruit new players."

"You want me to do this for you?"

He glanced at me as we stepped into the elevator. "Don't kid yourself. I know everything about these players from the size of their skates to who their peewee coach was. This exercise is for your benefit. Until you understand the team we have, you'll have no chance of being an effective member of my team."

Roger that.

He gave me a big smile. "Come on now. Don't look like that. You used to love watching hockey."

"Yes, I did."

When I was 10 years old.

He walked to our box. "What are your thoughts on traveling these days?"

"What do you mean?"

"Are you still afraid to fly?"

I thought about getting on a plane. I had zero reaction in my body. No fear. No anxiety. Nothing. My lifelong fear seemed to have disappeared. Go figure. "No. I don't think so."

He nodded. "Good. Tell Julie that you'll be traveling with the team for all away games. You'll need ice level seats and hotel arrangements, and clearance on all flights."

I groaned. I had walked into that one.

———

FROM OUR FAMILY BOX, we spent two hours watching the team practice. I didn't even crack the files. My dad talked, and I listened and made notes. He discussed playing styles. Past injuries. Cited contracts and numbers. The man knew his team, I would give him that.

"Check out number 33," Dad instructed. We watched as 33 did a two-on-one breakaway. His teammates couldn't keep up with his speed and agility and he scored with ease. "He's a sniper. He has a brilliant track record on ice. One of the fastest players in the NHL and feared by all, during any fight."

I could hear my dad's tone. He was holding back.

"What aren't you saying?"

"He's a wildcard. His off-ice antics have created havoc for his last team, so we bought out his contract at a basement bargain price."

"What antics?"

"Last year they arrested him for joyriding a Porsche, but he got off with community service. He got caught, by the media, locked out of his hotel room in the buff. Those unfortunate photos made the front page. He's more than a lady's man. Social media sites are filled with indelicate photos of himself in compromising pictures."

"Not good for a team's image, but he's hardly in a class of his own in this league." Hockey players were notorious bad boys.

My dad glanced at me. "He was permanently benched during the final round of playoffs last season. By his own coach."

"During playoffs? For what reason?"

"He was in a full-on brawl with one of his own teammates. The fight was not only brutal, it spilled out of the locker room after a game and a syndicated television station managed to record it."

Oh. That was bad. I made a mental note to look up that fight online. "What was the fight about?"

"No one knows, and trust me, I tried finding out before we bought out his contract. They would have won the cup if he had been playing. They lost because he sat on the bench."

"That's a coaching decision."

"He hospitalized one of his own teammates."

That stunned me. Even more that my father had bought his contract. "Why did you take him on when he's such a risk?"

"Because he's one of the best players in the league and if we can tame him, he'll be a huge factor to getting us the cup."

Tame him. I realized that this year I would see the not-so-pretty, inner workings of my dad's mind. Who even talked like that? Everything for him was about control and power. He was never happy unless he was the puppet master, negotiating the strings.

"How do you plan on doing that?"

He glanced over at me. "I don't. You're going to."

My mouth dropped open. "What? How?"

"We'll meet him after practice. You'll start by reading him the riot act. Then you'll monitor his behavior. You will be the monkey on his back."

Now that was a visual I could do without.

"Dad..."

"Rory," he interrupted. "We have a lot to teach you this year. Your training starts now."

"Now?"

He stood up. "Come on. Let's go down to the ice. I want to introduce you. This introduction is about dominance. You let the team know you own them. You let them know you have all the power and hold all the cards."

This was insane. "How do I do that?"

He stopped and stared at me. "By understanding that you do own them and by realizing that you are their boss and you have all the power. Is that clear?"

Jesus. "Crystal."

CHAPTER 8

WE WALKED DOWN to ice level. One of the assistant coaches skated over to us.

"I want the team in front of me in the next minute," my dad spoke without lifting his eyes up from his notes.

The whistle screamed, and I watched as the players all stopped whatever drills they were running.

"Team meeting, 30 seconds. Hustle!" the assistant coach yelled.

I could feel my heart pound as the players and coaches skated over to the gate where we stood. My dad didn't even look up as 32 players and eight coaches skated up and formed a semi-circle on the ice in front of us. I was so nervous I had to work to keep my legs from shaking. I glossed over the team and saw a sea of sweaty faces and wet hair beneath helmets.

I did not understand how to radiate power but decided that a good pissed off vibe was better than a scared vibe. I tried to think about world hunger. And how I didn't want to be here.

Get angry. Find that inner bitch.

My dad bent down and spoke into my ear while everyone stood and watched. I knew this tactic. He was holding everyone captive.

This was one of his classic moves. His message was that they could stand and wait until he was good and ready.

His instructions in my ear were clear. "I will introduce you. Then you call #33 out and instruct him to come up for a meeting after practice."

I nodded, dying inside. I did not want to speak in front of these men. I worked to wipe all expression off my face. The less they could read of me, the less chance these men would realize that I was a big fraud.

My dad began his speech. "My name is Mark Ashford. I'm the owner and GM of the Vancouver Wolves. We will cut nine of you before submitting our opening day player roster to the league. I respect and appreciate the input I get from the coaching staff here, but make no mistake, I make the final decision on who stays and who goes, so work hard."

He stood there for a moment, letting that threat sink in.

I watched as players shifted on their skates, straightened up, looked more alert.

"I'm proud to introduce my daughter, Rory Ashford, who has returned from studying in New York. She is being groomed to be the next GM of this team. Do not underestimate her. She has been attending hockey games since birth and no one knows more about hockey and this game than her. I wouldn't be training Rory to take over this job if I didn't think she could handle it."

I felt 40 pairs of eyes move to me.

No emotion. Show no emotion. I stared back hard. No pun intended, but it felt like I was trying to stare down a pack of wolves. I tried to infuse anger and hate in my gaze, but I had no idea if it was working.

"I've put Rory in charge of monitoring your progress. She'll be at every single game this season including all away games. She'll be traveling with the team. She'll be my eyes and ears on your performance, your stats, your ability to get along with your teammates, and your office antics. At this moment, she holds all the power, so don't piss her off."

Laughter rippled through the team and then died off when they realized my dad wasn't joking.

"Rory?" my dad focused on me.

Oh my god. This was it. This was the moment that would decide whether these players respected or mocked me for the rest of the year.

I stood, paused, and looked over the entire group and collected my thoughts. My voice rang loud and clear.

"Number 33."

The entire group froze while everyone glanced around. Movement from the back and the players in the front parted so the player could skate to the front.

Holy fucking fuck.

I stared at Max.

Max was here. None of this was making any sense. How was he here? On the ice? He was a hockey player? For the Wolves?

He stared back at me. Dripping sweat. Impossibly big in his uniform. Stupidly hot. Defiant. If possible, more pissed off than me.

You hurt me. You left me in a hotel without saying goodbye.

The entire group held their breath while we stared at each other, neither of us blinking.

I didn't have to channel any emotion. It was all there. Like a red haze in front of my eyes.

"You'll report to a meeting in my office after practice." My command was crisp, edged with scathing scorn and a heavy dose of indifference.

His nostrils flared, but he didn't speak.

I added, viciously. "Make sure you shower."

I turned and walked up the cement steps. Dad moved with me.

"What's the meeting about, Rory?"

Max's tone was challenging, taunting and arrogant.

My dad stiffened beside me, but before he could respond, I spun around in Mom's $800 heels.

"Thirty-three, you'll address me as Miss Ashford. Is that clear?" My voice dripped hate. Because right now I hated him. On so many levels. With all my heart.

"My name is Max Logan."

Blue eyes challenged me. He hated being called by his number.

I took pleasure in responding with an arctic tone. "When you earn my respect, you'll earn your name. Until then, you're just a number. Don't be late."

I glanced over the faces of the group of men. Shock, surprise, and respect showed on their faces. And then I turned away.

———

DAD, not big on praise, said nothing about that little moment, but he puffed up with pride. I had shown the world my Ashford backbone and my dad loved it.

The minute I got back to my office, I shut the door. My entire body trembled. I put my hands on my burning hot face while tumultuous emotions churned through my body.

Max was here.

He was a player on this team.

We would work together this year.

Fuckfuckfuckfuck.

I was now his boss.

I paced the length of my office, freaking out. He knew I was a fraud. He knew I didn't want to be here. Worse, he had an intimate, carnal knowledge of my body.

Flashes of the night in the hotel blinded me. The things he had done with his mouth. Cold sweat washed over my body. If my father ever found out I had fooled around with one of his precious players, hell would know no fury. It'd be the end of Max's career on this team.

I stood at the window and stared down at the ice below. Practice was winding down. I couldn't make out players' faces but I had no trouble tracking him. He was one of the largest players on the ice and the fastest.

My dad had made a good choice in buying his contract out, any idiot could see he would be an asset to the team, but all the other stuff? That would be an issue.

My issue.

He could call me out to the world. He could degrade me in front of the team, put me in my place, make me small. But that would put him at risk. If my father ever found out about our history, Max would be gone. So, I felt reasonably confident that Max wouldn't tell anyone about our time in North Dakota.

But this situation was a nightmare.

Judging by his cocky and defiant response on the ice, I knew he hated the power I held over him. I understood his response. That is how I behaved when Dad put the screws to me.

How would this meeting go?

The skaters were leaving the ice.

I needed to prepare.

I returned to my desk and pawed through the files until I found the one with Max's name on it. I flipped open the cover and read. Max was 26 years old. He stood 6'4" tall and weighed in at a solid 220 lbs. His stats on ice were impeccable. His performance off-ice were dismal.

He got drunk at a gala event and got into a brawl with one bene-factor, who pushed him into a chocolate fountain. An incident that left both Max and two women covered in chocolate. That had made front page news.

He picked fights with reporters.

He picked fights in bars.

There was photo evidence of him with multiple puck-bunnies who seemed to enjoy posting pictures of him in their social media accounts in various states of dress in random hotel rooms. I studied each photo with my heart in my throat. The implications of those pictures were clear. I was not the only one who had enjoyed the Max factor.

Mortification burned the back of my throat.

There was a knock on the door.

Dad opened the door and surveyed me.

"So, what do you think?"

I dropped the file on my desk. "I think I need your help."

CHAPTER 9

MY NERVES WERE PULLED SO tight, I felt like an elastic band, stretched taut and quivering, ready to snap. Dad stood facing the glass window of my office. He played casual observer, but I knew he'd be listening to every word, taking in every nuance of this meeting.

Did Max know how important it was to not broadcast we knew each other?

Even worse, I was about to read him the riot act, ruthlessly citing a list of points that my father laid out for me. Yes, I was angry that Max had left me in a hotel room without saying goodbye, but it didn't warrant how I was about to speak to him. Max had been good to me, and now I would verbally crush him.

I had argued over every point with Dad, but he had been adamant about how I address Max.

A slow knock sounded at the door. Our eyes met. Max looked wary.

I stood up from behind my desk. "Please take a seat."

I motioned for him to sit at the chair in front of my desk, but I was also trying to establish the formal nature of this meeting, willing him not to speak like he knew me.

He moved across the room with athletic grace and I wondered how I had missed that he was a professional athlete. I'd grown up with hockey players. I knew how they moved, I knew their body types and Max was 100% a hockey player.

It was laughable that I had thought he was a fireman.

I watched as he lowered himself into the seat. He took a moment to glance at my father, who stood with his back to us.

My father told me to go for the jugular. He wanted me to take Max off guard and to let him know I was in charge.

Those blue eyes returned to my face.

I cleared my throat. "Number 33, do you want to tell me why you're such an idiot?"

He froze, his eyes widening. "Excuse me?"

"You're a brilliant hockey player. Arguably the best player in the league, but we paid more for some of our third string players than we paid for you. Do you know why that is?"

He straightened in his chair and his eyes narrowed on my face, but he didn't answer.

"You either haven't figured it out, which makes you an idiot, or you know better, but you can't control yourself, which makes you an even bigger idiot. So, are you the clueless idiot, or the idiot who can't control himself?" That last line was Dad's. He had insisted I speak to Max like this.

Max's jaw tightened, and his nostrils flared, but his only response was to hold my gaze in a cold stare. I could feel myself sweat as I checked my notes.

"Maybe you don't care about money. Players inferior to your skill set are laughing all the way to the bank. And yet, you almost didn't get re-signed after Minnesota put you up for trade. Do you care about money?"

His blue eyes were like slits. He remained motionless, but emotion rolled off him in waves. "Yes."

"How much?"

"Excuse me?"

"The question, number 33, is do you give enough of a fuck to play for this team? That's the question I want to know. You can make a lot of money on this team if you follow our rules. So, do you give enough of a fuck that you can comply?"

He stared at me but didn't respond. His emotions crackled between us. There was so much frustration and so much anger being directed towards me.

I opened his file and grabbed a handful of the 9x11 glosses that depicted all the ways someone had caught him in compromising positions. I tossed them over the desk at him, and he leaned forward in a scramble to catch them.

His face darkened as he glanced down at the photos.

I cleared my throat again, but I couldn't erase the trace of hurt and disappointment in my voice. "I can't decide if I prefer your mug shot or the picture of you on your hotel balcony in the buff with not one, not two, but three naked women."

His eyes lifted from the photos to my face. I couldn't hold his gaze. I needed to hide how those pictures affected me. I fussed with some papers on my desk. "You will spend time with our media team for training and until we deem you ready to deal with the media, you will not talk to any reporters. No off-camera quips, no off-handed comments. You don't even glance at the cameras. You will stay off social media. Yours and everyone else's too."

I reached over the desk and handed him his schedule. "Here is a list of community charities we support. You will volunteer in the community for a minimum of ten hours a month. There is a list of charity events, like the kids skate-a-thon and the Autumn Gala that will be mandatory for you to attend. If you make the team."

Max studied the paper in his hands. Emotion bunched his neck muscles.

"Do you have anything to say?"

"No."

I glanced at Dad, wondering if he wanted to add anything, but he remained standing with his back to us. Silence settled in the room, colder than a January night in New York.

"Then you're dismissed."

With deliberation, Max stood up, towered over me, to offer me the photos. I glanced up at his face and my eyes widened at the stark expression on his face. He clenched his jaw. His muscles were rigid and his eyes were a turbulent sea of emotion.

I dropped my gaze, unable to face him. This man had been nothing but kind and I had drawn the line in the ice, letting him know that I owned his ass. This meeting had not been fair, and we both knew it.

"Keep the photos. I have wiped your slate clean, but we won't take kindly to you screwing up. We won't be as lenient as Minnesota."

He flinched when I mentioned his old team. He tossed the photos on my desk and then with deliberation, he turned and walked towards the door.

Dad turned his head and raised his eyebrow at me. He wanted me to take my final parting shot. A shot he had come up with and made me memorize. It was a low blow designed to install an emotional reaction in Max. My father wanted to see how much emotional control Max had.

Max almost made it to the door. I cleared my throat. "One more thing, thirty-three."

His entire body stiffened, but he didn't turn around nor did he speak.

"If you ever disrespect me again, like you did today you'll be cut. And a sad, lonely beer league will be the only hockey you ever see again. This is your last chance. Remember that."

He stood there, still, and for one heart-wrenching moment, I thought he'd turn around and give me a piece of his mind.

Go. Walk away from here.

Without saying a word, he walked out of my office and disappeared out of sight.

CHAPTER 10

I HAD HURT MAX, and that made my heart hurt. I had seen anger and pain in him and it killed me that I had been the person to put that expression in his eyes. I felt numb as Dad shut the door.

With his hands in his pockets, pride shone in his eyes.

"What do you think?"

I worked to cover how much that meeting had affected me. I took my time answering. "I think if he loves hockey as much as we think he does, he'll get in line."

"Keep me posted," he opened the door before glancing back at me. "You passed your first day with flying colors."

I nodded, with a lump in my throat. I couldn't remember the last time I had made Dad proud, but at what cost?

I waited until he closed the door before I dropped my face into my hands and groaned.

Max.

Being close to him had been torture.

He needed to be off limits. No one could ever find out about what had happened between us.

I had hurt him. After everything he had done for me, I had treated him unfairly.

We needed to keep our distance.

I needed to stop thinking about him.

So why did I want to fling myself at him, wrap my arms around him and beg him for another kiss?

———

DAD LEFT EARLY, to meet Mom at some charity event. I did not understand how he had the energy to go glad-handing after a day like today.

With guilt, feeling like a thief about to commit a crime, I walked down to human resources. The receptionist lifted her head.

"Do you have Max Logan's human resource file?"

"Yes," she sounded hesitant.

I gave her my brightest smile. "We'd like to send him a welcome basket since he's new to the team, but I need an address."

Her face brightened. "Sure."

I watched as she copied his address onto a sticky note and then handed it to me.

"Thanks," I smiled. "I appreciate it."

———

I PICKED up a gift basket up at a flower shop before taking a taxi over to the address that the HR admin gave me. I knew I was breaking about a million privacy laws, but I needed to talk to Max. Not only about the meeting we had today, but I needed reassurances from him that he'd tell no one about our night in North Dakota.

I also want to see him.

I questioned my sanity when I got to the lobby of his building. The doorman stood up as I approached his desk.

"I'm here to see Max Logan?"

"Sorry," the man apologized. "He requested that we allow no one upstairs without his express permission, but I can ensure that we deliver your basket to him."

Well, this was awkward. I needed to talk to him.

"Could you call him and tell him I'm here?"

The man picked up the phone. "What's your name?"

"Rory Ashford."

I stepped away from the desk while he phoned, feeling anxious. What if Max refused to see me? What if he reported me for coming to his home?

"Miss Ashford. You can take the elevator up to the 15th floor. His suite is 1509."

I debated leaving the basket and taking off, but we needed to talk in private.

Stepping off the elevator, I walked down the long hallway to his apartment. I almost tripped when I saw how delicious he looked standing in the doorway. He was wearing a pair of ripped jeans, a faded t-shirt and his feet were bare.

As I approached, I tried to gauge how he was feeling. Judging by the dark expression on his face, I realized that this meeting would not be easy.

He didn't speak, he just held the door open for me. I stepped into his place and my eager eyes took in his place. For Vancouver, it was a substantial apartment. Twenty-foot ceilings, huge glass windows that overlook False Creek. It had a modern feel, made even more stark because Max had almost no furniture. He had two bar stools at the kitchen island. In the sitting area off the kitchen, there was a single expensive looking brown leather couch and a huge screen television. From what I could see the main living room was devoid of furniture. A lone coffee maker decorated the counter.

Max stood there, watching me look around.

I flushed and set the basket down on the island. "This is for you."

He continued to stare at me. Unimpressed.

Nerves made me babble. "The basket is from me. Not from the

Vancouver Wolves. Although come to think of it, the Wolves should have sent you a welcome basket. They should send all new players a basket."

"What are you doing, Rory?"

He sounded pissed.

"I wanted to apologize."

He didn't move or speak.

"Max. How I talked to you in that meeting was inexcusable. Especially after everything you did for me in North Dakota." *He gave me an orgasm.* I flushed. "I mean, how you calmed me down during the flight and gave me your life vest and then you carried me off the plane and took care of me."

His stillness unnerved me.

I continued to flail in this one-way conversation. "I owe you so much."

"You owe me nothing."

"My dad scripted that entire meeting."

"I know."

"You knew?"

"I'm not pissed about that meeting."

"Why not?"

"I'm aware of the circumstances in which I'm coming to this team. I expected some version of that conversation."

Now I didn't know what to say. "What are you pissed about?"

"Doesn't matter."

"But you admit you're pissed."

"Are we done here?"

His coldness cut me to the bone. I forged on. "I also wanted to mention one more thing. In private. Which is why I showed up here."

He answered by crossing his arms across his broad chest.

"I think it'd be best if we told no one what happened between us."

"No shit."

I dropped my eyes down to mom's pumps. Shoes that were

pinching my toes to the point of pain. "My dad wouldn't be too happy if he heard what happened."

"I figured."

Without speaking, I turned on my heels and started towards the door. It was stupid that I had shown up here. Stupid and reckless. I don't know what I had been expecting, but it wasn't this. I worked to keep my emotions under control.

I squeaked when a big hand grabbed my wrist and spun me around.

"Rory."

"What?"

He ran a hand through his hair. "My career is hanging by a thread."

"I know."

"I shouldn't have touched you that night."

"I asked you to."

"It wasn't right."

"Don't tell me it was wrong."

"It was a mistake."

I worked to keep my bottom lip from trembling. "What are you saying?"

"You're a complication I can't afford. You need to forget about what happened between us."

"How can I? We survived a plane crash together," my eyes searched his face. "We shared something that night."

He pushed his hand through his hair in frustration. "You saw those photos of me. I'm not the guy for you. I'll never be the guy for you."

"People change."

"You don't know me and it's in your best interest to stay away from me."

What could I say to that? Max wanted nothing to do with me. My shoulder drooped. I searched his face one last time before I turned to go.

"Don't look at me like that."

I didn't turn around. "Like what?"

But he didn't respond, so I gathered up my shredded pride and walked out.

⊏⊐

THAT NIGHT, I lay in bed, my arms curled around a pillow while I thought about Max. He was so damn hot. Which is why I needed to stay away from him. He was a big, muscular, hockey player. A player in general. Scared of commitment. Bossy. Dominating. Alpha male. And a royal mess off the ice.

He was no Baby Man and if I made a checklist of everything I didn't want in a relationship, he would check off every single box.

Yet, I liked his surly attitude. I liked how he didn't seem to give a fuck. I loved the shape of his lips and the way his eyes seemed to always be on my mouth. That he was the ultimate bad boy made me want him even more.

I groaned and buried my face into my bed.

I needed to forget about him.

I needed to keep this professional. I needed to put a stop to this intense attraction that I felt for him.

The only problem? I wasn't sure how to do that.

CHAPTER 11

THREE WEEKS DRAGGED by without me talking to Max again. My job comprised of shadowing Dad on everything he did and learning everything I could about our players. I sat in meetings with Dad. I met with the media market team who explained their strategy for the year. I didn't contribute. My sole job was to learn. And learn I did. I listened, made notes, and asked hundreds of questions.

I was developing a greater respect for Dad. He had built his business with talent, business acumen and a lot of guts. Even if this was not something I wanted, it was teaching me what he wanted and what he had done to achieve it. Dad was not afraid of hard work.

The best part of my workday was when we sat together and watched the daily practice. He talked about how the game had changed. And we discussed various players, their strengths and weaknesses.

When Max was on the ice, it was difficult to not give him my undivided attention. Although, my father couldn't fault me if I did, because he was everything we wanted in a player. Max was the fastest player on the team. He had incredible accuracy when he shot and he was a phenomenal team player. You could see how he reacted during plays, that he could think on his feet. No matter what scenario the coaches ran him through, he excelled.

My dad talked about everyone, but he rarely spoke about Max.

We watched Max make an exceptional shot at the net, during a drill, placing the puck where no one else could. I felt pride for how well he was shooting. Dreaming of other times. Dreaming of when he had looked up at me from between my spread legs with that intense, I'm-going-to-blow-your-mind look. I had delicious daydreams about him. I wanted him to come to my office late at night after everyone had gone home. I would wear a skirt, without panties and he would push that skirt above my hips, spin me around against the wall and then I would hear the zip of his pants come down. I would spread my legs farther and then he would trace his fingers over my...

"How's it going with 33?" Dad's question ripped me out of my daydream.

Oh my god.

Mortified, I worked to gather my thoughts.

"According to Katrina, from the media team, he's attended three media meetings."

Dad nodded. "Katrina knows her stuff."

Katrina was stunningly beautiful with dark hair and a tall, model-thin body. The best part about Katrina is that she was a married woman.

"Max requested to change his volunteer duties."

He glanced at me. "To what?"

"He loves kids. So, with my approval, most of his volunteer work is with disadvantaged kids in the form of hockey camps and mentorships."

My dad failed to keep the surprise off his face. "And he's been doing his hours?"

"Yes. According to Katrina both the kids and the parents love him."

"How's the media behaving?"

"Seventeen calls this week alone. Everyone wants to discuss Max and his past."

My dad made a short noise in his throat.

"Do you have any reservations?" I asked, dreading his answer.

My dad crossed his arms and watched as Max made a remarkable shot on the net during the drill. He was thinking. "I don't know. There's something about him."

I could feel my heart pound in my throat. "What do you mean?"

He shook his head. "He reminds me of someone."

"Who?"

His eyes followed Max down the ice. "Someone I didn't like."

"Dad, you can't dismiss Max because he reminds you of someone."

"Yes, I can. It's called intuition."

I rolled my eyes at Dad's back. "He's doing what we've asked him to do."

"We'll see."

Those two words terrified me. My dad ruthlessly protected his team. I made a mental note to remind Katrina to follow up with Max before our first pre-season game about Max avoiding the media.

━━━

IT WAS the first game of the preseason and Dad had filled our executive viewing box with his friends and colleagues. It was a bois-terous affair with plenty of food and booze. I wasn't in the mood. Before the game started, I glad-handed with his guests before slipping down to the family seats we always had reserved at ice level.

I'd never admit this to anyone, but I wanted to watch the game in peace. I didn't want to make small talk with business executives while trying to concentrate on the game.

This was a big night for our players. We still hadn't cut the roster, and a lot was riding on the game for several of the players. Not that I cared about most of those players. I was only worried about one.

Max.

It shocked me that Katrina was sitting in one of our eight private family seats that were off limits to everyone, including staff.

"Hi." I sat down beside her.

Her delicate features were marred with shock at my arrival. Her beauty always stunned me.

At least she was a married woman.

She gave me a cold glance but didn't say a word. For the life of me, I couldn't figure out why Katrina didn't like me, but from day one, she had remained reserved around me. Perhaps this was an opportunity to warm up our professional relationship.

I waved over one of the personal attendants that stood off to the side.

"Could you please bring me a lager beer," I glanced at Katrina. "Can I offer you something to drink?"

She didn't glance at me. "I'll have a white wine."

The attendant disappeared.

"So, fresh new season, hey?"

She ignored me.

Perhaps she had trouble hearing.

I waited until the attendant returned with our drinks. I passed Katrina her wine and then signed off on the receipt, leaving the attendant a generous tip.

Katrina didn't thank me for her drink, nor did she thank the attendant which I found rude. Mom had ingrained impeccable manners into me from a young age. You always say thank you.

I gave her one last shot. "Your husband is always welcome to come to the games. You know we can get you some good seats."

"My husband and I separated this summer."

Instant retribution. Mom was always warning me you never knew what someone else was going through. Perhaps this is why Katrina seemed so distant.

"I'm sorry to hear that."

"Glad the dick is gone."

Or perhaps Katrina was simply an unpleasant person.

Music thundered around the stadium. Players spilled onto the ice for their pre-game warmup. I hadn't seen Max close up in weeks and now I couldn't seem to take my eyes off him. His skates and helmet added inches to his 6'4" frame, making him look like an ice warrior. He talked to another player, took a few shots on goal and appeared at home and relaxed on the ice.

So *why* was I so damn nervous for him and his first game?

The entire arena stood for the Canadian and American anthems.

The game started out rough. Players shoved and pushed to get control of the puck. The plexiglass shook every time someone got body checked into the boards.

I would die before I admitted it to my father, but I loved hockey. I loved the sound of skates cutting on the ice. I loved the speed and intensity of the game. I loved how blood-thirsty this sport was.

Five minutes into the game, Max got a breakaway. He skated around the opposing defense and approached the net with unfathomable speed. He slapped the stick and shot the puck so fast, my eyes couldn't follow it. The deep goal horn reverberated throughout the stadium and then the goal song played.

A few of his teammates crowded around him, hugging and congratulating him. The crowd's response concerned me. They cheered but didn't go wild.

Well, it was the start of the season. Perhaps the crowd needed warming up. Regardless, it thrilled me that Max had gotten the first goal of the pre-season.

Max, breathing hard, skated toward the bench. He appeared impossibly big and sweaty. As if he could sense me, his eyes lifted to where I sat. My breath caught in my throat as he held my gaze for an extended couple of seconds before he moved to the bench. I crossed my arms over my waist, thrilled that he had noticed me.

Which was silly and so school-girlish. Still. It elated me far more than it should have.

"So, how long have you been working here?" I tried again to make conversation with Katrina.

"Look, Ro-r-y." She used a disdainful three entire syllables to say my name. "We don't have to do this."

"Do what?"

"I don't need another ass to kiss and you don't have enough room on your ass for another pair of lips."

My face flamed as I stared at the ice. Her rudeness shocked me, but for all I knew, Dad set her up to test my ability to maintain professionalism in the face of extraordinary rudeness. "A professional relationship is fine with me, Katrina."

She snorted and rolled her eyes.

No one could be that rude, could they?

I focused on the game, studying the various plays they made. I made a mental note about which player lineups worked and which lineups struggled. The crowd roared with every breakaway. It was a thrilling game and every time Max stepped onto the ice, I felt pride at his extraordinary speed and agility.

During the end of the first period, another player, with an assist from Max, scored. The stadium went wild. They screamed so loud, we couldn't hear the goal song.

Heading into the back of the 3rd period, the Wolves tied the game up. It was neck-to-neck with equal shots on goal. Max, two against one, battled his way down to the end of the ice. He needed someone to pass to, but the rest of the team lagged. He swung to one side, gave a fake shot and then slid the puck in between the goalie's legs.

It was a brilliant goal.

The horn echoed, reverberating throughout the stadium.

People cheered, but it sounded muted, unlike when the other player had scored.

My heart sunk. The crowd didn't like Max.

I glanced up behind me, at the family box. My dad stood on the balcony, his arms crossed, with a hard-to-read expression. He sensed it too.

I swung back to Max who skated back to the bench. His eyes

were on the ice and he didn't look up at the crowd.

Katrina seemed oblivious. She spent most of her time on her phone uninterested in the game that played out in front of us.

Two minutes later, Dad appeared and sat down beside me.

"Hi Katrina," Dad offered a friendly smile.

"Mr. Ashford," her voice sounded warm.

"Your name didn't show on my list of guests approved to sit in my private seats."

She flushed a deep red. "Rory invited me. At the last minute."

I turned, wide-eyed to stare at Katrina. She wrapped her arm around mine. "We've become friends, haven't we?"

I had no response. I didn't want to make it awkward for her, but I refused to lie to Dad on her behalf. Especially after she had been such a bitch.

Dad saved me from answering. "That's great. Would you mind giving us some privacy?"

She beamed a smile at him and stood up. "Of course. And thank you both for your generosity. Are we still going to talk to Max after the game, Rory?"

I worked to keep the shock off my face. "I don't know."

Her voice sounded patient. "You promised we'd talk about releasing his media ban."

What was she even talking about? "Wait for me on the Concord. I'll be right up."

She gave Dad another inculpable smile. "Night."

Dad watched her walk up the stairs and then turned back to me. "You didn't invite her to sit with you, did you?"

I shrugged. "She was here when I got here."

"Did you tell her this was off limits to staff?"

"I thought it'd be an opportunity to bond."

"How did that go?"

I ignored him. "What did you think about tonight?"

"You tell me."

I discussed my concerns with our second offensive line.

"Anything else?"

I sighed. "The fan's reaction to Logan concerned me."

"You noticed that too. What is this nonsense about lifting his media ban?"

"It's the first I've heard of it."

"Thoughts?"

I weighed my response. "If we lift the media ban, the media will only focus on Logan's past. What he doesn't need is more bad press." I pressed my lips together. "I think we need the fans to gain an appreciation for him first before we release the hounds on him."

"Good, I agree. Are you able to enforce that?"

I glanced up at Dad. "Yes."

"You have any trouble, you come to me. Let no one push you around on that."

"Another test?"

"Yes," his dark eyes found mine. "I want to know if you can hold your own."

The game ended. We stood as the players left the ice and the announcer called the star players. With two goals and one assist, they named Max first star.

I watched as he came back onto the ice and skated in a short circle. The crowd remained silent and didn't cheer or clap. The deafening quiet was eerie. Max glanced up at the crowd and the fleeting expression on his face made my breath catch in my throat.

Sadness etched his features.

He dropped his eyes and stepped off the ice.

My heart was in my throat. I felt for him. What a lonely position to be in.

Why didn't the crowd love him? He was our most valuable player. Anyone could see that.

Dad interrupted my thoughts. "I'll be a couple hours. Do you want to ride home with me?"

I didn't want to wait around. "Don't worry about me."

He nodded. "See you at home."

CHAPTER 12

WHEN I MET up with Katrina on the Concord, she didn't even bother to apologize for using me to lie to Dad. Which annoyed me to no end.

"How long do you think Max will be on a media gag?" She asked, as we moved towards the team locker room.

"When I can trust him."

She threw me a haughty look. "He's trustworthy. He's ready."

"The ban needs to remain in place."

Max wanted to play hockey and therefore he would toe the line, but he had left Minnesota under a cloud of dark secrets. And now the media was circling him like sharks hunting for blood instead of focusing on his hockey game. I had grown up in the glare of the media and I knew firsthand what a struggle it was. This was the least we could do for him.

The press grumbled their displeasure. They knew there was a secret to reveal, and they were relentless in their pursuit. We allowed his coaches to discuss his progress with the press. After that, he was off limits.

Katrina and I stood in the private back hallway, outside the locker room, and waited for Max to come out.

"I think you're making a big mistake," Katrina spoke with force. "He's ready."

I didn't get the sense that Max missed the camera time.

I blinked at Katrina. I knew she only saw daddy's little girl playing at an undeserved role. I was young and she probably thought she could easily push me around. What no one seemed to realize was I had been taking on my dad, one of the greatest forces in this industry, since I could talk. No one was more qualified to stand up for myself or my convictions than I was. Not to mention that Dad had requested I stand my ground on this matter.

I took a deep breath. "I don't think Max should mix with the media yet."

She defiantly stared at me. In her expression, I saw resentment. "Why? He's ready. He can take on the media. He's been working hard."

"If I find that anyone advises against that ban, they'll answer to me."

She crossed her arms. "I'm the media expert."

The locker room opened and four players came out. They all glanced between Katrina and me, but no one spoke to us.

She pushed, "What is the reason for this ban?"

"We want to give Max some room to breathe before needing to deal with the media."

Her eyes narrowed and her voice was caustic. "You're not being fair to Max."

I tempered my desire to respond in the same tone. "Why don't you tell me why you think Max should talk to the media."

"He's a star. And he works hard for his place in this world. Your gag on him is stealing his limelight. You should be letting him shine. We both think it's disrespectful that you'd take that away from him."

"Who's we?"

"Max and myself."

"Max wants his media gag lifted?"

"What he doesn't want is a daddy's girl who has no life experience making decisions about his career."

The audacity of that statement shocked me. The problem was, she was right. I was new to this job, walking around in mommy's shoes and playing at this game. What she didn't realize is that I was carrying out Dad's orders.

Max chose that moment to step out of the locker room.

He wore an expensive, black suit, and a crisp white shirt open at the collar. His gaze zeroed in on both of us. His expression didn't shift, but he was astute in assessing the funky energy between Katrina and me.

"Good game." I forced neutrality into my voice as he approached.

"That was phenomenal," Katrina gushed. "Two goals and one assist? You were perfect out there."

His blue eyes studied me. "Thanks."

My stomach spun under his intense gaze. He felt like a stranger. So why did it feel like someone trapped a thousand butterflies in my throat? I worked to settle a neutral expression on my face.

A long pause hung between the three of us.

"Do we have an agreement, Rory?" Katrina asked.

"About what?"

"You agreed to lift the media ban on Max."

"No, I didn't!"

Katrina turned to Max. "It's lifted and now we've got a lot of work to do."

"It's not lifted!"

Max sounded bored. "Is it or isn't it?"

Katrina rubbed his arm. "Your ban is lifted."

"No, it's not," incredulity marred my tone. I peeked up at Max. "For the record, the ban will be lifted only by myself or the GM. If you proceed without that, do so at your own peril."

Katrina scoffed. "Are you now threatening Max?"

"No, I'm trying to make it clear to Max that I haven't authorized him to talk to the media."

She rolled her eyes. "Max, she doesn't have the authority to make these decisions."

I couldn't take it. "What's your issue, Katrina?"

She spun around to face me. "My issue is that I don't take orders from a teenager who thinks it's fun to play in Daddy's world."

Humiliation flooded my cheeks with warmth.

"Have a good night," my stupid voice quivered on the last word. I walked away to the sound of Katrina's amused laughter.

CHAPTER 13

ALL I WANTED to do was go home but catching a cab so soon after the game would be impossible.

I swiped my key to access the locked executive offices and made my way to my office.

I made a gin and tonic and then stood at my window and studied the near empty arena. Only a few straggler fans remained, while a Zamboni circled the ice and men with shovels scrapped the ice up from along the boards.

I shut my eyes and put my forehead on the cool glass. Tears blurred my vision.

What had I expected? I knew this job wouldn't be easy but in my naïvety I thought it'd be hard because I'd be working for Dad. I hadn't imaged that I'd come against the likes of Katrina.

"You want to tell me what is going on?"

I stiffened at the sound of Max's voice. "How did you get up here?"

"A security guard let me in."

I stood still, watching a father and daughter. They remained in their seats, laughing every time the Zamboni drove by their corner. It reminded me of better times when my dad and I used to watch hockey together. When had I started to fight him and his world? I missed how close we used to be.

"Are you okay?"

I took a deep, calming breath and lied. "Fine."

"So, what did I witness between you and Katrina?"

I stared down at the arena. Father and daughter put on their coats. She chatted and her dad listened with rapt attention. Would my dad and I ever be that close again?

The Zamboni made its final lap.

"Katrina wants us to lift your media ban."

"I got that part."

I turned to him. He stood with his feet planted, and his hands in the pocket of his suit. The guy could be the face of Armani. He had the body and the bank account of a professional athlete and the face of a model. No wonder he wanted to keep on playing the field. He could get any woman he wanted.

Which made it even more embarrassing that I had thought for a fleeting moment he'd want me.

"I don't want you to talk to the media yet."

"And the GM?"

"He agrees with me."

"Why?"

"Why what?"

"No other player has a media gag. I'm wondering why I have one?"

"Do you want to talk to the media?"

"I don't give a fuck about the media. That's not what I asked."

"You told me you don't want any distractions."

He sounded pissed. "You're protecting me?"

"I'm helping you shut out the noise."

"Why would you do that?"

"Because if I shut out the noise and you can focus, you're the best player on this team. I want you to go far. I want you to be the best."

"Are you for real?"

Anyone else would express their gratitude. Not Max.

"Yes. I'm for real."

His eyes drifted down my body and back up. "What's the catch?"

"It also works to our club's benefit to avoid any undue media storms."

"You mean bad press."

I choose my words with care. "We are concerned with the overall health of the club's image."

He stepped up next to me and took the glass from my hands. A faint sweet, woody fragrance, that was distinctly Max, teased my senses. It was subtle but masculine. I watched as he drained my glass.

"You know, you're the only one around here who's honest with me?"

I stared up at his eyes, in particular his eyelashes. They were sooty black and thick.

He glanced down at me and frowned. "Were you crying?"

"No."

His big hand moved up to my face, and I felt his thumb smear a lone tear from beneath my eye.

I swallowed as I stared up at him, feeling vulnerable. Didn't matter that less than a month ago, I had been doing the ugly cry in front of him when our plane was going down. Now, my tears were an admission of weakness. It spoke about how over my head I was in this job, and about how much my conversation with Katrina affected me. We were no longer strangers facing death together. Now, so much more was at stake which meant that tears could no longer be on the menu.

His blues dropped to my mouth. "Fuck I'm going to regret this."

"Regret what?"

His hand slid around my neck and then he tugged me closer. My breath was a staccato in my ribcage as he dropped his head down towards mine. And then his mouth moved over mine, stealing my breath. He tasted like gin and warm male. His playful kiss coaxed me until my mouth opened beneath his. I moaned, and he groaned in response. I felt him tug me closer as he deepened the kiss. It languorously combined wicked sensation and shameless desire.

My heart slammed in my chest, and I swear my knees were shaking.

I was in fucking sensory overload. My mind didn't seem capable of keeping up with the sensations that assaulted me down to my toes.

I gasped when he lifted his mouth and stepped back. His blue eyes, with blown pupils, lingered on my mouth.

"I should go."

"What?" I sounded as stunned as I felt.

He didn't answer and without saying another word, he turned and walked out of the office.

My fingertips fluttered to my lips. Max had kissed me. It shouldn't make me this happy, but I couldn't stop my heart from zinging with joy. We didn't have a future. He was a player, and I was the GM's daughter and there was no possibility of pursuing anything between us.

But my stupid heart didn't care.

THAT NIGHT, I crawled into bed with my laptop. I would watch the one video I had been avoiding since I had heard about it. The video of the famous fight between Max and Joseph, his old team member.

This fight was the real reason no one cheered for him. This fight is why thousands of people judged him by withholding their praise. I needed to watch it.

It took less than a second to find it. It was the most viewed hockey video with over 19 million views.

I clicked play. The video footage was raw. A cameraman from a known sports news station, ran his film, while he waited for players to come out of the locker room.

Off camera, you could hear reporters talking about the game.

A faint shout.

And then another shout.

Voices yelling. Muffled. A fight from behind closed doors.

The reporters all stopped talking.

The cameraman shifted the camera to the door of the locker room.

Something banged against the door.

The shouting got louder. It sounded like a complete brawl.

The excited murmurs of the reporters.

The door flew open. In a blur, two hockey players tumbled out.

One was Joseph Flanynk, and the other was Max. Both still in uniform. Both wore their skates.

Joseph got a wild punch that connected with Max's face.

Max's head snapped back and blood splattered. His lip split.

Max's face was a mask of pure rage.

He all but lifted Joseph up off his skates and body slammed him into the cement floor. He lost his own footing and landed on Joseph.

Reporters hustled out of the way, blocking the camera.

The door yanked open and three more players piled out.

Someone lifted the camera and moved closer.

Max was on top of Joseph. He hit Joseph with a savage violence that shocked me.

Voices off camera. "He's going to kill him. Get Max off him."

A flurry of arms and legs and hard wrestling. Max fought being lifted off Joseph, but his teammates restrained him and shoved back into the locker room.

Joseph was unconscious and his face was unrecognizable.

"Call an ambulance."

"Turn off that camera."

The video ended.

Horrified, I sat with my hand over my mouth.

I knew the facts. Max had broken Joseph's jaw in three places, smashed his nose and broken two of his teeth. Joseph's injuries were so extensive he required restorative surgery to his face.

Max hadn't been charged, but the coach had benched him. According to my father, it was a move made by his team to buy time, so they could wrap up the paperwork and remove him from the team.

As soon as the playoffs ended, Minnesota had put Max up for trade. Not a single team had wanted him, except my father.

It baffled me that no one from his old club talked about what the fight was about. There were plenty of news articles written about the fight, filled with speculation, but no one from his old team talked. Which was unusual. Hockey lips sank ships, but in this case, no one breathed a word. Which showed how bad the secret was.

No wonder there was such a feeding frenzy around Max.

What had happened?

Why had he lost his cool and beat his own teammate?

I couldn't reconcile the Max I knew with the barbarian who seemed determined to destroy Joseph. My question was, what had Joseph done to Max? Max wasn't a fiery hothead. He didn't have a hair-trigger temper.

Now the hockey world held Max's past against him. I had promised him a clean slate and I would grant him that. This video only validated my decision to protect him from the press. And the public. Without speaking to anyone, the media couldn't twist and turn his words against him. Without sound bites, reporters had nothing to write about.

I needed to find out what secret he was hiding. I needed to know what that fight was about.

CHAPTER 14

THE NEXT MORNING, dad called me into his office. I faltered when I saw Katrina, smug as fuck, sitting on my dad's couch.

"Come in," my dad motioned me into the room.

I eyeballed Katrina, but didn't speak. I could read my father better than anyone and something annoyed him. I chose the other end of the couch.

He picked up a file and then tossed it on the table. "What's going on with Logan and the press?"

"I think you already know."

"Excuse me?" my dad raised his eyes.

"Isn't that what this meeting is about?"

Katrina's smile was smooth. "Max is ready to speak to the press."

"I disagree," I shot back.

My dad glanced between both of us. "Katrina, why do you think he's ready?"

"He's done a phenomenal job of studying media training. We've been through dozens of dummy interviews. He's charming, personable and his career deserves to shine. It's not fair for this team to hold him back."

I bite back my retort.

"Rory?" my dad eyeballed me.

"Right now, Max's focus is on his game. Why bring the media into his life when they only want a scandal?"

"You don't know that," Katrina cut me off.

"Yes, I do."

"Ladies." Dad had a bored expression on his face.

"You told me Logan was my player to protect and work with. Don't take this decision away from me."

"I'm the media specialist here," Katrina reminded.

I turned to her. "Max has one shot here. If this goes sideways, it's his career that gets hurt, not yours. When this blows up in his face are you going to take responsibility for this?"

"It will not blow up," her voice was stubborn.

My dad stood up. "Let him talk to the media."

I wanted to tip my head back and howl.

"Thank-you," Katrina stood up. "I knew you'd see my side."

This was the wrong move for Max. I knew it in my bones. It frustrated me so much I couldn't even handle it. I started towards the door.

"Rory, a moment, please," Dad commanded.

I turned around. I wanted to wipe that self-satisfied smile off Katrina's face with a slap.

My father waited until we were alone. "Want to tell me what's going on?"

"What do you mean?"

"Katrina barged into my office, all hot and bothered."

"If I ran to you with my problems behind the backs of others, people would accuse me of abusing our relationship."

"Trust me, she won't make it a habit."

We stared at each other.

"After the game, Katrina talked about setting Max free with the media. I was adamant that this was the wrong decision."

"Is Katrina sleeping with Logan?"

His words felt like a shiv between my ribs. "Excuse me?"

"Are they a couple?"

I worked to keep all emotion off my face. "I have no idea."

"I want you to get close to that situation and find out."

I sputtered, "How do you expect me to do that?"

"I have confidence in you that you'll figure it out."

If this situation wasn't such a mess, and if I wasn't the one who kept messing around with Max, I'd find this conversation amusing, but it terrified me that Dad was turning his focus onto Max's sex life.

I switched gears. "Why didn't you back me up with Katrina?"

"What are you talking about?"

"Yesterday you told me that the media ban would continue, yet this morning, you're taking her recommendation over mine."

"She thinks he's ready."

"And you agreed that we should get him on the right side of the fans before he faces old gossip. So why didn't you back me?"

"My biggest concern is that you're accepted by the staff."

"And not backing me up will do that?"

"It sends a message I don't favor you."

"By siding with someone else even though you know I'm right?"

"Exactly."

This was so frustrating. "Next time put our players first. I can handle myself."

"Keep your eye on Logan. He's your responsibility."

God. Help. Me.

He checked his watch. "Your meeting starts at 9 AM."

"What meeting?"

He stood up. "I want you to get to know the game better from the ice level. I want you to sit in on the weekly coaches meeting. It'll give you a great oversight of the players from their perspective."

"Are you coming?"

He smiled. "Nope. This meeting is all yours."

"Do they know I'm coming?" I checked my watch. The meeting started in three minutes.

"Baxter won't mind. The meeting is in boardroom B."

I rushed to my office to grab my portfolio along with my copies of the players files. By the time I got to the boardroom, the meeting had already started.

When I opened the door, eight sets of male eyes turned towards me.

Baxter, the head coach, stopped speaking. Annoyance laced his voice. "Can I help you?"

I glanced around the table. There were no empty chairs at the table. I grabbed one chair from along the wall and wheeled it to the table while trying to balance my papers and coffee. No easy task in 4-inch heels. "I'm here to sit in on your meeting."

"Like hell you will."

I realized that Baxter had no idea who I was. The last time we had met was on my first day, when I stood at the edge of the ice with Dad in front of the entire team, but until now, there had been no one-on-one interaction.

"It's at the request of the GM I attend all your meetings going forward."

Don, the assistant coach moved his chair over so I could squeeze in beside him.

Baxter gave a humorless laugh. "Are you his new admin?"

Two coaches dropped their eyes to the table. I set my coffee and files on the table before speaking.

I chose my words with care. "I don't have an official title, since I'm learning the ropes. My name is Rory Ashford."

His eyes widened as he realized who I was. "This is still a closed-door meeting."

I hated this. Why was everything such a battle around here? I didn't lift my eyes as I opened my portfolio and clicked on my pen. "If you have an issue with my attendance, please take it up with the GM."

He tossed his papers on the table and stomped out of the room. The rest of us sat there in uncomfortable silence, waiting for his return. Don leaned forward and passed me his meeting agenda. He pointed at a name on the top. "That's the admin for the coaches. You can ask her to put you on the mailing list for meeting minutes and the agenda."

"Thanks."

Baxter returned, and without addressing my attendance, he instructed, "Let's get this meeting started."

Our eyes met, and I almost drew back at the level of resentment and loathing in his expression. I steeled myself against his unmasked fury.

One year. I can survive anything for one year, can't I?

CHAPTER 15

I WALKED OUT OF THE COACHES' meeting feeling conflicted about what I had observed. Seven out of the eight coaches loved Max and his performance, and the head coach, Baxter, could not stand Max.

The biased negativity I heard color all of Baxter's comments concerned me enough that I made a note to observe some player/coach meetings and to get closer to the ice for practices. I needed to know if he was professional enough to hide how he felt from Max and could remain impassive and professional.

Now I needed to find Max and ward off any impending disasters that could result with him talking to the media. I saw two players walking down the Concord.

I approached. "Have either of you seen Logan?"

"Think he's in the weight room."

The weight room was the one place I avoided. With dread, I made my way down to the state-of-the-art fitness center designed for our players. From the hallway, I could hear the music and the clank of metal bars. The overpowering scent of sweat, deodorant, and antibacterial cleaner assaulted my nostrils as I stood in the doorway. Huge screen televisions lined the front wall. Everywhere I laid my eyes, players in various states of undress, worked alongside our hired sports trainers to the point of dripping sweat.

Hockey players in their full gear were intimidating, but stepping into the weight room, felt like I was stepping into the wolves den. The slicked wet skin and masculine grunting felt way too intimate. It also made me feel like I was at a disadvantage.

My eyes located Max in the corner doing squats with a big weight bar. I waited until he dropped the bar before I approached. He lifted the bottom of his t-shirt up, to wipe the sweat out of his eyes and in the process revealed a wall of rippling muscles and smooth skin.

It took all my effort not to linger my gaze on his body and to focus on his face.

He instructed his trainer. "Give me a sec, Ken."

I watched as Ken walked off.

"You look tidy." His eyes took in my spiked black sandals, tight black cigarette pants, and a black and white striped, wrap around sweater that hugged my waist. I wasn't sure if tidy was a compliment, but the way his eyes lingered at my waist, made it feel like one.

"Sorry to interrupt your workout."

He shrugged.

I got distracted by a lone rivulet of sweat that trickled down the side of his face. "I wanted to let you know we've dropped your media ban."

"Katrina told me."

Of course, she had.

"Well, you have her to thank for that. She went all the way to the GM to fight on your behalf."

His eyes narrowed. "I didn't ask her to do that."

"I know."

"Anything else?" His eyes moved to my mouth.

"Are you sleeping with Katrina?"

"Not yet."

My eyes widened with shock and hurt. I stumbled back a few steps before turning to flee.

"Rory." He grabbed my wrist and stood too close. He spoke in a low voice. "That was an asshole thing to say."

I stared at the space over his shoulder. "The question was too personal."

"I told you. I'm not doing distractions this year, but if I was..."

Our eyes met. His gaze was so infused with heat, it made me blush.

I dropped my eyes. "Are you ready for the media?"

He shrugged. "Don't worry about it. I can handle a few reporters."

"They want to get personal."

He smiled. "So, let them."

"Take this seriously."

"Has anyone ever told you that you're cute when you're worried?"

"Okay. That's my cue to leave."

I spun around and started towards the door. I could see him in the reflection of the wall-length mirror. He stood with his hands on his hips and his eyes watched my ass.

━━

EXACTLY EIGHT HOURS, I stood in my PJs in my bedroom in front of my television.

I was going to *kill* Max.

No. I would kill Katrina first and then I'd kill Max.

Max had shoved a reporter. Eight hours after our talk, Max *freaking* Logan lost his cool and shoved a reporter into a cameraman.

The bite was on every syndicated sports news channel.

It had made the top five worst plays of the days.

Anchors were talking about it.

People were doing memes about it.

A strangled noise ripped out of me as I yanked on the first thing I could find. Skinny jeans, a tank top, and a hoodie.

Max Logan was a dead man walking.

"Rory." Dad roared from his bedroom.

I walked down the long hallway and composed myself before I tapped on the bedroom door.

My dad, clad in his housecoat, stood in front of his television. We made eye contact.

"You saw the news?"

"Yes."

"Where is he now?"

"The reporter is threatening to press charges. He's at a police station."

"Are our lawyers involved?"

"Brian is on his way."

"Go fix this."

If we'd done things my way in the first place, we wouldn't have anything to fix, but my dad hated it when I reminded him that he was wrong and I was right.

⊏▭⊐

AS I WALKED up the steps of the police station, Brian, our lawyer, caught up.

"Brian, thank you for coming."

"Katrina also called me." He worked to tighten his tie.

"I hope we didn't drag you away from anything too important."

He gave me a tight smile which meant we had. "Lead the way."

Katrina sat in the waiting room.

"Go do your magic, Brian," I veered toward Katrina.

She stood up when she saw me. Lord, her dress was tight. That was a date dress, not a work dress. So why did that feel like a hot knife in my gut?

Her eyes lifted up to me. "Is the lawyer here?"

"Keep your voice down," my voice sounded harsh. "What happened?"

She glared at me. "Max and I were out for dinner. The reporter and cameraman appeared out of nowhere."

"And?"

"And they got nosey about Max's past and he lost his cool."

"How did they know you'd be at that exact restaurant?"

"I don't know. Maybe they followed us."

Highly unlikely. I suspected there was more at play here.

"It makes no sense that a reporter would follow Max and push for an interview when we had only removed his media ban this afternoon. There are only four people who knew about that ban being lifted."

"Are you suggesting that I tipped off the media?"

"Did you tell anyone?"

"Go to hell."

I pinched the bridge of my nose. "Go home."

"I came here with Max."

"And now the Vancouver Wolves and our lawyers will take it from here. So please go home."

"I'm not leaving here without Max."

"After this, Max will head down to the stadium to meet with our legal team," I lied. "When he's finished, I'll tell him to call you."

"I want to be part of that meeting."

I took a deep, uneven breath. This woman was a barracuda. Why was I the only one who saw this? "Even if Max wants you to be part of that meeting, the Vancouver Wolves do not. Go home."

She eyeballed me. "Is there a car here?"

"No."

She crossed her arms. "I saw you arrive in a company car. I'm taking it home. After the night I've had, I deserve it."

I despised her. So much. This time my smile was real. "I'm sorry, the only car and driver that is here is my personal family car, not a company car. Would you like my driver to call you a cab?"

She shook her head at me in disgust. Like I was the problem.

I watched as she walked away.

CHAPTER 16

AN HOUR LATER, Max and Brian appeared from the back. I didn't get up from my seat while they signed papers at the counter. Max towered over Brian. He wore a pair of jeans and a faded, army green t-shirt. Over that, he wore a thick gray hoodie. Odd outfit for a hot date.

Max had lied. When I asked him about Katrina, he told me he would not do any distractions this year and only hours later; he was on a date with her. I couldn't decide if I was angry or hurt.

I stood up as they walked towards me. Max wore a pissed off expression.

"What's the damage?" I asked Brian, ignoring Max.

"Reporter is unwilling to drop the charges. We have a court date set for three weeks from now."

"Brian, can you please email me copies of your files as soon as you get home?"

"Of course."

"Thanks for coming on such short notice."

Max and I walked outside in silence. We stood outside my car.

I was so annoyed, I couldn't even make eye contact. "Where is your vehicle?"

"At the stadium."

"Do you want a ride?"

He nodded and then opened the door for me. We got in and the car pulled away from the curb.

"Where's Katrina?" he broke the silence.

"I told your date to take a cab home. She also wants you to call her as soon as possible."

Blue eyes met mine. "It wasn't a date."

I worked to keep my voice devoid of emotion. "I don't care about your personal life, but I need to discuss what happened."

"Tonight?"

I rubbed my forehead. The Wolves needed to do damage control on this, but I wasn't sure how. "It'd help to get your side of the story."

The rest of the drive was silent. He was unnaturally still. Aside from his hands curled into fists in his lap, he did nothing but stare out the window of the car.

We arrived at the stadium and made the silent walk up to my office.

"Want a drink?"

"Yes."

Without asking him what he wanted, I poured us both generous portions of scotch. He stood and studied the dark stadium.

"Why don't you tell me what happened. From the beginning." I handed him the drink.

Silence from him.

"I need you to tell me everything, so I can help you."

"After I saw you in the gym, I met with the media team about the gag being lifted."

"What happened?"

"It ran late. Katrina's assistant left and it was only Katrina and myself."

"How late?"

"Our meeting finished around 7 PM."

"Then what happened?"

"In celebration, she wanted to buy me dinner."

"And you agreed?"

"I thought it would be a burger in some pub. She said she would change, and she came out wearing a dress."

"I saw that dress." I paused. "That was a date dress."

He rubbed the back of his neck. "I know."

"But you went anyway."

"I don't know. I figured it was just dinner."

"So, you were on a date."

"No."

"She sure seems to think different."

He took a deep breath and looked at the ceiling. "Fine. It was an accidental date."

I ignore the emotions churning in my gut. "Then what happened?"

"I offered to drive to the restaurant, but she wanted to take a cab."

"Did you pick the restaurant?"

"She suggested it. She said she knew all the secret, great places to eat in Vancouver."

"Then what?"

"We arrived at a restaurant and out of nowhere this reporter was in my face. Screaming shit at me. Taunting me."

"What was he saying?"

"You saw the tape."

I walked over to the TV and pulled up the PVR. Our office recorded and catalogued all sports channels on a nightly basis.

"This is what we saw on the news."

Max came to stand beside me.

The film showed Max and Katrina walk up to the restaurant.

The next clip was the reporter shouting, "You owe the public answers."

Max moved forward and shoved the reporter hard against the

cameraman. You could hear Max say, "I'll kill you." The view of the camera went towards the sky and the film ended.

Max stared at the television. "That's not what happened."

"What do you mean?"

"The guy was in my face and he was saying shit. They cut so much out."

"They do that."

"That doesn't even show the truth."

I debated our options. "Did you tell anyone that your media ban had ended?"

"What? No."

"How did the reporter know that you'd be at that restaurant?"

He ran his fingers through his thick hair. "I don't know."

I narrowed my eyes.

His eyes widened. "Are you suggesting that Katrina had something to do with this?"

"She's the one pushing to get you in front of a camera."

"Fuck."

"Max, you need to learn to control yourself around these reporters."

"I know."

"You say that but look at the shit storm you're in."

He sounded pissed. "I said I know."

"Yet you still got into an altercation."

"You had to be there, okay?"

"Go home. Get some sleep. Go to practice. Don't talk to the media. Let me handle this."

"Rory."

"I mean it. I'll handle all of this, but going forward, I need your compliance."

He radiated defiance and frustration. I wanted to reach out and touch him. I wanted to comfort him. Instead, I crossed my arms. "Do you trust me?"

"You're the only person around here that I do trust."

"Then let me take care of this for you."

"Rory," he spoke with emotion. "I'm not ready to give up hockey."

"You won't have to," I made a promise I wasn't sure I could keep.

Blue eyes held mine and then he walked out.

***

"YOU LOOK LIKE HELL," my dad walked into his office carrying his morning coffee.

Probably because I hadn't left the office yet. I still wore my clothes from the night before. "I need you to see something."

He moved to stand beside me in front of his huge 72" TV. I pressed play. It was the raw footage from the night before.

The unedited version.

The camera zoomed in on Max and Katrina getting out of the cab.

The NCR station reporter stared into the camera. "No matter what, keep filming. I'm going to get Logan to hit me."

The cameraman spoke from behind the camera. "Gary, are you sure that's a wise idea?"

"It'll get me the ratings I need."

"Well you won't get ratings if you're badgering him."

"I can edit that out, plus if he hurts me, I can sue him and the Wolves."

Gary, the reporter, walked towards Max.

"Max, what happened in Minnesota?"

Max blinked in the bright light of the camera. "I'm a Vancouver Wolf now, I prefer to focus on my future not the past."

"Max, I heard the fight with Joseph Flanynk was over a woman."

"No comment."

"Max, my sources tell me that you lost your cool because one of your teammates said you couldn't get it up for a woman."

"No comment."

"She said you preferred men."

"No comment."

"Our sources tell us that the only reason you're here is because you're sleeping with Mr. Ashford. They say you both prefer men."

Dad stiffened beside me.

Max gave the camera his attention. "Mr. Ashford is one of the greatest GMs in the league. He's happily married to his wife. Leave him out of this mess."

"That's not what I heard. I heard that after practice, he likes a big strong guy like you on his knees in front of him."

Max stared at the camera. "Go ahead and badger me, but please talk about Mr. Ashford and his wife with the respect they deserve."

"You sure seem protective of your lover, Max. Is that why you got kicked off your last team? You molested one of your own?"

"Back off," Max growled.

"If I suck your cock, will you give me some answers?"

"No comment."

"What happened in Minnesota? Maybe I should try to get an interview with Mr. Ashford's daughter, Rory? I'm sure she'd be more than happy to give me some answers, or even better, get on her knees. Isn't that how it's done in that family?"

"Leave the Ashford family alone." Max ground out before turning to walk away.

The reporter shouted, "You owe the public answers. I can make Rory give me the answers I need. She's a nice tight piece of ass and I think she'd love to suck me off."

Max turned around and shoved him hard. You could hear him say, "Touch her and I'll kill you."

The film ended.

I clicked the TV off. My dad rocked back on his heels. He wasn't happy.

"Where did you get this footage?"

I took a deep breath. "I found someone who knew someone who worked at the station. I paid five thousand dollars for this footage."

My dad's eyes widened. "Interesting."

"I talked to Brian, and he said that we can threaten to counter-sue to get the reporter to back off his charges."

"Agreed. What else?"

"I think we make an official statement and post this footage up for the public."

My dad's eyes narrowed at me. "Why?"

"It shows Max not responding until the reporter threatened you and your family. That shows that Max is a team player and I think it'll go a long way with the public."

"It goes a long way with me, but I think it'd upset your mom. So, the answer is no. I want this tape buried."

I bite back my argument. My dad was protective of my mom and he'd never budge on it. "What about Katrina?"

"You think she tipped the reporter off?"

"Don't you?"

My dad let out a weary sigh. "Keep your eye on her."

"I want us to reinstate Logan's media ban and when I determine it is the right time, I want him to have a sit-down interview with a friendly reporter."

My dad shook his head, but admiration tinged his voice. "You're learning fast."

"Failing pisses me off."

My dad laughed. "Give our legal team the green light to go after that reporter and his news station. Tell them not to hold back, but I mean it. That tape stays buried."

"Okay." I gathered up my papers.

"Rory."

I turned back. "Yeah?"

"Good job."

CHAPTER 17

BY NOON, our legal team had banned the reporter from entry to our stadium until further notice. They also threatened to ban the entire NCR news station from our stadium and all future events, unless Gary, their reporter, dropped his charges and their network posted a public apology.

The news station responded within thirty minutes and complied. Gary gave a heartfelt apology for misleading the public and they suspended him without pay.

I couldn't wait to tell Max. I brought my lunch down to the rink to watch the team practice, hoping to catch Max afterwards to tell him the good news. I studied Max as he worked. Despite what happened last night, he worked hard while they skated speed drills. It did not surprise me that Max led the team with his speed.

A sharp whistle blew.

The team stopped, all of them breathing hard.

Baxter, the head coach, called out, "Since Logan is dragging his ass, we will start from the beginning."

Groans sounded from the players.

Baxter continued to ride Max's ass. I watched Max push himself harder than anyone else, but his best was never good enough for Baxter.

"Logan, you look asleep out there."

"Logan, how hungover are you?"

"Logan, why do you bother to show up, if you won't do the work?"

They did the same drill again. And again. And again. Until they were all dripping with sweat and heaving for oxygen.

When they moved to an offense drill I breathed a sigh of relief.

Three offense players with the puck, played against two defensive players and a goalie.

I watched as Max wove up the ice with the puck. Max waited to pass but the defense covered the other two players. Max shot the puck and easily hit the net.

The whistle pierced the air.

"Logan, you think you're a one-man team? Learn to pass the puck. This isn't the Logan show." Baxter yelled, shaking his head in disgust. "Again."

I watched as Max started with the puck again. The defense covered the other players. Max took advantage of a split second that his teammate was free. The pass was perfect and the other player scored.

The whistled echoed.

"Logan! Why would you pass? You were wide open," Baxter yelled, his face red in anger.

The players exchanged glances. Baxter was being a complete dick. We all knew it.

Max circled back to Baxter.

Baxter ignored him and blew his whistle. "We're done for today. Thanks to those of you who mentally showed up to this practice. Your commitment to our team has not gone unnoticed."

The team and the other assistant coaches filed off the ice. It concerned me that Baxter could not remain professional with Max.

Baxter called out. "Logan."

Almost off the ice, Max made eye contact with me with an empty expression. He stopped short and skated back towards Baxter.

At that moment, I realized that Baxter had no idea I was listening.

"I don't give a shit who you are or how many goals you score, you can't come to my practices and act like you don't give a shit." Baxter skated around him and then stopped in front of his face. "You think you're such hot shit, but you're a washed-up loser."

Max visibly swallowed but didn't speak.

"If you don't get your ass in gear and act like you're part of this team, I will ensure you get cut. Do you understand that? Everyone is sick of your spoiled and lazy attitude."

Max's eyes narrowed.

"Watch your back. I don't want you on this team and I can't wait until you're gone."

Baxter skated away, leaving Max to stand there. I waited until Baxter disappeared off the ice before I headed down the stairs to the ice level. Max met me at the gate. His jaw was tight, and he seemed to be holding back a lot of emotion.

"What was that about?"

"Nothing," he took off his helmet. Sweat ran down his face. His hair was dripping wet. Not the picture of someone who was lazy or coasting.

"Max, I saw you out there. You work harder than anyone else out there."

"It's fine."

"I don't know what kind of head games Baxter's playing but he's talking bullshit. Everyone else raves about your performance in practices and games."

His eyes met mine. He was trying to gauge if I was telling the truth.

"You're our most valuable player. Let no one tell you otherwise!"

"Max!" a voice called. From behind me, Katrina headed down the stairs. She wore nude heels, a black pencil skirt, and her blouse was almost see-thru. I clenched my teeth.

"Hey Katrina," resignation traced in his voice.

She didn't even glance my way. "I have great news."

"Could use it."

"Well, I did my magic behind the scenes and the reporter has dropped his charges against you and issued a public apology!" Her cheeks were flushed.

What the hell. She was taking credit for my work?

His blue eyes lit up. "That's amazing. Wow, I owe you."

She gave a cute little shrug. "You can count on me."

I snorted, and they both turned to me.

I wanted to speak up and let Max know that I had been the one who helped him. My tired brain tried to think of a response.

She didn't help you, I did.

I'm the one who had the reporter banned.

I'm the one who really has your back.

Everything that came to mind sounded stupid and petty.

Katrina's lips curled. "Someone should have told me that it's casual Tuesday."

I felt myself flush as I watched Max's eyes drop to my jeans and sneakers.

Without saying a word, I turned to head up the stairs.

Max's voice made me pause on the steps. "What did you want to talk about?"

"Nothing important." I kept walking.

———

I STOMPED BACK to my office. I couldn't believe that Katrina took credit for all my hard work, and worse, I couldn't believe I had said nothing. I had a million responses, five seconds after the fact, but at the moment, my tired brain could not come up with anything that sounded intelligent.

Katrina drove me crazy. There was no doubt in my mind that she had tipped off that reporter. The question was why? She pushed to have him in front of the media and then set him up to fail. If I hadn't gotten to the bottom of last night's incident, who knows what would have happened to Max? And now she took credit for fixing the issue? It was so infuriating, I almost couldn't stand it.

I read about twenty emails and then decided that my heart wasn't in the game. I needed to cut out of work early. I was so tired I couldn't see straight.

I started packing up when a knock sounded at the door. Max filled the doorway. No matter how many times I saw this man up close and in person, I never got used to how big he was. I could smell his intoxicating fresh scent from my desk, and I thought he looked hot with his freshly showered wet hair.

"What?" my tone cut.

He stepped into my office. "Are you heading home?"

"Thanks to you, I haven't been home since last night, so I think I deserve to go home a few hours early. If that's okay with you." My voice was sharp. I knew my comment wasn't fair, but I couldn't seem to stop myself.

He tipped his head to the side. "You were here all night?"

"What do you want?"

"What did you want to talk about?"

Silence ticked between us while I dumped my wallet and keys into my bag.

"What's going on?" Dad's terse voice sounded from my office door. He trained his eyes on Max, who visibly stiffened under his gaze.

"We were talking about last night," I swung my Louis Vuitton purse over my shoulder. "And I'm heading home."

Dad rocked on his heels and crossed his arms. "Did Rory tell you everything she did for you last night?"

Max scratched the side of his neck. "We hadn't gotten that far yet."

I could tell that answer annoyed Dad. "Rory somehow managed to get her hands on the raw footage of your interview. Then she worked with our legal team to use that tape to gain some much needed leverage. She banned that reporter from this arena and by threatening to do the same to the station, they have issued a public apology. That reporter has dropped all charges against you and they have suspended him without pay all because of Rory's hard work."

It was anticlimactic that my father had to sing my praises. Especially after Katrina stole my thunder. I stepped from around my desk avoiding Max's all-seeing eyes. "Just doing my job. Now if you'll both excuse me, I'm heading home."

I made it down to the Concord before I heard Max calling my name. "Rory."

Ignoring him, I skipped down the steps towards the entrance.

He moved as fast off the ice as he did on it.

"Rory."

His big hand grabbed my arm and held me until I stopped walking.

"What?"

Frustration marred his expression. "Why did you let me think Katrina fixed this?"

"I didn't want to get into it with Katrina."

He studied me. "You're tired."

His concern was almost too much to bear. For one terrible moment, I thought I might start to cry. I forced myself to steel my expression. "I need to go home."

"Let me give you a ride."

I shook my head. "Unnecessary."

"Come on," he walked with my arm still in his grasp. "I'm not taking no for an answer."

I didn't want to wait for a cab, and a small part of me, really wanted to be near Max.

"Fine," I huffed, making it sound like I was doing him the favor.

His lips twitched. "You're cute when you're grumpy."

HE DROVE a brand new black Lexus SUV.

"Where to?"

I gave him my address which he punched into his GPS. We crawled through the congested downtown traffic and pulled to a stop at a red light.

Max glanced over at me. "How are you?"

"Fine."

His long fingers tapped on the steering wheel.

The question blurted out of me. "Do you ever think about the plane crash?"

He took his time answering. "Every day."

"I don't talk about it with anyone. They all ask about it, but I don't want to talk about it."

"Because no one understands."

"Yeah." I turned to him. "But you get it. You were there."

He swallowed and stared out the windshield. "I have dreams about it."

"Really? What do you dream?"

"I dream that we crash, I go to pick you up out of your seat but you're not there and I can't find you. And then I wake up."

Max dreamed about me.

It sounded more like a nightmare, but it thrilled me that I was in it.

The shrill sound of his phone on blue tooth interrupts us. The screen on the dashboard said: *Uncle Ronny Calling.*

"I have to get this." Max threw me a sidelong glance.

To give him some privacy, I focused my attention out the window.

"Ronny!"

"Hey, Kiddo. How ya doing?" A deep male voice boomed through the car.

"I'm good."

"Saw your last game on TV. You're on your game."

"You're my only fan, you have to say that."

The man's laughter filled the car. "This call has to be short and sweet since I'm on a break, but I wanted you to know that your mom's car broke down last week."

"Oh shit."

"She's taking the bus now, but I was wondering..."

"Anything. Buy her a new car and send me the bill."

"She'll know it's from you."

Max drew his hand over his mouth but didn't speak.

"I thought maybe we could do a work around," his uncle added.

"Anything."

"You wire me the money. I'll tell her that my mechanic friend owes me a favor and I'll secretly pay the mechanic and get her back on the road."

"That works. I'll send you the money tonight."

"I'll make it happen." Uncle Ronny cleared his throat. "So, are they treating you right out there?"

"Absolutely."

"How about Baxter Nicols? I heard he's tough on his players."

"Nah," Max lied. "He's been great."

My mind raced as I listened to his conversation. Why didn't his Mom want his money? And why did they have to trick her into letting Max help her?

I listened as they joked around before the call ended. My insatiable curiosity about Max drove me to prod. "So, that was your uncle?"

"Yup. My mom's brother."

What about Max's dad? Was he around?

"He sounds like he's a good guy."

"He's the reason I'm here."

"What do you mean?"

"My mom hates hockey, but he paid for my gear and drove me to my practices."

Oh wow.

"Well, if he ever comes to a game, be sure to tell me so we can give him the royal treatment."

"Thanks."

I wracked my brain, trying to think about how I could ask him more about his mom without coming across as being snoopy.

He turned onto my street. I didn't want this drive to end. I could never quite get enough of this guy.

He pulled up into the driveway and whistled under his breath as he took in the massive 8,000 square foot Greystone that was more mansion than house.

"Well, this is me," I announced unnecessarily. "Thanks for the ride."

"Rory," his expression was hard to read. "Thanks for helping me out."

I gave him a tired smile. "Last night wasn't your fault."

"I should have kept my cool."

He lost his cool when the reporter threatened me. "Thanks for standing up for me."

Anger flashed in his eyes. "That guy was out of control."

"I'm reinstating the media ban. I don't want you to talk to the media. When I think you're ready, I want to set up an interview with a friendly reporter."

"Yeah, sure."

I watched him. He stared pensively out the front windshield. What was he thinking? What did he need? What was going on with his mom? Why couldn't I get this guy out of my mind?

"I should go."

His smile was tight. "Yeah. Thanks."

He was thanking me? He drove *me* home. "Thanks for the ride."

"Anytime."

I climbed out of his vehicle and turned back to Max. Something passed between us. Without speaking, wishing that I could spend more time with him, I shut the door and moved to the house.

Max was off limits. I needed to remember that.

CHAPTER 18
TWEET

Hockey Gurl @hockeygurl
  Rory Ashford is a spoiled little brat who doesn't have a clue. The only reason why she has a job with the Vancouver Wolves is because Daddy knows she can't manage real life. @VancouverWolves @rory_ashford

CHAPTER 19

4,798 TIMES. That is how many times the offensive tweet had been retweeted. Who was Hockey Gurl and why did she dislike me so much? I tossed my phone on my desk. It wasn't public knowledge I worked for the Wolves, so I suspected that this tweet was from someone who worked in our club.

Nepotism is the worst, and I blamed no one for resenting my position, but I wasn't strutting around, acting like a queen bee and making nefarious demands of people. I only wanted to get through this year unscathed.

I packed up my office. Dad stepped in.

"Hey, Dad."

"Hey," he was vibrating with energy. I did not understand where he got it. This place drained me.

He looked thoughtful. "Your mom is waiting in the car. She's bound and determined to have one last weekend getaway before the regular season gets underway. You want to come? We've booked a house on the water outside Seattle."

"Thanks, but I have plans with Ola tonight."

He winked at me. "Well, make sure you enjoy your last weekend of freedom. Once the regular season starts, you will not have a life."

Wow. That sounded like so much fun. *Not.*

"I guess the same advice goes to you. Enjoy your freedom."

He put his hands in his pockets. "We're taking the car this weekend. Are you going to be okay without a ride?"

I found it ridiculous that my dad insisted we get driven everywhere. In New York, I had only used the subway. "I can take a cab."

"Okay," he nodded. "Have a good weekend."

"You too."

He turned to go.

"Max."

My head whipped up. Max was passing by my office, and at the sound of my father saying his name, he stopped in the doorway.

"Mr. Ashford."

Icy blue eyes glanced at me for a nanosecond before focusing back at my dad.

"You have homework."

My dad had his polite tone. The one he saved for people he was about to crush. I got anxious.

Max considered the package in his hand. "Coach wants me to watch some videos from last season."

My dad rocked on his heels, but didn't speak.

To Max's credit, he didn't react. He lifted his eyes up to Dad with a benign expression on his face.

"Do you feel you're learning a lot?" My father's tone patronized.

I felt myself go still. Like a deer standing between two wary wolves.

"Yes, sir," Max used the word sir, but there wasn't an ounce of respect in his voice. How he sounded insolent and amused with only two words was beyond me.

"That's great," I interjected, trying to defuse.

Max's eyes moved to my face.

Dad made a noise in his throat. I recognized that noise. He wanted to pick a fight.

What was going on? What was Max triggering in him?

I needed to break up this conversation before it escalated. "Well, I hope you enjoy watching those videos."

Max held onto my father's gaze for a moment too long. There was a challenge in his gaze. Two alphas, sizing each other up. Together they would make an incredible team. Pitted against each other, they had the potential to destroy each other.

Max broke his gaze with my dad and he glanced at me. His eyes dropped to my mouth.

I widened my eyes at him, telling him to obey.

Dad's voice patronized. "Our regular season game is Monday. Make sure you're rested."

Translation. Don't party this weekend. Which was insane because this was notoriously the biggest party weekend for all the hockey teams. The last hurrah before the season started.

"I'll be rested." Annoyance replaced the calm expression on Max's face.

Before my father could say anything, I stepped closer and worked to calm down Dad. "I can't wait until the regular season starts."

Liar, liar, pants on fire.

My comment distracted Dad. He turned towards me with a smile on his face. "Really?"

"Really. We have such a strong team this year. I think we can go all the way."

I could see Dad relax. He loved talking about winning. "Yeah, I think you're right."

I flashed my gaze at Max, needing to get him out of here. "I hope you have a nice weekend, Max."

You're dismissed.

His blue eyes looked between my father and me. Seeing far too much. "Have a nice weekend."

Without letting either of us reply, he stepped back and disappeared.

A long moment passed before I had the nerve to speak.

"Dad, what was that about?"

"What?"

I blinked at him in disbelief. "Why were you goading one of our players?"

My dad flushed. "I wasn't."

"Yes. You were goading Max Logan and trying to get a reaction out of him. I want to know why?"

"Why do you care?" he threw back. My dad had a hairline trigger.

"Because you gave him to me as a project. I don't appreciate you taking shots at him and setting him up to fail."

My dad stared at me for a long moment and then a smile broke over his face. "God, you remind me of your mother some days."

Thinking about Baxter, I replied, "He's got enough coming against him."

Dad's eyes narrowed. "What do you mean?"

But a call from Mom interrupted us. He kissed me on the cheek and then I was alone.

◁▭▷

OLA, one of my best friends from grade school, met me for dinner in Gastown. After dinner, we walked down the street to a high end bar that promoted subtle glam and yet had the same buzz as a New York bar. The decor was black with muted lighting, low couches, and secretive booths and beautiful waitresses. We found seats in a curved booth that overlooked the entire bar and ordered over-priced cocktails.

We caught up on life and although I didn't tell her about Max, I shared how tough it was to work for my dad. I even elaborated on some of my less fortunate run-ins with Katrina.

"She sounds awful."

"From the moment I met her, she seemed to dislike me."

I pulled out my phone and showed her the hockey gurl tweet.

"Who would write that?" Anger flashed in her eyes. "Do you think it's this Katrina chick?"

"I don't know, but if it is, how do I prove it? If I can make it through this season, I can move on. I won't be anyone's daughter. I'll just be a person making it on my own."

Ola's phone rang. "Sorry. This is my boss. I'll answer outside."

Waiting, I sipped my drink and almost choked as I watched a group of huge men walk into the bar.

It was the Vancouver Wolves.

Holy shit.

My eyes sought out Max. He walked between two of his teammates and laughed at something they said. He looked beyond sexy, with his black button shirt and a pair of dark jeans. He reminded me of the Max I had noticed in the airport bar. Expensive and confident.

The group sprawled out in a reserved section of low couches and glass coffee tables. They attracted a lot of interest from the rest of the bar patrons and no less than four waitresses appeared in front of the team to take their drink orders. I leaned back, so the shadows obscured me. The last thing I wanted was for them to notice me.

Max smiled up at one waitress. All heat and sexy male. Did he know how gorgeous his smile was? It was lethal. The waitress touched her neck and flushed.

"Sorry that took so long," Ola slid into the seat beside me.

"That's okay."

"What did I miss?"

"The Wolves just came in."

"Ooh, where?" she twisted around, craning her neck.

I ducked my head. "Be subtle. I'd prefer if they didn't notice me."

Her eyes went wide. "So, we're spying?"

"Let's just say we're doing an anthropological study of a group of red blooded, testosterone-filled males."

"I love it."

We ordered more drinks and talked about old friends. Ola was a connector. She knew everyone and their business. She was also the vault and could keep a secret better than anyone I knew, but anything that was public knowledge, she was happy to share.

Max laughed at something someone said.

I worked to listen to Ola, but I didn't hear a word she said.

Two women approached the group of men. Max took a sip of his beer and glanced up at them. Both of the women had killer bodies, clad in skin tight dresses and stiletto heels. Puck bunnies, whose main goal was to secure themselves a hockey player.

I gritted my teeth. And smiled back at Ola.

She was still talking. I worked to concentrate on her words.

Geez. Max now held one of the women's hand and stared up at her.

Jealousy licked my soul. I forced myself to nod at Ola.

The puck bunny sat down next to Max and stared up at him.

I could feel sadness settle over me.

I blinked unseeing at Ola, while I tried to cool my reaction, but my stomach was so hard it hurt.

Ola, unaware that I wasn't listening, continued with her story.

My eyes averted to Max. *He smiled at the floor, listening while Blondie whispered something in his ear.*

This was my future. I needed to accept this. Max didn't want me. He wanted his player lifestyle.

"You'd think they'd be kicking his ass to the curb but they're still fighting over him," Ola finished with a flourish.

I stared at Ola as I worked to get all my erratic emotions under control.

"Are you okay?" she asked, amused. "You have that same look on your face that you did when Ruby stole your science project idea in grade 7."

"Sorry." I tried to focus. I needed a moment alone to think, so I didn't blurt out my secret about Max. "I need to use the washroom. Do you know where they are?"

She pointed to the corner. To get there, I would have to walk past the Wolves.

No! I could not walk past him.

I debated suggesting to Ola that we leave, but pride wouldn't let me. I stood up and took a deep breath. I knew I looked good with my mile-high heels and wrap around navy dress. Yet, I felt petrified.

I survived a plane crash. I can walk to the washroom.

With my head held high, and confidence in my stride I started the long, lonely walk past the three couches filled with the Wolves.

I focused on my phone, pretending not to see any of them. I could sense the moment they all noticed me. One by one, I could feel the group still and watch as I walked past. Nerves strummed my body but I couldn't acknowledge them. If I did, it would force me to stop and chat, and that was not an option.

I could feel him staring at me.

I tried to resist, but I failed. I lifted my gaze and looked at him. Only him.

The cute blonde was curled up next to him, talking in his ear, but he tracked me as I walked past him.

I felt myself flush hot. I ducked my head and disappeared into the washroom.

CHAPTER 20
TWEET

Hockey Gurl @hockeygurl

I heard that Rory's dad not only paid her tuition, but when she failed every class, he needed to buy a new library to ensure she graduated. She really is that #dumb.

CHAPTER 21

I DIDN'T EVEN NEED to use the washroom. I washed my hands, touched up my lipstick and gave myself a pep talk.

Max is a free agent. He can date or sleep with anyone he wants.

We have a professional relationship.

I am not jealous.

My only job is to make sure he succeeds on the ice.

I patted my hair into place and then took a deep bolstering breath. I could do this.

I opened the door and paused. Leaning against the wall, across from the door, was Max.

"Hi, Max!" I sounded way too high pitched and chipper. I cleared my throat.

"Having a good night?"

"Um, yup."

His eyes traveled down the length of me. His voice sounded casual. "How's your date going?"

I rapidly blinked not sure how to answer. Not sure if I wanted him to know I wasn't on a date. "You're here with the team?"

"I am."

I did not understand why he was waiting for me or why he wanted to talk.

He let me know when he asked, "Did your parents go out of town?"

"How did you know?"

"I saw your dad with a suitcase."

My stomach did a slow flop. "Yes. They went down to Seattle for the weekend."

He stared at me for a long moment. "Phone."

"What?"

"Give me your phone."

I didn't even ask why he wanted it. I unlocked it and handed it to him.

I watched as he typed something in before passing it back. I peeked down at the screen. He had entered his phone number in my contact information.

My breath caught in my throat. Why had he given me his number?

OMG! Did he want a bootie call? Did he want to come over? Is that why he was giving me his number? My heart raced in my throat.

"Do you want me to call you later?"

"Text me when you get home safe."

I stopped, confused. "What?"

He pushed himself off the wall, looming over me. "I want to know when you get home safe. Text me when you do."

My lips parted, but before I could answer he disappeared into the men's room.

I shut my eyes in mortification. It was laughable that I had thought for even a fleeting second he wanted to come over later. He had a puck bunny salivating over him. It embarrassed me that I had thought he'd want to see me.

With my head down, I made my way back to Ola.

She gave me an apologetic smile. "I'm so sorry, but I need to leave. My boyfriend called. His car broke down in Surrey and he needs me to come and get him."

"That's fine. I'm not feeling that great."

We paid for our drinks. As we walked out, I glanced over my shoulder. Max stood with his back to me. The cute blonde was all but glued to his side.

The whole thing depressed me.

I took a cab home, letting myself into my childhood home. I sighed as I stood in the dark foyer of the huge silent house. Friday night and I was home by 10 PM. So much for having a social life.

Time for soft clothing, popcorn, and Netflix.

While the popcorn popped, I checked my phone again.

Max had given me his number. Not because he wanted a bootie call, but because he was treating me like a kid sister that he needed to take care of. It kind of made me happy that he was thinking about me, but he wasn't thinking about me in the way I wanted him to.

I started to text him that I was home, but then stopped myself. How lame would I seem if I texted him at 10 PM? I could envision him, at the bar, with some puck bunny sitting on his lap and then his phone would buzz with my text. A text that would scream sad loner.

I tossed the phone on the counter. It wouldn't hurt for him to believe that I was on some hot and heavy date. I'd text him after the movie.

—

CHIMES WERE PLAYING *in my dream. Long, echoing chimes on repeat.*

I sat up straight in bed, heart pounding. The chimes sounded again.

The doorbell.

The clock read 3:21 AM. *Oh no!*

Oh no, oh no, oh no.

No one rang the doorbell at this time of night unless something bad had happened.

I ripped the covers off and raced down the stairs. I stood there, for a long moment, while my heart hammered in my chest and I braced myself to face whatever I would need to face. Was it the police? Had something happened with my parents? Whatever it was, I needed to face it.

Heart in my throat, I swung the door open.

There stood Max with a stiff posture.

"Max." I sounded thick and stupid.

His nostrils flared as his eyes went up and down, taking in my yoga pants, droopy ponytail, and bare feet.

"Are you alone?" He spoke through a clenched jaw.

Was I dreaming?

I nodded, confused and disoriented.

His eyes narrowed. "I didn't get a text."

I looked to his vehicle that sat in the long driveway, and then back to him. "You know where I live?"

"Your address was in my GPS. Why didn't you text me?"

The tone of his voice made my eyes widen. He was not a happy camper.

I put my hand on my forehead, trying to process this. "It's the middle of the night."

"Exactly."

I hadn't texted him, but in my defense, I thought it was too pathetic to be texting him that I was home alone while he frolicked with some hot bunny.

"Were you worried?"

He glowered. He ticked off his points with his fingers. "Home by yourself. On some date. Didn't text."

In that moment, I made the game time decision to not tell him that I hadn't been on a date. "So, you drove here to check up on me?"

A muscle in his jaw ticked. Finally, he spoke. "I wanted to go to bed, and I got tired of waiting."

It dawned on me that Max had been waiting for me to text him that I was okay. And when I hadn't, he had gotten into his vehicle, to drive across town to check on me. That fact staggered me.

"Max." My voice had more feeling than I wanted it to.

He turned and stalked back to his truck. He slammed the door of his vehicle and then the engine roared to life.

He unrolled his window and called something to me.

"What?"

He pointed at the door. He wanted me to go back inside. I nodded but stood there, waiting for him to drive off. A moment passed before I realized that he would not drive away until I moved inside.

Confused, I stepped inside and shut the door. Only then did I hear the roar of his vehicle.

What had just *happened*?

I LAY IN BED, replaying that Max had been so concerned about my safety that he had driven to my home in the middle of the night to check on me. Did that mean he cared? It must mean a small part of him cared.

I picked up my phone.

Me: Sorry I didn't text. Thank you for checking up on me.

Max: Why didn't you?

I curled up on my side, thinking. The guy had gone out of his way for me. He deserved my honesty.

Me: I came home early and fell asleep in front of a movie.

Max: What time?

Me: 10 PM

Max: What happened to your date?

Me: I was with my girlfriend and she needed to leave early.

I lay there for a long moment, wondering if he'd text back.

Max: So, no date?

Me: No date. How was your date?

Max: I wasn't on a date.

Me: Didn't look that way to me

Max: I came home alone

I smiled. Now that made me happy.

Me: Night

Max: Night

I SAT in the executive box with Dad and watched our fifth regular game of the season. I had packed my bags and tonight I would travel with the team for their first set of away games. Dad had accompanied me and the team for all our pre-season games, so this would be the first time I traveled alone with the team.

We were only three weeks into the regular season, and Max was the second highest scoring player in the NHL league. Although he single-handedly ensured we won most of our games, the Vancouver fans refused to accept Max. Tonight he had already scored two goals, but the fans refused to show their appreciation. I studied the sea of faces. There were no homemade signs in the crowd, scribbled with his name or number, nor did they chant his name like they did the other players.

"Come on, go, go," Dad yelled at Max.

I sat clenched and tight, watching as Max took advantage of his breakaway. With speed he moved up the ice, weaving past the opposing defense.

Slap!

Max scored his third goal of the game, and the goal siren sounded across the stadium.

A hat trick.

In the rare event of a hat trick, when a player scores three goals in one game, fans show their appreciation by throwing hundreds of hats onto the ice. In response, the player would skate around the ice, pick up a couple of hats with his stick and bask in the love of the crowd. Dad and I watched in horrified silence as seven measly baseball hats drifted to the ice. Seven hats was worse than insulting. It was the fan's declaration that they didn't like Max.

In response, Max didn't even acknowledge the hats. With an indifferent expression, he skated back to the bench. The Jumbotron flashed his accomplishment, and the announcer's voice boomed over the speakers, trying to drum up enthusiasm, but the crowd remained mute.

Dad and I exchanged glances.

"They hate him," he stated.

"They're stupid."

Dad shook his head in disgust. "What does Katrina say?"

"She wants to get him in front of the media."

That was an understatement. Katrina was relentless in her pursuit to get Max back in front of a camera. She emailed me, messaged me or phoned me daily about getting Max's media ban lifted.

"And?" Dad pushed.

Anxiety rolled through me. "The media will only focus on his past and his fight with Joseph Flanynk. Max needs to win the hearts of our fans. Unless he can do that, he is bad for our brand because the media will only focus on the negative."

Dad gave a sharp nod. "I agree."

I sagged in relief, but I wasn't sure if it was because of Dad's approval or if it was because it meant I had bought Max some more time out of the limelight.

He continued, "We sell tickets because the fans love hockey and they love this team. Max needs to win over the love of these fans, or else...."

"Or else what?"

Dad shrugged but didn't answer me. "How do you feel about these upcoming away games?"

"I'm fine."

Immediately after the game, we were taking a bus to the airport to catch a red-eye.

"Ottawa first?"

"Ottawa, Boston, Buffalo, Minnesota and then Detroit."

"Tell Max to watch his back in Minnesota. In fact, the entire team needs to be vigilant. Their hatred there for Max runs deep, and that translates into angry fans and dirty plays."

I shook my head, feeling sad for Max. "Everyone seems to hate him."

"They used to love him. He was a star there."

"And then he beat up Joseph."

"They lost the Stanley Cup and turned on him. The entire city turned on him."

"How?"

He cleared his throat but didn't speak.

"Dad, tell me."

"I heard that he got death threats."

I worked to cover my gasp. "Serious death threats?"

"Enough that it involved the police. He needed police security until he left the city."

This shocked me. "Do you think he'll be in danger there?"

Dad sounded thoughtful. "It might be a good idea if you sit this trip out."

"Why?"

"It will get rough in Minnesota."

"Forget it," I argued, surprising myself. An hour ago, I had been dreading this trip. Now I was pushing to go?

"It doesn't hurt if you don't go."

"I'm not a coward. This is my job. Let me support the team."

Dad stood there for a long moment before nodding. "Be careful."

With my father's warning ringing in my brain, I sat back to watch the rest of the game. Max's focus on the ice and the bench was absolute. He seemed completely indifferent to the fact that our fans didn't seem to like him. How did a person survive going from celebrated celebrity to being hated by the public? Most people I knew would have gone into hiding. It was a testament to his character that he could block out that energy.

CHAPTER 22

WHEN PEOPLE THINK about being a professional hockey player, they only see the huge pay cheques, the celebrity status, and the countless number of hot women ready and willing. What could be better than playing hockey for a living?

I saw firsthand the other side of the profession. I saw the bruised faces, the iced knees, the injuries and the high physical price each player paid. No one talks about how, after playing a 90 minute game, a player needs to get dressed in a suit, talk to the media, get on a bus, wait at an airport, get on a flight and check into a hotel room in some strange city.

Away games were an act of endurance. There was a lack of sleep, long flights, practices in strange arenas and a different hotel room every night.

Tonight, we were in Minnesota. It was our fourth game on the road, and it promised to be a tough one. I sat four rows up from the ice, and the vibe in the arena differed from the previous three games. There was an indescribable energy in the air.

The second Max stepped onto the ice, the Minnesota fans booed. In response to their anger, Max played with unbelievable skill. With my hands pressed over my mouth, I watched as he fought his way to the opponent's net and tipped the puck in.

He scored!

Around me, the fans went batshit crazy. Garbage rained down on the ice including water bottles, garbage, and hot dogs.

Referee whistles screamed as they halted the game to clean up the ice. Attendants tried to throw people out of the game which resulted in a brawl in the stands. Police officers waded into the mess to help remove the worst of the offenders.

Our hockey players stood beside the bench, talking amongst themselves, watching and waiting for the game to begin again.

Dad: What is the hold up? We've been on commercials forever

Me: The fans won't stop throwing stuff on the ice

Dad: Assholes

It seemed like that was the tipping point for the fans. The gloves were off, so to speak. And after that, the game became ugly, rough and bloody. Illegal hits, fighting, and unnecessary force marred the game, which resulted in the penalty boxes being crowded with players.

Dad: Am I watching a boxing match or a game of hockey?

Me: Not sure

Dad: Tell the three blind mice they have for refs to call some of these shots!

Me: I'll get right on that

Dad: Smart ass

Even worse, Joseph Flanynk and his enforcers made it their mission to hit Max every chance they got. Max did his fair share of taking players out against the boards, but all of his hits were legal. Devastating but legal.

The whistle blew. I watched as someone from the opposing team skated up behind Max and slammed him on the back of the head with their stick. He dropped to his knees on the ice, with his arms over his head. I huddled in my seat, scarcely breathing, willing him to move. Another player skated over to help him off the ice. The fans screamed and cheered their pleasure at his exit. Around him, a full-blown brawl started with three of our players and four of theirs.

Dad: Tell me someone will pay for that hit

Me: Game misconduct. Is 33 okay?

Dad: Trainer texted that there is no concussion, he'll return to game

Part of me had almost hoped that he wouldn't. I hated how Max seemed to be the target of every abuse imaginable.

Ten minutes later, when Max returned, I watched in disbelief as fans dumped more garbage over the plexiglass onto our players on the bench which resulted in another pause in the game.

Dad: Tell me that did not just happen

Me: They are posting police around the plexiglass of our bench

Dad: The refs should end the game

Me: Agreed

But we both knew they wouldn't. The NHL was notoriously lenient with their fans and it'd take a lot worse for them to call the game off. NHL fans have rioted in the streets to show their displeasure. Food dumped on players would not stop anything.

The game raged on and with three minutes to go, we were in a tie. Max looked fierce and focused. I held my breath during an amazing breakaway and then he scored a goal that put us ahead. In frustration and rage, Joseph jumped off his bench and skated towards Max wanting to fight. Six Minnesota players against five of our own. By the time the refs pulled both teams apart, everyone was bleeding including two of the refs. They removed Joseph from the game for the second game misconduct of the night and the penalty boxes were overflowing.

The crowd was becoming increasingly insane. People screamed

and jeered. Everyone was standing. I saw a group of guys start to brawl one section over.

Dad called my cell phone.

"Hello?" I shouted.

"What the hell is going on?"

"It's bad."

"The crowd acts like they are about to riot."

People screamed like savages around me. "They might."

"Are you near the ice?"

"Yes."

"I want you to get yourself to the green room. Now."

I didn't need telling twice. "Okay."

"And tell Baxter I want him to call me the second he has a chance."

"Okay."

We won 5-4, and once our team was off the ice, I met up with Baxter.

He wore a pissed off expression. "What?"

"The GM wants you to call him." It sounded marginally more professional than saying, "Call my dad."

CHAPTER 23

THIRTY MINUTES LATER, the players and management gathered together. Baxter wanted everyone to move out to the bus as a group.

Dave, the assistant coach, instructed us. "We head straight to the bus. You keep your head down. Now we can't do anything about the fans lined up, but you can ignore them and whatever they shout at you, is that clear?"

No one said a word.

We opened the door and filed out. The Minnesota fans that were lined up behind waist-high metal gates, went ballistic when they saw the Wolves file out of the dressing room.

"Max, you dumb fuck, why don't you come over here so we can show you how we feel about you?"

"Hey, Max. I heard the reason Flanynk fought you is because you tried to suck his cock."

"Max. Who paid you off to lose the cup for us?"

I kept my head down, willing myself not to acknowledge the angry men that lined up on the other side of the short fence. Baxter shoved past me, knocking me towards the angry men. I righted myself and hands grabbed me. Hands from the other side.

I screamed as more hands yanked at me. My feet lifted off the ground and I felt myself being pulled over the gate. I fought with panic, but they were all too strong, too big. Someone pulled my hair. I could feel my shirt ride up as more of my body got dragged over the gate.

I felt a pressure from behind me as a big body slammed against me. Warm mist sprayed my face. Something connected with my cheek, a fist or an elbow, perhaps. It hit me so hard, I saw stars. People jeered and screamed around me and then, two big, warm hands, from my side of the fence, lifted me. Above the grabby hands, above the fence.

Someone set me down on unsteady legs. I blinked up at Max. Around me chaos ensued. The Wolves reined punches at the men on the other side of the fence. Baxter screamed. Police and security valiantly tried to break everyone up.

I burst into tears.

Max scooped me up into his arms. I covered my face with my hands while he walked me outside towards the bus. He sat me down on one of our boxes. One trainer rushed over.

"Is she cut?"

Max carefully pulled my hands off my face. Concerned blue eyes stared into mine. "I think she's only shaken up."

"Is that her blood?"

"No."

The trainer opened one of our Medi-kits. "Rory, we're going to clean you up."

"Sorry," I managed.

Max grimaced. "For what?"

"Everyone is fighting."

"This wasn't your fault."

I nodded, but tears continued to leak down my face. I felt horrible about what had transpired. One by one, players came trickling out of the stadium. Most of them were bleeding. After the most brutal game, they ended up getting into another brawl, because of me.

The trainers moved into motion. They butterfly taped cuts, provided gauze for nosebleeds and checked pupils for concussions.

Baxter strode out of the stadium with a bloody nose and a ripped suit jacket. He stopped and pointed at me. "This is your fault, and this is why there is no place for women in hockey."

My eyes dropped to the ground. I was the only woman, sitting amongst the wounded, men who had all taken part in a brawl because the opposing team had mauled me.

"That's bullshit," some player called. "I was hoping to get into it with the fans."

"Yeah me too."

"That fight was the best part of my night."

Oh geez. I fought more tears as these men, this team, stood up for me.

Max put a familiar hand on the back of my neck. "Why don't you go get on the bus?"

I nodded and avoiding eye contact with everyone, I climbed onto the bus. I crawled into my seat when something outside caught my eyes. Max was toe-to-toe with Baxter and he wasn't backing down. Baxter screamed. Max responded with a look so lethal it scared me. Apparently, it scared Baxter too because he shook his head and walked off.

I huddled in my seat and held the ice pack to my cheek. I still felt like crying, but because everyone had come to my defense, I sucked it up hard and put on a brave face. No one spoke when they got onto the bus. We drove in complete silence to the airport.

When we got to the airport, we found out that our flight had been delayed due to shit weather. Usually, when we waited for a flight, our team took up residence in the airport bar. Not tonight. Everyone hunkered down in the private security room provided by the airport. The bruised and cut faces of the players gave the impression that they had been to war and lost.

On the corner TV, the sports channel played.

"And now some breaking news from Minnesota, where the Wolves get into a brawl with angry fans."

"Turn it up," someone yelled.

Players stood and watched the screen.

There we were. Walking out of the green room. I looked like a tiny child, surrounded by massive hockey players. And then, for everyone to see, Baxter rushed up behind me, knocking me without care against the fence. Big men, from the other side, reached and grabbed, trying to haul me over the fence.

Max appeared out of nowhere. He somehow shielded me from the worst, holding my body while using one hand to fight off those that worked to pull me over. His fist reigned blows on surprised faces. Responding fists connected with his face, yet he never let go. He kept punching until those angry hands let go. Other players scrambled to get into the mix. Fists flew. Blood sprayed. And then the camera zoomed back to the reporter.

"The female in the middle of that mix was none other than Rory Ashford. She is the daughter of the Vancouver Wolves' GM."

"Turn it off." A player shook his head in disgust.

The television snapped off.

All the eyes shifted to me. I swallowed, feeling stupid.

"You okay?" a player asked.

I nodded.

"You're all right. If that had been my girlfriend, she'd be hysterical right now."

"Same," someone else agreed.

I nodded, working to keep all the emotion off my face. "Thanks."

I made my way to the farthest seat away from everyone. I curled up on the seat and turned my body away from the group. I felt vulnerable, weak, and on the verge of my own hysterical tears.

My phone was blowing up. Two calls from Dad and about a million texts.

Me: I'm fine

Dad: Tell.Baxter.To.Call.Me

The last thing I needed was Dad coming to my defense.

Me: Dad. Please. It's tense right now

Dad: I knew it was a mistake to let you go

Me: If it wasn't for Logan, it could have been way worse

Dad: Call me

Me: I have to go, they are boarding

A slight lie, but I knew if I talked to Dad, I would begin to cry and I probably wouldn't stop. My cheek was on fire, and I felt dirty, angry, and completely overwhelmed. I avoided making eye contact with anyone.

I sat there, pretending to work on my phone, until they called us for boarding.

I USUALLY SAT in the front, in business class, with the rest of management. When I walked to my seat, I saw Baxter sitting in the seat next to my assigned seat.

Yeah, that wasn't happening.

I carried on, heading to the back, where the players sat. I picked a random seat, jammed my bag in the baggage bin and crawled over to the window seat. I put on my seatbelt and covered myself with the blanket I stole from business class. The players filed in after me. Everyone left me alone. No one sat beside me, probably because I was curled up in a tiny ball and staring out the window. My body language screamed 'leave me alone'.

Someone shoved their bag in the bin above my seat. Then a familiar masculine citrus scent hit my nostrils.

I glanced up at Max. He had the start of a black eye and a split lip.

We didn't speak when he eased his big body into the seat beside me. I watched as the flight attendant walked us through the usual safety procedures.

"You okay?" Max's voice was low.

I knew he was asking about the fight, but I pretended he was talking about the takeoff.

"I still don't like to fly."

The plane screamed down the runway and my hands clenched around the armrests. Beneath the blanket, Max peeled my hand off the cold metal and squeezed it in his big, warm hand.

"Thank you," I breathed, keeping my eyes on my lap.

"So, have you been avoiding me?" his voice was low.

"No." I glanced at him and saw a true question in his gaze. "Yes. Maybe."

"Why?"

"Because you told me to."

Blue eyes clashed with mine, but we didn't speak.

I wanted to ask him how he was doing after tonight. Tonight, his old team, men who used to be close friends, had done everything in their power to hurt him. Fans who used to adore him showed their hate. If that was me, I'd feel crushed.

I fell into a fitful sleep, and when I woke up, my hand was still in his.

CHAPTER 24
TWEET

Hockey Gurl @hockeygurl
Cleaning up the disaster in the wake of Rory is a full-time job. Not only can she not do her job, but she makes everything a hundred times harder for everyone around her. #MinnesotaFight

---

CHAPTER 25

IT WAS ALMOST the middle of the night when we got to our hotel in Detroit. I took a shower as soon as I got to my room, but despite feeling overwhelmed, I refused to let myself cry. I felt violated, vulnerable and alone.

I will not cry.

Ashfords do not cry.

I pulled a tank top and a pair of thin pajama bottoms on and studied my reflection in the mirror. A faint bruise was beginning to show on my cheekbone. My appearance was as sad as I felt. Baxter was right. I didn't belong here. This job was so beyond my skill set, it wasn't even funny.

A slow knock sounded on the door.

"Who is it?"

"Max."

I swung the door open. He wore a pair of jeans and a blue t-shirt. He stood there, taking in my night attire. I crossed my arms over my chest, feeling both vulnerable and exposed beneath his intense observation.

"Can I come in?"

I held the door open wide and watched as he walked into the room. I shut the door after him, wondering why he was here.

He stood there, studying me. "I wanted to check up on you."

"I'm okay."

He stepped closer and tilted my chin up, so he could study my cheek. I struggled to hold onto my emotions in the face of his concern. Light fingertips grazed around the bruise.

My bottom lip trembled.

I shook my head, unable to meet his eyes. "Don't, Max."

"Come here," he pulled me against his chest. I felt his big arms wrap around me, making me feel safe and protected. And then I burst into noisy tears.

He moved us to the bed and pulled me onto his lap. I wrapped my arms around his neck and wept. All the fear, anger and indignation of the night poured out of me. A big hand rubbed my back while I released all my pent-up stress and emotion. I cried until there were no tears left.

I lifted my wet face from his neck, swiping away the tears with the back of my hand. "Sorry."

"Feel better?" His hand cupped my neck and his thumb rubbed tears from my cheek.

I drowned in his blue gaze. "Yeah."

"Come on, let's get you into bed."

I stood up and like that night in North Dakota, he moved to pull back the covers. I climbed in.

He pulled the covers up over me, tucking me in like a child.

"Night."

I grabbed his large hand. "Will you please stay with me until I fall asleep?"

What?

I did not understand why those words blurted out of me. I could see the hesitation on his face.

"Please, Max?"

He kicked off his shoes, clicked off the lamp and then I felt him move easily over me to the other side of the bed.

I squeaked when he grabbed me by the waist and hauled me back against his warm chest. I shut my eyes in complete bliss as I snuggled further back against his body.

"Thank you."

His lips were against my hair. "Just until you fall asleep."

A gusty sigh escaped out of me. Never in my life, had I felt more safe, more protected or more cocooned from the world.

"I like you," I mumbled. And then sleep claimed me.

When I woke up, he was gone.

CHAPTER 26

TWO DAYS after I got home, I sat in another insufferable coaches meeting. I dreaded these meetings. Baxter's hatred of Max was so plain, it was to the point of being uncomfortable for anyone required to listen to him vent about all of Max's shortcomings. Most of which Baxter made up.

At the end of the meeting, everyone stood up and gathered their things. Dad walked into the room.

"Baxter, may I have a word?"

Baxter paused, fear flitting across his face. "Sure."

The other coaches filed towards the door with haste. I made quick work of gathering up my papers and almost made it to the door when Dad's voice rang out. "Rory, you can stay."

I stared longingly at the door before shutting the door and turning around.

"Have a seat, Baxter." Dad's voice was deceptively casual.

Baxter sat. Dad leaned against the wall, his arms crossed. I hovered between the table and the door, in no-man's-land.

"Baxter, how do you think the last road trip went?"

Baxter's eyes widened. "We won four out of the five games. No major injuries. Despite the small incident in Minnesota, it went well."

Dad studied the floor and made a noise. "So, when you knocked my daughter into a crowd of drunk, angry men, and they dragged her body over a fence wanting to tear her from limb to limb, you'd consider that a small incident?"

Baxter's eyes flitted to mine. "I consider that everyone got away safe and there were no major injuries, so it was resolved."

Dad nodded again. "Twenty-three of my most valuable employees, whom I pay over $96 million dollars' worth of wages to per year, had to step in and engage in a full-on brawl over that incident."

Baxter held my gaze. Hatred sparked in his eyes. "Yes, they did."

"Did I not talk to you about getting extra security to escort our team out of the building?"

"We had it."

"Yet, you were the catalyst who pushed Rory into the crowd."

"This is Logan's fault."

Dad tilted his head, his face a mask of calm. I knew Dad. The cooler he appeared on the outside, the more volatile his emotions ran beneath the surface. "From what I could see on the tape, Logan is the one who stepped forward and saved Rory."

"I meant, none of this would have transpired if it wasn't for his sordid past in Minnesota. He's the reason the fans were so angry and worked up. And furthermore, I think it might warrant adding that we've never had a female accompany our team. Historically, we've had men who can handle those kinds of situations."

The bastard!

Dad nodded. "I see. So, you believe that perhaps Rory's job would be better suited for a man?"

Baxter flushed. "I'm saying that this world is rough. And no fault of her own, but because of her gender, she's an easy target."

"An easy target." Dad measured each word out.

"I'm not saying this is my opinion," Baxter protested. "I'm only voicing the common concern everyone has about this situation. I mean, there is even a twitter account tweeting about Rory and these issues. These are going concerns."

Dad ignored his comment about the social media. "I will not stop Rory from traveling with the team. So, if you're unable to protect her, then find someone on the fucking team that will."

"Yes, sir."

"Dad," I protested, finding myself siding with Baxter on this one. I was way over my head. I didn't belong in this world, no matter how much Dad wanted me to belong.

Dad turned his attention towards me. "Make this work, Rory, or I will hire a personal security team to accompany you on all these trips."

Which would be worse than hiring a babysitter.

I nodded.

Dad leaned onto the table and stared down at Baxter. "If you can't make this work, I'll find someone who can make this work."

Baxter sat frozen, staring up at Dad. "I'll make it work."

Dad straightened up. "Good. Good talk."

His phone rang. "I have to take this."

He stepped out of the room.

I stood there, clutching my papers to my chest, like a school girl. Baxter turned on me.

"Couldn't help but go running to Daddy, hey?"

"I didn't talk to him about Minnesota."

He rolled his eyes. "Do us all a fucking favor and walk. No one wants you here. Not the players. Not the coaching staff. No one."

My face burned, but I didn't speak.

Dad popped his head back into the room. "Are we good?"

I nodded.

He eyeballed Baxter.

Baxter nodded. "Got this covered, boss."

Dad didn't smile. "Great. Talk to you both later."

I turned to leave.

Baxter got one last shot it. "Try to stay away from the players. You get on their nerves."

I stiffened, but I didn't turn around. Face burning, I walked out of the room.

I hated Baxter, but I feared he was telling me the truth. I wasn't accepted by the team. No one gave me a hard time, but how did I know that they all didn't hate me?

I vowed to keep my head down and not bother anyone. Especially the players.

TWO DAYS LATER, Baxter sent me an email asking me to attend the next player meeting. The invite surprised me, but I decided that perhaps he was extending the olive branch after the awkward talk we had with Dad.

I felt excited. I hadn't seen Max since that night in the hotel. I was wearing a pink fuzzy angora sweater and a pair of skinny cigarette pants with spiky black heels.

"Rory, come sit at the front," Baxter motioned me to the front of the room. I preferred the back seats, in case I wanted a quick escape, but since Baxter was trying so hard, I weaved my way to the front of the room and sat in the front chair.

Players entered the room. I regretted the pink sweater. It was too fluffy and too feminine. I felt like a bunny in a roomful of wolves. I needed to rethink some of my wardrobe choices. Perhaps wear more neutral or dark colors that would help me blend in.

Baxter showed a video of last week's games. Then the offense coach talked to the players about two new offensive plays they wanted to try. With my head bent over my book, I made careful notes. I had some serious doubts that our third offensive line could handle the second play. I chewed on my pen and made a note to ask Dad about it later.

I could sense that someone was watching me. I lifted my eyes. Off to the side of the room, Max leaned against the wall. His penetrating gaze focused on me. I flushed and ducked my head back over my book.

The man was way too hot. I swallowed, remembering how he had held me while I sobbed before tucking me into bed. Being cuddled by Max was almost a life changing experience. The sheer size of him, surrounding me, protecting me had made it one of the best cuddles in my history of cuddles.

"What are you writing in your book?"

Baxter had paused his talk and now stared at me.

"Me?"

"You are bent over your little diary writing so intently." He glanced up at the room, with a smile on his face, inviting everyone into his joke. "We all want to know what kind of notes you write in there."

I shook my head.

"Yes," he motioned for me to come up and stand beside him. "Come. Come and talk to us. We're interested in what you have to say."

I could feel myself begin to sweat in my fucking angora sweater. Oh shit. Dad would kill me. He didn't want me to talk in these meetings.

"I'm not supposed to talk."

Baxter's face broke out into a huge smile. "That's okay. We won't tell anyone."

If I refused, I'd be dubbed a coward. But if took part, I might sound like a fool. I'd rather be a fool than a coward. With a flushed face, I stood up, and stared down at my notes.

"Well, I made notes about the second play for the third offensive line."

"Go on," Baxter was all smiles.

My shy gaze skimmed over the group. "Number 12 shoots left. And this play puts him far too deep in the pocket on the right side. It'd be an awkward angle for him. I thought we could flip or reverse the play, but if he doesn't get the shot, and he has to send it back to the center man, the angle would be so sharp, that I doubt the center could manage a slap shot. It'd be a serious disadvantage. But," I chewed on my pen. "It would work, if the leftie zipped around the net and took his shot on the other side."

I fanned my face with my book and squinted at the room. Players all sat there, stock still, staring at me.

I shook my head. "It's dumb. I wanted to ask my dad, I mean, ask the GM about it."

Baxter had his arms crossed, and he wore a scowl on his face.

The offensive coach stepped forward. "That's a brilliant idea. We had the same questions about #12 but we didn't know how it'd work until we ran the play." He stared at the whiteboard and then grinned at his two assistant coaches. "Why didn't we think of this?"

I glanced up at Max. His head rested on his chest, and his arms were crossed. His shoulder shook. Was he laughing?

Baxter stepped forward. "Well, I guess that solves that mystery." He sounded sour. "One more announcement, Rory."

"Okay."

He gestured widely to the men in the room. "On top of everything we ask you to do, the GM has come forward and asked for a volunteer to play personal bodyguard to Rory."

My mouth parted in horror. *That* is not what Dad had meant. Had he? The way Baxter said it, he made it sound so awful.

I shook my head. "Unnecessary."

"Yes, Rory. The GM insisted we babysit, sorry, we protect you."

I shook my head at the room. "Total misunderstanding. I think I'm more than fine to take care of myself. In fact, my job is to take care of you. All of you."

Baxter rubbed his hands together. "So, do we have any volunteers?"

One player spoke up. "We all have her back. That goes without saying."

I could feel sweat rolling down my back. My face was flushed hot.

"Thank you. That was proven the other night. Thank you."

I scrambled to my seat to grab my bag. I needed to get out of this meeting.

"I'll do it," a familiar voice spoke.

My back snapped up so fast, I almost gave myself whiplash. Blue eyes met mine.

"No!" I spoke with more force than necessary.

Baxter bestowed a cold smile between the two of us. "Logan, you have been assigned to ensure that Rory remains safe, as termed by the GM."

Mortified, I picked my way over a sea of big long legs, in a desperate attempt to leave this meeting.

I'd deal with Max later. And stop this ridiculous notion that I needed to be babysat.

I got to the back of the room and glanced over my shoulder. Max's eyes tracked me. I gave him my best "WTF" look and then fled.

CHAPTER 27
TWEET

Hockey Gurl @hockeygurl

Rory Ashford treats the hockey team like they are her personal bodyguards. She feels like the team is there to serve every one of her needs - including sexual. She makes everyone's life a living hell, but no one dares say no to her demands. #PlayersHateHer

---

CHAPTER 28

I MOVED along the cement corridor of the stadium. My heels echoed in the silence of the big dome. I needed to talk to Dad. This whole 'protect Rory' thing was ridiculous. He couldn't ask the players to babysit me if he wanted them to respect me. That whole meeting had been embarrassing and Baxter had made me sound like a joke. The more I thought about it, the angrier I got. Dad was half the problem. He couldn't expect me to work in a professional capacity when he treated me like a child in front of everyone.

"Rory." Max spoke from behind me.

I did *not* want to talk to Max. His knack in this world was to see me at my most emotional. Why couldn't he bump into me in the morning when my make-up was fresh and nothing had yet gone wrong? No, the guy was always there, observing me when my plane was crashing, or I was being mauled by a mob. How was he ever going to want more from me when I was a walking billboard of big emojis?

"Not now." I doubled my speed.

"Rory." I glanced over my shoulder. He moved with deceptive casualness, but he was gaining on me.

"What!" I spun around on him. "What?"

His eyes crinkled with amusement as he took in my flushed face. "In a rush?"

When I stopped running, all my emotions caught up with me. I put my hand on my forehead. "Gah!"

"What?"

"Everything! No one respects me."

His eyes narrowed. "What are you talking about?"

"Were we not in the same meeting?"

"Still not following."

I waved my hand around. "That whole thing with Baxter when he made me try to explain hockey to a bunch of professional hockey players?"

"You didn't just try."

I thought of all the players faces as they stared back at me after I spoke. "They all stared at me like I had three heads. It's obvious I don't know what I am talking about."

"I think you caught them off guard by showing them how much you do know."

"It doesn't matter because Baxter ruined everything by asking for someone to babysit me."

"No one sees it like that."

"How do you know?!"

"Because we talked about it."

I blinked and paused. "What does that mean?"

He shrugged but didn't answer.

I put my hand on my hip. "If you're talking about me, it matters."

"The guys want to keep you safe."

"Yes, because so many of them were rushing to volunteer."

"It's because of me."

I froze. "What does that mean?"

"They knew it's my job."

That caught me off guard. "What is your job?"

"To have your back."

This conversation was confusing me. "You don't have to protect me! I can handle myself."

"Rory, why is this such a big deal?"

"Because I don't want to be different."

"You are different."

"What does that mean?"

He thought about his answer. "You're not good in fist fights, so we watch over you. That's the difference."

"Max! There you are! Max!" A high-pitched female voice pierced the air.

We both lifted our heads.

Katrina was on the next level and she waved as she worked her way down the stairs towards us.

"I wish I belonged here," sadness tinged my voice.

"You do." He held my gaze.

Katrina ruined the moment as she rushed up to us.

"Max, I've been searching all over for you!"

"Katrina."

Katrina stared down her nose at me. I knew she wanted me to leave, but for that reason alone, I stood my ground.

She tossed her head. "So, as you know, the Autumn Ashford Gala is coming up and your attendance is mandatory."

Max didn't answer.

She reached out and put her hand on his forearm. "I know you don't love these events, so I thought we could make it a work event. I could go as your date and help you navigate the gala. You know, introduce you to the right people, that kind of thing."

Max winced. "You don't have to do that."

Her laughter echoed through the corridor. "Nonsense. I've reserved us two seats at one of the best tables."

I almost admired her for how she so effectively backed Max into a corner.

"Which table is that?" I joined the conversation.

She beamed up at Max. "It's the hockey royalty table. Rory and her plus one will be seated there."

What the hell? I hadn't been planning on bringing a date. "You must be mistaken. I haven't bought tickets for this event."

Her singsong voice grated on my nerves. "I ran into your mother. She said you had a hot date lined up, and she was picking up your tickets for you."

Oh *shit*. Mom was matchmaking again. She had told me that her friends had lots of nice sons who were worthy of dating me, but I had laughed her off. It appears she had taken that as a concession for her to proceed.

Max's eyes zeroed in on my face. "Sure, Katrina. I'll attend with you."

He might as well have sucker punched me. Excuse *fucking* me? I never thought he'd agree to go with her. I felt myself flush hot.

He held my gaze for a moment longer than necessary.

She batted her eyelashes. "Great because I have the most amazing dress I'm dying to wear."

I couldn't take another second of this conversation anymore. "I look forward to seeing you both at the gala. If you'll excuse me, please."

Without letting either of them speak, I turned and walked away. Katrina was worse than a puck bunny. Why couldn't I get this guy out of my brain? Now I would have to sit across from them for the entire night and watch them flirt. Maybe I could skip the event? Maybe I didn't have to attend?

"RORY, DON'T BE PISSED."

I stared out the car window and worked to control my frustration. "Dad, how do you expect me to gain respect in this industry if you treat me like your daughter?"

He gave a sharp laugh. "You are my daughter."

"If I was your son, would you ask someone on the team to have my back?"

"That's different."

"It's not!" I argued. "And not only was it embarrassing, but it undermined me. It made me seem childish and incapable."

"I'm sorry Baxter's delivery was so poor."

"Dad, you can't treat me like someone that needs to be protected with kid gloves and then expect me to be one of the guys."

"You need protecting."

"No! What I need from you is to show me how to protect myself."

We both did the stare down.

"Rory, when I saw you on the news getting almost attacked by that mob, I thought my heart would stop."

"Dad. You need to pick. Either you want me in this hockey world and you help me figure out how to survive, or you let me go. But you expect me to thrive in this world while being hog-tied in bubble wrap."

"Don't be ridiculous. I'm not trying to bubble wrap you." His words rang hollow.

"The position you've put me in is unfair. So, I am your protégée or I'm your daughter, but I can't be both."

Dad turned his face away from me and the rest of the drive home we sat in silence.

CHAPTER 29

"OH RORY," Mom stood behind me, her hands over her mouth.

"Do I look okay?" I turned and smoothed the fabric of my gown over my hips. My elegant, spaghetti strap, floor length blood-red ball gown fit me perfectly. I had piled my long hair up on the top of my head in an elaborate twist of braids and curls. My makeup was dark and dramatic, with red pouty lips and dark eyes.

Teardrop diamond earrings and a diamond bracelet completed the look.

Tears welled in Mom's eyes. "You're gorgeous."

"I want to stay home."

"This is the Autumn Ashford Gala! Staying home is not an option. What time is Calder picking you up?"

I rolled my eyes. I had been forced to invite Calder, the son of my parents' friends, because I lacked a social life and had no prospect of a real date. I grew up with Calder. When we were kids, he used to chase me around with his boogers. Calder was more annoying brother than date material.

"He said he'd be here at 6 PM."

"Helene," Dad's voice boomed from downstairs. "Time to go."

She leaned forward and kissed my cheek. "I'll see you there."

CALDER WAS 30 MINUTES LATE. He strolled into the house like the spoiled aristocrat he was with his $4000 tuxedo and coiffed hair. He was an heir baby, and he seemed to think that was his full-time job. He would have been gorgeous if he didn't have that life-is-so-boring sneer on his face.

"Hey, Calder," I stood watching as he pulled something out of his pocket.

"Your parents gone?"

"Yes."

"Want to smoke a joint?"

"Excuse me?"

"Marijuana."

My eyes widened. "Not really."

"Do you have an ashtray?"

"Do you mind smoking outside?"

He rolled his eyes. "Sure. Whatever."

I stood, shivering, outside the front step, watching as he smoked his joint.

"How's life?" he winced as he sucked on the thin burning rolled paper.

"Good."

"Heard your old man was making you work."

Oh, *freaking* hell. Tonight was going to be long.

"I don't mind."

"Yeah, you getting some on the side?"

"Excuse me?" My voice sounded like ice.

"Hey, don't get mad. Just repeating what I'm reading on social media."

My heart stuttered. "What have you been reading?"

"Hockey gurl's tweets about you always go viral. The last tweet was retweeted over 45,000 times."

I felt my stomach twist into a ball. "What was the tweet?"

He shrugged. "Something about how you like to fuck hockey players."

Oh, sweet baby Jesus.

Calder squinted at me. "Ready to go?"

Actually, I want to go hide under my bed.

I took a fortifying breath. "Ready."

THE AUTUMN ASHFORD GALA was one of Vancouver's most elite and expensive charity events. Tickets sold for $1000 a seat and every year, the tickets sold out within hours.

Arriving unfashionably late, Calder and I walked into the foyer of the huge banquet hall. The front was empty as most of the guests had already moved to the dining area.

"Hold up, Roar." Calder used my childhood nickname, as he pulled me towards the champagne bar.

He downed two glasses of champagne before we made our way into the main hall. People were all seated and talking, but thank fuck the dinner prayer hadn't started.

Despite the fact that Calder was a complete hooligan, his manners were impeccable. He first greeted Dad and Mom and then, gave his own parents, who sat at the next table, a nod before he turned his attention on me. He helped me sit down and then, with a small flourish, sat down next to me.

I glanced up at the table and the breath nearly sucked out of my chest. Max in a tuxedo was more than breath-taking. It almost hurt how gorgeous he was. His dark, unimpressed gaze focused only on Calder.

When Max turned his attention to me, I could see the question in his eyes. I raised one eyebrow and motioned to Katrina with my eyes.

He had no right to judge my date, not when he had a barracuda sitting next to him.

Dinner started. Calder ordered two double scotches in succession, but managed to sound both intelligent and business savvy when he discussed the market with Dad.

Mom leaned over and whispered in my ear. "Calder is very handsome."

I whispered back. "Mom, stop it."

She reached out and squeezed my hand. "Is Katrina sleeping with that hockey player?"

I froze. "Max?"

"Yes, that's his name." Her smile grew. "He's handsome and she seems besotted with him."

The irony! It was *killing* me.

"I don't know if they're dating."

"Well, they make a gorgeous couple."

I glanced over at Katrina and Max. As she leaned over Max to talk to the person on the other side of him, she pressed her entire body against his. I mean, she might as well climb into his lap. Bitterness washed over me. Mom was right. They were a gorgeous couple.

I thought about that night I saw him flirting with the puck bunny. *This* was who he was. He told me that he didn't want to settle down. Seeing him with another woman was torture, but seeing him with Katrina devastated me. Anyone but her!

Calder slung his arm around me and put his lips to my ear. "So, is the guy you're fucking the one who is giving me the death stare from across the table?"

"Calder!"

He pulled back and his face was only a couple inches from my face. He stared into my eyes like a lover. "Just wondering. Since the brood he's with is a fox."

I put my hand in his chest to push him back. Instead, he captured my hand and pressed it against his chest.

"What are you doing?" I whispered, annoyed.

Calder smiled and stared at me for a few more seconds before he spoke. "I'm making your lover jealous hoping he comes after you, which will give me a decent opening to fuck the fox."

The thought of Calder and Katrina disappearing, made me feel more happy than it should.

"Why would you do that?"

His eyes dropped to my mouth, like a lover would do. "Team work, Roar. Team work."

"I'm afraid your Fox has eyes only for him."

Calder laughed and pulled back. He grabbed my hand and without taking his eyes off my face, brought my hand up to his lips. "Is that a challenge? Do we want to put a wager on that bet?"

He was being so ridiculous, I couldn't help it. I burst out laughing. "What is the bet?"

"If I can fuck her, you get me and my boys some tickets to the game the next time Minnesota comes to town. Close up to the ice. We want to see lots of blood."

"You're sick, but yeah. Deal."

He winked at me and mouthed, "Thank me later."

I was still smiling when I glanced over at Max.

Max stared at both of us, with unabashed hostility directed toward Calder. His jaw was tight and his gaze was flat and cold.

Katrina, as if she could sense the tension between us, leaned over Max. "Would you mind accompanying me outside?"

CHAPTER 30

CALDER LIFTED HIS HEAD, like a predator catching the scent of his prey. "You know, I was going to get a touch of fresh air. Would you like me to accompany you wherever you are going?"

Katrina's eyes widened. I could tell she was both flattered and impressed. She was weighing her options between a disinterested hockey player and an interested member of an elite world she so desperately wanted to be part of. Her ambitions won out. "That'd be appreciated."

Calder stood up with a flourish and walked around the table to pull out her chair. I watched as he tucked her arm over his. As they walked away, I could hear her girlish giggle.

Max continued to give me the death stare.

I took a sip of water.

He continued to glare, all riled up.

I glanced around the table. We were the only ones that remained sitting. Most people were mingling before the dance portion of the evening started. The band started the first song of the night.

"Max, why are you trying to kill me with your gaze?"

"Your date is a complete punk."

I played indifferent. "Calder?"

His eyes looked away from me for a long moment before returning to my face. "He's one of the Baby Men."

"You and Katrina make a lovely couple."

"We're not a couple."

"She doesn't seem to have gotten the memo."

He stood up and walked around to my side of the table and offered me his hand. "Would you like to dance?"

His shift in mood threw me. Nerves jangled in the pit of my belly as I placed my hand in his and let him lead me out to the dance floor where couples already moved together to the music.

The song changed to *Unforgettable* by Nat King Cole and Natalie Cole. I stifled my gasp when Max swung me into his arms. One hand wrapped around my waist, and the other hand held my hand. I tentatively put my hand on his shoulder. Together we started to dance. Max was light on his feet, and confident in his ability to guide me around the dance floor.

I stared up at him in amazement.

"What?" His eyes caressed my mouth.

"You're a good dancer."

White teeth flashed in amusement. "You're surprised?"

"A bit."

"I've got a few talents."

"What else?"

He spun me around. "Well, I make a mean grilled cheese."

I tried to imagine Max cooking. The thought of him in the kitchen with a pair of oven mitts was somehow both domestic and intoxicating. "You should try my pancakes."

"I guess we have breakfast and lunch covered."

I could feel the heat of his hand on my back through the thin fabric of my dress. "It appears we do."

His blue gaze clashed with mine. "What about you? Any secret hidden talents I should know about?"

"I used to belong to a marching band."

A smile spread over his face. "A marching band?"

"I'll have you know that in grade 6, that was the epitome of cool."

"Did you play an instrument?"

"No, I twirled the baton."

His smile was close to a laugh. "That's adorable. Was that a life-long passion of yours?"

"The tassel boots and sparkly outfits drew me in."

"Will you baton twirl for me?"

"Only if you make a grilled cheese sandwich for me."

His eyes were on my mouth again. "I think we could make that a date."

I gasped as he spun me around again. I clung to his shoulder.

"You need to warn a girl."

"And miss that little noise you make?"

Our eyes met again. "Max."

"So, not sure if I mentioned this, but your date's a punk."

My smile broadened. "Funny. He was hand picked by my mom."

"So, you're not dating him?"

"Not that I know of."

"How do you know him?"

"Old family friend. I've known Calder since we were toddlers. Why do you think he's a punk?"

He cleared his throat.

"What, Max?"

I could see his internal debate on how much he wanted to tell me. "I think your date is trying to sleep with my date."

"Yes, he told me his plan."

Shock crossed his face. "You don't mind?"

"Do you?"

"Couldn't care less."

"Same."

"Oh."

"Yeah."

We both smiled.

"Excuse me," Dad's voice spoke from beside me. "But I think this next dance belongs to me."

"Absolutely." Max let go of me and stepped back. "Thank you for the dance, Miss Ashford."

"Thank you."

Dad swept me into his arms. We moved across the dance floor in silence.

"Rory, how is your night?"

"It's good."

"Where did Calder disappear to?"

"Not sure."

His eyes were on my face. "Be careful."

"Dad, I'm not actually dating Calder. You do know that Mom set us up tonight?"

"I'm not talking about Calder."

"Who are you talking about?"

He raised his eyebrows at me.

"Max?" I sputtered. "That's ridiculous. He's a hockey player."

"Yes, and you'd be wise to remember that."

I felt my heart sink at his warning while working to cover up my feelings. "I think he felt bad for me that Calder took off."

"Even if Max wasn't part of our team, I wouldn't approve of him."

"Why don't you like him? He's an incredible hockey player."

"He reminds me of someone."

Oh, this old story again. I refrained from rolling my eyes. "Who?"

"It's in the past."

He piqued my interest. "Was he a hockey player?"

"Come on," he led me off the dance floor. "Your mom is waiting for me."

I wanted to tell Dad he wasn't giving Max a fair chance, but this was not the time nor the place for that conversation.

"I'm going to the powder room."

Dad kissed me on the temple.

I made my way to the ladies room to freshen my lipstick. Voices from behind stall doors were talking.

"Did you see the latest tweet by Hockey Gurl?"

I froze and listened.

"No what?"

"Apparently Miss Stuck Up has been fucking her way through the entire team."

"Shut up."

"Someone told me she threatens the players with their contracts, forcing them to service her. They said one night she had three different guys."

"Are you serious?"

"Yeah, and even though she's cute, the players hate her. They see her coming and they dread it when it's their turn."

"That's disgusting."

"Yeah, well, I heard she's a total nymphomaniac."

I heard a toilet flush. I tossed my lipstick in my bag and fled. Tears blinded me. *That* was the rumor that was going around about me? Mortification washed over me. Did Dad know?

I bumped into a broad chest and lifted my head when two strong arms grabbed my shoulders.

"Rory."

I stared up at Max's concerned face. Did he hear these rumors? Did he believe these things about me?

"Sorry, excuse me."

"Rory," he took my hand and pulled me off to the side. He leaned against the wall. "Talk."

I shook my head. "Nothing to talk about."

"You're upset."

I steeled my lip, willing myself not to cry. "It's nothing."

"Did someone say something to you?"

"Not to my face."

"What?"

"Have you heard of Hockey Gurl?"

Max's face darkened. "Don't tell me you're buying into that shit."

"You've heard of her?"

"Rory, everyone knows she's some idiot spouting her mouth off."

My shoulders sagged. "She says such terrible things about me."

"Lies. Everyone knows they are lies."

"How do you know?"

He shrugged. "Why do you think anyone believes that shit?"

"I heard two women talking about it in the washroom and trust me, they believe what they are reading!"

"Fuck em."

I swallowed. Thinking.

"I mean it. You're tough-as-nails-Rory-Ashford. You're not going to let a tweet take you down."

I squinted up at him. "We both know I'm not tough."

"Why do you say that?"

"You've seen me at my worst."

"And that's how I know you're tough."

I took a long-winded sigh. "Thanks."

"No one believes that shit."

I knew he was lying to make me feel better, but knowing he didn't believe those lies, made all the difference.

"Okay."

He studied me. "You okay?"

"Yeah. I guess I should get back to the table. In case my date shows up."

He snorted. "You do that."

Without turning back, I walked away from Max, but I felt strong. He was right. There was no reason for me to get wound up about lies that were being posted on social media.

When I returned to the table, Calder and Katrina had yet to return. Dad was off to the side, talking to someone and Mom sat by herself.

"Hey, Mom."

"Darling," she smiled up at me. "I saw you dancing and might I say that you were gorgeous out there."

"Thanks."

"Come," she stood up. "Time to do the rounds."

I protested. "Mom."

"Rory, when you host a gala, you need to be a gracious hostess."

I groaned.

The next two hours, I worked the crowd with Mom. She knew everyone. She said hello to various players and their significant others. She talked to the coaching staff and their wives. She tried to speak to everyone. I admired how she seemed to have a personal connection with everyone, but it was exhausting following in her wake.

I stiffened when we approached Baxter's table.

"Helene!" Baxter's face was red, compliments of the amber liquor in the glass he clutched.

"Hello Baxter and Carly," she bent down to kiss a woman who wore a sour expression. "You look lovely tonight."

"I see that you are as gorgeous as ever, Helene." Baxter ogled my mom through his whiskey goggles. "Hey," he caught sight of me. His tone sounded jovial despite the cold glint in his eyes. "How's my favorite assistant GM in training?"

"Hello, Baxter." I tried to infuse warmth into my voice.

Mom turned towards me. "Have you met Baxter's wife, Carly?"

I reached forward and shook her limp hand. "Pleased to meet you."

Instead of responding, she vacantly stared at me.

After a few minutes of painstaking conversation, we moved away from their table.

"You missed your calling," I could not keep the dry tone from my voice.

She smiled at me. "And what is that?"

"Politician."

"I enjoy talking to people."

"I could move to a deserted island and I don't think I'd miss talking."

She touched my face with her palm. "Rory, you look exhausted."

I yawned. "I could sleep for a week."

"Why don't you take the car home and send it back to us. We will be here for a couple more hours."

I glanced around, wondering if I should find Calder. "Yeah, okay."

"Let me walk you out."

We got to the front foyer, and I saw Max leaning up against the bar. He was talking to another player. Calder and Katrina were nowhere in sight.

"Mom, did something happen between a player and Dad?"

"What do you mean?"

"Dad doesn't like Max Logan, because he says he reminds him of someone."

Mom's eyes studied Max and then it was like the ball dropped. She put a hand over her mouth. "Oh no."

"Mom! What is it?"

She shook her head. "Nothing."

"You know who Dad is talking about? You know who Max reminds him of?"

Mom squeezed my hand too tight. "Don't go there, Rory, please."

"Go where?"

"Leave the past in the past. And stay away from Max Logan."

I protested when someone put their arm around my waist.

"Calder!" Mom gave a relieved smile to my dinner date. "We were searching for you."

I unwrapped his grabby hand from my waist. "I'm going home."

"Great," he pulled out his phone. "Let me text my driver." He lifted his head up. "He'll be out front in ten minutes. Just going to get a drink, want one?"

I shook my head. "No thanks."

Mom and I watched as he made his way to the bar. I turned back to Mom. "Please tell me what you are talking about, Mom. This is important. Dad is so biased against Max for no reason other than he reminds him of someone? This is Max's career, Mom."

She shook her head. "Sorry, Rory. I can't."

"Mom. That's not fair."

"Please, Rory. I'm asking you. Drop it."

"Fine."

She gave me a quick hug. "Have a good night."

I watched as she moved away from me. What had happened? And who did Max remind them of? What was going on? And why wouldn't they talk about it with me?

A shout sounded behind me. I spun around in time to see Calder shove Max against the chest. Max didn't budge and stepped closer, towering over Calder. Calder wasn't backing down. Another hockey player stepped in between them and pushed Max away from the bar. Max lifted his hands in disgust and walked away.

I rushed to Calder's side and hissed. "What are you doing?"

He smoothed his hair back off his forehead. "Your lover is feisty."

"Okay, let's go. Right now."

"I'm not done with my drink."

I pulled the glass out of his limp fingers. "You're done."

"You're so bossy." But he slung his arm around my shoulder. "Lead the way."

Once we got into the car, I turned on him. "What happened between you and Max?"

"Loverboy?"

I ignored his jab. "Did you say something that upset him?"

"He seems quite protective of you."

"Calder!"

"Relax. It's not my fault if your boyfriend can't take a joke."

I rolled my eyes and stared out the window.

"Roar, don't be like that." He tossed something towards me. "What is this?"

I picked up something lacy. In horror, I realized that I was holding a pair of female panties. I tossed them back at him, hitting him on the face. "Calder!"

"I have a secret about the fox," he taunted as he held the fabric to his nose and breathed deeply.

"Those are Katrina's? You slept with her?"

"Let's say, based on my performance tonight, you owe me tickets for more than one game."

"Ewww."

"She's not the innocent she pretends to be."

My mind was still trying to comprehend that Katrina hooked up with Calder. "What are you talking about?"

"The fox has been in the chicken coop."

"Can you please speak English?"

"She's sleeping with a married man. Hot and heavy. Her marriage broke up over it."

My heart zinged with joy over the fact she was not sleeping with Max. "Who?"

"Baxter."

My mouth dropped open. "The head coach? Baxter Nicols?"

Calder shrugged, already bored with this conversation. "Yup."

My mind raced. "But I met his wife."

"He wants to leave her."

"You're shitting me."

"The fox is up in arms because he hasn't left his wife yet. He was supposed to get a promotion, but he didn't so he refuses to leave his wife until that happens."

"Promotion? What promotion? He's already the head coach!"

"No clue." He shrugged and shut his eyes. "Wake me when we get home."

My mind raced as I tried to process what Calder has told me. What promotion was he talking about? I couldn't even comprehend that Katrina and Baxter were sleeping together. So why was she always making such a big play for Max? I thought back to the media fiasco that had transpired. I had thought she had called the media so she could be seen as his girlfriend. Now it appeared she had tried to set Max up. Was she doing that to help Baxter?

Calder snored beside me. The driver pulled up to my family home. Without waking him or saying goodbye, I let myself out of the vehicle. I wondered if Max knew about Baxter and Katrina? I decided, even though I didn't like to spread gossip, it warranted talking to Max about. Perhaps he could shed light on Katrina's motivation. If anything, he needed to be on his guard with her.

CHAPTER 31

I STOOD IN MY OFFICE, at the window, watching the practice below. I should be at my desk working, but I couldn't seem to pull myself away from watching Max skate. A week had passed since the gala and I hadn't seen Max other than from watching him in practice.

I pressed my forehead against the cool glass.

Why couldn't I get Max Logan out of my brain?

No matter how hard I worked to avoid him, I couldn't stop thinking about him.

A knock on my door pulled me back to reality.

"Rory?" Dad and a young woman stood in the doorway. "Rory, this is Andrea. She's from Digital Dream."

My mind was blank. "I'm sorry, did we have an appointment?"

Dad cleared his throat. "Andrea tells me that you are doing the final sign off for the outfits for one of our players?"

"For what?" I asked in confusion.

Andrea's expression was perplexed. "I'm sorry. They told me that this was a formality."

I sat down on the couch and motioned for her to join me. "Why don't you start at the beginning?"

"We are putting together a photo calendar of Canadian hockey players from the NHL. All proceeds go to a charity that supports women in need. Katrina reached out to us and asked if Max Logan could be part of the calendar and naturally we were thrilled."

Dad sat across from us with his arms crossed.

I spoke slowly. "This is the first I've heard of it, but it sounds like a good cause."

"It's an amazing cause. Last year we raised enough money to keep the doors open for eight women's shelters across the country for twelve months."

"That's very impressive. What do you need from me?"

"I need you to sign off on the outfits for Max. Our policy is to get approval from the GM or assistant GM." She handed me the file. "These are the possible outfits that we would like him to wear. He'll be the month of December, which is quite an honor since that is our most popular month."

My eyes widened as I took in the three proposed sketched outfits.

The first was a sketch of black underwear and a pair of skates.

The second sketch was nothing more than a white sports towel around the waist.

The final sketch showed that he'd model naked except for a helmet strategically held in front of his private parts.

I looked up at Andrea with concern. "Where are the clothes?"

Dad coughed, covering his laughter.

"Max would be positioned so that his photo would remain tasteful. This isn't Playboy, this is a charity calendar."

"Max approved this?"

"Katrina approved it."

I stalled. "Has Max seen these?"

Dad reached forward and grabbed the sketches. The smile on his face grew. "He'll do it."

"What?" I lifted my head. "Don't you think we should confirm with Max?"

"Nope. He's in."

"That's amazing." Andrea stood up. "The photoshoot is on Friday and Katrina said she'd attend with Max. We really appreciate this."

Dad stood up and shook her hand. "It's my pleasure."

After she left, I turned on Dad. "Why did you approve that? I don't think Max has seen those sketches."

"I know he hasn't."

"Why is this funny to you?"

"Rory, you're the one who said you wanted him to win the public over. This is for a good cause."

"Not like this!"

"The guy needs to learn that we have rules. This should have been approved."

"That's a Katrina issue."

He ignored that fact. "One more thing. I don't want Katrina to attend this photo event."

"Why not?"

"Because she has an agenda with Max and I don't like it." His voice sounded thoughtful. "You go with him instead. Let them both know."

"Dad!"

The last thing I needed was to see Max naked wearing nothing but a towel.

Dad stood up. "I gave my word, so make sure Max takes part. That's an order."

I sagged back against the couch. God help me.

"WHAT THE HELL IS THIS?" Max sat in front of my desk, holding the sketches like they were contaminated.

"Those are your proposed outfits for the charity calendar you signed up for."

"Like fuck I did."

Katrina leaned towards Max and put a possessive hand on his big forearm. "Max, remember the woman's shelter project?"

His eyes widened. "You said I'd be wearing a uniform."

"I said you'd be in a variation of a hockey uniform."

He sounded incredulous. "This dude is holding a helmet in front of his junk. That is not a fucking variation."

"I think you'll be sensational."

He tossed the sketches on my desk. "This is bullshit. Pull me out."

My voice was dry. "It's for a great cause."

Accusing blue eyes lifted to my face. "You approved this? Without asking me?"

"The GM approved it. He believes in the cause, and he wants you to do this."

"Tell him I want out."

"He wasn't asking."

Max ran a hand over his face. "Fuck me."

"Max," Katrina coaxed in a soothing voice. "It'll be fine. I'll be there to walk you through every step."

There were days I hated my job, but right now I was enjoying myself.

Too much.

"Katrina, the GM has requested that you don't attend this event with Max."

Katrina's eyes went wide. "No. I set this up. This is my project. Max needs my support. I have to go."

"Those were his orders."

"He needs someone to be there," she argued. "Max can't go to this alone."

"He won't be alone. Someone will accompany him."

"Who?" Her voice was shrill. "Who is going in my place?"

I worked to keep an impassive expression on my face. "I am."

Max winced.

Katrina shot up off her seat. "You preordained this."

"Trust me, I have better things to do, but the GM requested I attend."

"I don't think so," she gathered her bag and focused her attention on Max. "I promise you that I'll be there, okay? You can count on me."

She strode out of my office.

Max leaned forward and pleaded. "You need to get me out of this."

"I can't."

"You can talk to your dad."

"I already tried, and he's adamant this will happen."

"Why?"

"Why do you think?" I parlayed back. "You're banned from the media. You should have sought special permission before doing this."

"Katrina set this up."

"She should have then."

"But I don't even want to do this."

"And that's why he is making you do it."

"He's punishing me."

"He's teaching you that there are rules in this club."

"How was I supposed to know that?"

"We pay you 1.2 million dollars a year. For that amount of money, we expect you to know the rules."

"This is bullshit."

I lifted my hands up. "My hands are tied. You'll be excused from practice on Friday so we can go get your photo taken."

His eyes studied the sketches. "I don't think I can do this."

"Why not?"

"I'll be naked."

"You've had plenty of photos of you in the buff."

Anger flashed in his eyes. "You can't be in the room when this happens."

"That's fine. I will accompany you there and wait outside."

He gave me another angry glance and then stood up and walked out.

———

FRIDAY MORNING, at an ungodly hour, Max and I arrived on the set. The room was a hub of activity. There was a white screen set up, and half a dozen lights were being adjusted by two men. The photographer fiddled with a camera while another two assistants set up his gear. A make-up artist sat talking to another woman at a make-up counter. Two women talked at the back and a young man carried coffee. There were two more men in suits, standing and talking around the breakfast table.

"I'll wait for you outside," I yelled over the loud techno music.

A big hand shot out and grabbed my wrist. Max turned to me. "Don't leave me."

"Max."

He radiated tension. "Stay."

———

TWO HOURS LATER, the set was ready to go. Everyone stood around waiting. The only person missing was Max.

"Where's our sexy model?" the photographer yelled.

Someone scurried up to him and then he turned around and roared, "Rory?"

"Yes?"

"Max wants to talk to you. He's in the dressing room."

The entire room watched as I walked across the room and knocked on the door.

"Come in." Max's voice sounded terse.

I stepped into the room and had to work to keep my mouth from dropping wide open. Max looked like a hockey god wearing the

equivalent of hockey lingerie. His skates added 3 inches to his 6'4"
frame. He wore a pair of short black boxers that showed off his
powerful legs and his impressive bulge. His hard, muscular body
sparkled with oil and glistened in the light. His hair was messily
tousled. I had never seen anything so sexy in my entire life. My
mouth felt dry and the rest of my body felt hot.

"You need to call this off."

"Max."

"Do it."

"Tell me what is going on?"

His fists clenched at his side. "This is bullshit."

His Adam's apple bobbed as he swallowed.

"Max. Talk to me."

He breathed hard through flared nostrils. I'd never seen him this
rattled.

"Max, talk to me."

He waited so long I thought he wouldn't answer. "They hate me."

"Who?"

"The fans."

Suddenly I realized what was going on. Max's armor against the
haters was his skill and talent on the ice. Now he stood here in his
underwear. No armor. No protection. He felt vulnerable.

"Max, I don't hate you."

His gaze held mine.

"Not only do I not hate you, but I respect you. You haven't been
given a fair shot in this town and I wish that was different, but despite
that, you persevere. Your commitment is absolute and your talent as a
hockey player is flawless."

"What's your point?"

"After giving everything of yourself to the game, here you are,
giving even more of yourself. This calendar raises enough money so
that eight women's shelters can keep their doors open for a year. And
that makes me proud."

Annoyance seethed from his pores. "Fine."

"You'll do it?"

"After that fucking speech, do I have a choice?"

"Okay. Let's do this."

"Stay where I can see you." He demanded before he stalked out of the room.

⸻

"MAX, LOOSEN UP."

"Max, can you crack a smile?"

"Max, baby. You look like you're about to kill someone."

"Max, this is a sexy calendar. You look like you're posing for your passport photo."

The photo shoot was a disaster. Max's movements were stiff and uncomfortable. The photographer barked commands at him, and I heard grumblings they weren't getting any good shots.

The photographer turned to adjust his lens, and I took that time to walk over to Max.

"How's it going?"

"How the fuck do you think it's going?"

He sounded so pissy about it, I resisted the urge to smile. "What's wrong?"

"I hate this music."

"What else?"

"There's too many fucking people in this room."

"Would it help if they left?"

"Anything would help at this point."

"What else?"

"I'm wearing my skates and a pair of underwear. Some clothes would be nice."

I chewed on my lip, thinking about what I would need to hear if I stood in his place. I would need someone to encourage me. Did Max need encouragement? That would mean I'd need to put myself on my line. The part of myself that I tried so hard to hide from him.

I stared at my sneakers and then, in an act of bravery, lifted my face to his. "You look sexy, okay? Women everywhere will get all hot and bothered when they see your photo."

His eyes widened and then there it was. The start of that smile. "Bullshit."

I leaned closer. "You're so hot it's unfair to all the other dudes in this calendar."

I turned to walk away, and he reached out and grabbed my wrist, spinning me around.

"People, are we ready?" the photographer called out.

Max's eyes were on my mouth. "Get rid of everyone."

"I will."

TEN MINUTES LATER, the music was off and only three people remained. Max, the photographer and myself.

I stood behind the photographer.

"Okay Max. I want you to think of sex."

"Excuse me?"

The photographer was bent over his camera. "Try to imagine that I'm the chick you need to fuck. Not want, but need. This chick is the one that got away. You burn for her. You long for her. And when you see her, all you want to do is grab her and have your dirty way with her."

Max stared at me.

I stared back.

"Be sexy for her, Max," the photographer was taking photo after photo. "Tell her how you feel about her with your eyes. Try to let her know how much you want her."

Max's eyes never left me. I struggled to breathe. I could feel my body respond to his smoldering gaze. I was on the receiving end of his I-want-to-fuck-you stare and my traitorous body responded. My nipples hardened and my stomach clenched, but for the life of me, I couldn't drop my gaze from his.

The camera whirred, and the photographer called out directions, but Max never took his eyes off me.

I imagined him wearing only those skates, lifting me up against a wall, while I wrapped my legs around his waist. His face would be against mine. Those eyes would burn for me. And then he'd roughly push his big...

"That's a wrap."

I blinked. In a daze, I turned to the photographer. "What?"

"We're done here."

I turned back to Max. He continued to stare at me with an intensity that made my insides quivery. I tried to smile but instead, my lips trembled.

His wolfish smile grew on his face. I crossed my arms and tried to appear nonchalant as his gaze leisurely perused my body as if I was the one standing in my underwear. I lifted my chin. There was no question he knew what effect he was having on me. He gave me one more taunting, heat-filled gaze that made my knees weak before he strode back towards his dressing room.

What just happened?

"So, the photos turned out?" I babbled, trying to cover up how much Max had affected me.

The photographer paused. "I've been doing this for twenty years and I just took some of the sexiest photos of my life. Your sex life must be off the charts."

"Excuse me?"

He shook his head. "The way he was looking at you? That was pure, mind-blowing lust."

"We aren't sleeping together!"

He snorted. "Not yet. You're not sleeping together *yet.*"

"I'm his boss."

He lifted his head and took in my sneakers and skinny jeans. "Seriously?"

I crossed my arms over my still puckered nipples. "Yes. I'm his boss and we will not be sleeping together."

The photographer snorted. "Says you."

CHAPTER 32

MAX and I walked out to his vehicle in silence. We didn't speak. A line between us had been crossed. I didn't know what that meant, but it both scared me and thrilled me at the same time.

"The photographer said those were the best photos he's ever taken."

Max huffed as he tossed his bag in the back. "I'm glad that I didn't need to do the shot with the helmet over my junk."

Funny because I had been excited about that outfit.

We got in and Max started the vehicle. His phone rang. On the dashboard, it said: *Lolita calling*.

Max grabbed his phone and stepped back out of the vehicle. "Give me a minute."

What the hell?

Baffled, I watched him, as he stood in front of his SUV and laughed at something *Lolita* said.

Who was Lolita?

I observed him. He had a gentle smile on his face. His smiles were born from amusement, playfulness or sexual heat. He didn't give gentle smiles. Why was he smiling a gentle smile? A burning sensation flooded my chest.

Who was she?

Was he dating her?

Why did he get out of the vehicle?

The call lasted three long minutes while terrible questions and thoughts raced through my mind. He climbed back in beside me.

"Do you want me to drop you off at the stadium?"

He wasn't going to tell me who she was, and worse, it wasn't any of my business.

I stared out the passenger window. "Sure."

Was he dating someone? Was he hiding that fact from me? Why hadn't he wanted me to hear the call? Maybe he had been thinking about her at the photo shot? Maybe she was the one he burned for? Maybe he longed for Lolita?

I tried not to feel defeated. It shouldn't matter. It wasn't like he and I would date. I should be happy for him. I should be happy that he had one other person in his corner.

So why did I feel sick to my stomach?

"You're quiet." Max interrupted my thoughts.

"I think I'm tired. Early morning."

"Thanks for coming today."

"I didn't do anything."

"You helped."

We lapsed into another silence. When he pulled in front of the stadium and I climbed out, I felt his big hand wrap around my wrist.

I glanced over my shoulder at him.

"You okay?"

No. You're taking private calls from someone named Lolita.

I gave him a short nod before scrambling out. I felt stupid. Why was I torturing myself with this ridiculous crush when it was so obvious that Max wasn't interested? I vowed to steer clear of him. No matter what it cost me.

———

THREE WEEKS PASSED, and I had almost perfected avoiding Max. I came to all meetings a few minutes late, slipping in the back and strategically chose a place in the room that was as far away from Max as possible. During our away games, I sat up front with management, getting on the plane after Max boarded and getting off before him.

This meeting was no different. It was a coaching meeting, and I was deliberately running a few minutes late. I walked towards the boardroom when an arm grabbed me, spinning me around.

"Max," I breathed, avoiding his gaze.

"Haven't seen you around."

"I've been busy," I stared at my shoes.

He didn't speak, so I stole a glance up at him through my lashes.

"You avoiding me?"

Think of Lolita. Lolita.

I shook my head, and gave him a small, fake smile that made my cheeks feel like they would crack. "No, don't be silly. Come on, we're going to be late for the meeting."

He didn't budge, so I stepped around him and hurried into the meeting. I chose a seat along the side of the room that had no seats nearby.

I sensed him coming into the room, but I forced myself to keep my gaze either on my notes or towards the front of the room, but I could feel him watching me.

Don't look up. Don't look up.

My traitorous eyes turned towards him. Blue eyes held mine. Flushing, I ducked over my books.

Think of Lolita.

By some miracle I managed to not glance his way again, but I could feel him watching me for the rest of the meeting. Max was off limits. I knew that, he knew that. I didn't understand why he kept blasting me with his intensity, but I vowed to keep him at arm's length. I had spent way too much time thinking about him when he'd already told me that he wasn't able to have any distractions this year.

Except he seemed to make an exception for Lolita. Every time I felt myself weaken, I reminded myself of his gentle smile when he talked to her.

CHAPTER 33
TWEET

Hockey Gurl @hockeygurl
I was told that when the Vancouver Wolves hockey players see Rory coming, they are suddenly busy. An unnamed player said she's embarrassingly immature. #GrowUp #SpoiledBrat

CHAPTER 34

I FOUND Mom in the kitchen, talking to the catering staff. In less than an hour, a hundred guests for my parents' annual Christmas staff party would fill the house.

For as long as I could remember, my parents hosted the entire Wolves hockey team, the coaching staff, and the admin staff along with their significant others for a festive party to celebrate Christmas.

Mom always had the house professionally decorated. And she had hired six bartenders and over a dozen wait staff.

"Rory, come here and taste this," Mom motioned me over to the island in the kitchen. Around us, staff worked overtime getting the food ready.

"What is it?"

"Jeff, what is this again?" she asked the chef.

"That is the sautéed polenta cakes with mushroom Ragu and micro greens."

I put the tiny appetizer in my mouth.

Flavors exploded in my mouth. "That's delicious."

Mom smiled up at me. "Your outfit is lovely."

I glanced down at the red tartan dress that had a fitted bodice and flirty skirt. I had paired it with black high-heeled boots. My long hair was tied back into two messy French braids that twisted in a knot at the base of my neck.

"I invited Calder and his parents."

"Mom!"

"Calder is a nice young man."

I refrained from snorting. "Oka-aay."

"Rory, you know I'd love to see you with a boyfriend. Don't you want a boyfriend?"

The chef leaned over the island and offered me a mini-burger.

"Thanks," I took the plate from him. "Mom. It's kind of hard to find a boyfriend when I work 12 hour days."

"But that is my point," she watched me bite into the burger. "You don't have time to find a boyfriend, but Calder doesn't need finding."

I talked with my mouth full to the chef. "This is delicious."

He grinned at me.

"Mom, I love you, but you are way off base with Calder."

She squeezed my arm. "I think you are writing him off with far too much haste."

I loved Mom for her innocence. I could ruin her image of Calder by telling her he was the king of debauchery with his wild drinking, recreational drugs and salacious appetite for casual sex, but I didn't want to. I loved that she still saw only the good in people. "I promise to spend time with him."

Which reminded me. I need to ask Calder what else he knew about Baxter and Katrina.

━━━

TWO HOURS LATER, I stood in the huge family room, surrounded by guests. I had positioned myself to see the front foyer, so I would know if and when Max arrived.

I chewed on my bottom lip. What if he brought Lolita with him? I had already resigned myself to the fact I'd have to pretend to be super happy for them and make friendly chitchat with her. I imagined Lolita to be tall and blonde with an angelic face and the body of a supermodel. The thought more than depressed me.

"Why so glum, chum?"

I lifted my chin at Calder. Judging from his glassy eyes he was either drunk or stoned.

"Hey, Calder."

"Waiting for someone?"

"Why do you say that?" My tone was sharper than intended.

"Because," he took a long sip of his beer. "You've been eyeballing the front door like my dad's basset hound stares at his treat jar. With longing and anticipation."

"I'm surprised you showed up tonight. This party doesn't seem like your style."

"You know that our moms are playing matchmaker. They expect us to procreate because they are both so desperate for that little patter of feet."

"I think I just threw up in my mouth."

He laughed. "That's why we are having Christmas together."

"No."

"Yup. The raisins, as I affectionately like to call my parents, have rented a woodsy cabin in Whistler for the Christmas vacation. We get to spend four blissful days together as one big happy family for a big festive vacation."

"No one mentioned it to me." The last thing I wanted to do was spend the Christmas vacation with anyone other than my parents. I had been eagerly anticipating my PJs, Netflix and at least six books I had stockpiled.

"Don't worry, I have an escape plan planned for us."

He had my full attention. "What does that mean?"

"You'll see."

I wasn't sure I wanted to know. "Seems like you had fun at the gala."

"Katrina is one hot smoking piece of ass."

It did not go unnoticed that he called her by her name and did not reference her as the fox.

"Seems like her social calendar is already booked up."

He rolled his eyes. "With the old dickwad that won't leave his wife for her? She can do better."

"So, it's true. She's actually sleeping with Baxter?"

"Keep your voice down."

Baxter, although not hideous, was in his mid-forties. He kept himself in shape and was technically good-looking, but his personality could use a transplant. I caught sight of his wife. She stood off to the side, next to the Christmas tree. She wore a plain cotton dress with a slouchy cardigan and she exuded misery. I couldn't believe she was Baxter's wife, but then again, I also had no comprehension how someone as beautiful as Katrina could end up with someone like Baxter.

"How are they even together?"

Calder's expression was dark. "Kat could do much better than him. He treats her like crap. He expects her to stop and drop her life every time he wants to get laid."

Kat?

"Too much info, Calder."

"It's true. He gets her to do his bidding at work and she sits around and waits for him to call. It's depressing."

I tilted my head. "You got all of that from spending time with her at the gala?"

"We might have hooked up a few times since then."

My mouth parted. "Calder!"

"What? She deserves to be treated better than he treats her."

"What kind of stuff does he get her to do at work?"

Calder took a long sip of his beer. "Just watch yourself."

"Excuse me?"

He turned his bleary gaze onto my face. "I've got your back, Roar. Don't forget that."

"Why?" I found this conversation bewildering.

"Your dad bailed me out of a tough situation, a couple years back and that bought a lot of my loyalty."

"He did?" I couldn't keep up.

"And for that, I've got your back."

I wanted to ask him who or what he was protecting me from, but before I could ask, he slapped me on the back. "Go get him, Tiger."

Calder walked away from me and disappeared from view. I swung my attention back to the front door.

Max was standing in the front foyer.

He was alone!

The coat check attendant took his coat, and I held my breath as he glanced around the room. His gaze sucker punched me. I should have done something like give him a flirty smile or a small wave, but instead I stood there staring at him like the lovesick idiot I was.

Someone moved to greet him. He laughed, and I caught a flash of those perfect white teeth. I took that time to study him. He wore a black cashmere sweater that showed off his broad shoulders. He also wore a pair of dark jeans that sculpted that ass.

It was pathetic how the moment Max showed up, I became acutely aware of my heart and how hard it beat in my chest.

I forced myself to pull my gaze off Max. I chatted with people like my life depended on it. I laughed at everyone's jokes. I ate appetizers and drank two glasses of white wine.

Unable to stop myself, I kept lifting my head and searching the room for him. Each time I did so, it was as if he could sense my stare, and he'd lift his blue eyes to me. We didn't smile or wave or do anything you're supposed to do when you met someone's eyes repeatedly across the room.

I drank in the sight of him and in turn, he blasted me with looks so intense, I thought I might self-combust.

It was unnerving and thrilling.

The party got more boisterous. The copious amounts of alcohol flowing made the laughter grow louder, and the conversation was at such a fevered pitch it was almost difficult to hear.

I set my wineglass down and made my way through the kitchen. Congregated around the kitchen table, the wait staff feasting on the leftover appetizers while the cooking staff cleaned up the kitchen.

They all froze when they saw me.

"Don't mind me," I kept on walking. "Only passing through."

No one spoke while my boots echoed on the hardwood floor, but the moment I stepped through the hallway that led to the laundry room, library and gym, I could hear the chatter start again.

I was finished with this party. Done with small talk. Done with smiling until my face hurt. It was almost midnight. These parties lasted into the wee hours of the night. I was already counting the hours until I could climb into bed.

I stepped into the library and didn't bother turning on the light. I knew this room like the back of my hand. I sank into the big leather couch. The cool leather against my bare legs made me gasp.

"I'd recognize that sound anywhere." A deep voice spoke from behind me.

CHAPTER 35

I SPUN around to see shadowy Max standing in the doorway of the library. I reached over to the lamp and clicked it on.

We both blinked in the light.

"What are you doing here?"

He stepped into the room, as his eyes took in the expanse of bookshelves, the expensive leather furniture bought for comfort and reading and the cozy touches that were distinctly Mom's touch. My eyes, on the other hand, watched only him.

"Just wanted to see where you were stealing away to."

I flopped back against the couch. "Welcome to my favorite hideaway."

His eyes didn't move from my face. "I like it."

"Are you having fun?"

"Define fun."

"A jolly good time?"

"Christmas isn't my favorite holiday."

"Who doesn't like Christmas?"

He avoided the question. "Have you read all these books?"

"Only the ones on my bookshelf."

"You have your own bookshelf?"

"Of course."

"Show me."

I walked around the couch and like Vanna White, caress the edges. "This is my bookshelf."

He stepped forward and scanned all the neatly lined up titles. "You've read all these?"

"Every single one."

"Quite the eclectic collection."

"What do you mean?"

"Harry Potter, Agatha Christie, James Joyce, Nora Roberts."

"These books all have one thing in common."

His eyes moved to my face. "Oh yeah? What is that?"

"They all tell a great story. Why don't you like Christmas?"

"Christmas is a holiday built for families."

"You're not going home for Christmas?"

He dropped my gaze and pulled out *Harry Potter and the Deathly Hallows*. "I'm staying here for the holidays. Is this book any good?"

Max was going to be around for our time off. For some stupid reason that made me so happy. "What do you mean?"

"I've heard about this series."

"The Harry Potter series is one of the greatest stories I've ever read."

He put the book back. "If you're a kid."

"It's for adults too."

A smile teased his lips. "You're really cute when you get passionate about stuff."

"You *have* to read Harry Potter."

His eyes were on my mouth. "I'm not a huge reader."

"These books will make you a reader." I pulled *Harry Potter and the Philosopher's Stone* off the shelf. "Try the first book. Get through three chapters and if you hate it, you can stop reading."

"For a kiss."

"What?" I froze.

What about Lolita?

He stepped closer and put his hand on the shelf up above my head boxing me in. "I said, I'll read three chapters if you give me a kiss."

"What about your... girlfriend?"

His blue eyes widened. "Who said I had a girlfriend?"

I ducked my head down. "It was something I heard."

"Then you heard wrong."

My heart soared through my chest. "Because you don't do distractions."

"I'm looking at my only distraction. So, do we have a deal?"

I lifted my eyes. "About what?"

"Three chapters for a kiss."

Yes. Hell yes!

I caught my bottom lip between my teeth, pretending to debate my choice. "All right, but only because I really believe you'll love this book."

"What makes you think that?"

"They sold 500 million books in this series."

"That's a lot of books."

"People love this series. If these books don't make you a reader, I don't know what will."

"Before or after?"

"What?"

"Do I get my kiss before or after I read my chapters?"

I stared up at his beautiful face. "Well, maybe we could do it before..."

His mouth came down over mine. I moaned. His kiss reminded me of that first night we kissed. He took his time. He didn't rush our kiss. It was simply an experience in pleasure.

I pushed my fingers into his hair and sighed when his mouth moved along my jaw bone, nipping my neck. "I think if you read five chapters, you will get another kiss."

He murmured against my neck. "And if I read ten chapters?"

"Well, that would definitely qualify you for a third kiss."

His arm snaked around my waist pulling me hard against him. I sighed when his mouth found mine again. I lifted my arms around his neck to anchor myself from the way the entire world spun.

He spoke against my lips. "How many chapters does this book have?"

"Lots."

"What if I finish the book?"

I gasped when his mouth grazed down my neck. "Oh, if you finished a book, that would qualify you for a bonus."

He lifted his head, his eyes were dark. "What's the bonus?"

"It's good."

"I believe you. What is it?"

I gave a half scream as he picked me up and swung me around. Laughing, I buried my face in his neck while he carried me to the couch.

"Rory!"

We both froze. I lifted my head and squinted at Mom who stood in the doorway of the library.

"Mom!"

Her eyes narrowed onto Max. He unhurriedly lowered me to my feet.

His tone sounded polite. "Mrs. Ashford."

Mom, ever the experienced socialite, nodded at him. "It was a pleasure to have you in our home, Mr. Logan. So sorry you have to leave."

"Mom!"

He didn't move a muscle and then said. "Thank you for your hospitality."

My face burned. I felt like a high school student whose parent had busted up a hot kiss with an unapproved boyfriend.

"Mom, if you'd excuse us for a moment, I'd like to take a moment to say goodnight to Max."

She didn't like it, but she nodded. "I'll be waiting outside."

She shut the door behind her.

"I'm so sorry," I turned to him. "That was inexcusable."

"Winning over the parents has never been my strong suit. Are you okay?"

Terrible thoughts went through my mind. What if Mom told Dad? "I'll make sure she doesn't tell my dad."

He flinched. "I should go."

"Wait," I bent down and picked up the book from the floor. "Your book."

He lifted the book up and down as if to test the weight. "If you wanted to make me a reader, you should have picked a shorter book."

"You only owe me three chapters."

He bent down and pressed a hot kiss against my mouth. "If it kills me, I'm going to get my bonus."

"You're only supposed to read it if you like it."

"I like to win."

"I've noticed that about you."

"I should go." He kissed me one last time.

"See you later."

He opened the door, and I heard him thank Mom for her hospitality again before he disappeared out of sight. Mom stepped into the room and shut the door.

The words blurted out of me. "Are you going to tell Dad?"

"Rory." That one word held so much disappointment and hurt.

"Mom, please."

"That man is all kinds of trouble."

"He was on the plane crash!" My secret spilled out of me.

"What?"

I sat down on the couch, feeling defeated. She moved to sit down beside me. I felt her take my hand into hers. "You never talk about the crash."

I shook my head. "It's too awful to talk about."

"Oh, baby."

"He was there. I didn't know who he was, but Max was sitting beside me." I glanced at Mom's concerned expression. "He got me through that."

She squeezed my hand.

"The plane was shaking and tilting. People around us were screaming and crying. I was so scared, Mom. I was on the verge of losing it and Max, who was a complete stranger sitting next to me, he calmed me down. He talked and held my hand. And at the end, I was so terrified, I fainted. He carried me out of the plane and took care of me. He got me to the hotel and checked up on me."

Mom's concerned eyes studied my face as I talked.

"We became friends. No one understood what I went through. But he did. And everyone thinks he's such a bad guy, but before I knew about his past and his reputation, he acted like a pretty great guy."

"Oh, Rory." Mom's empathetic tone soothed me. "I didn't know."

"Don't tell Dad about tonight, please?"

"You know you can't get involved with that man. This doesn't have a happy ending no matter how you feel about him."

I bowed my head. "I know."

"I won't tell Dad, but please promise me you'll end whatever is going on between the two of you."

I didn't want to promise *that*. It hurt my heart to even think about that.

"Rory," her concerned look almost blew my heart to smithereens. "If your dad ever got wind of this, you and your dad's relationship would survive but how do you think Max's career would fare?"

My heart felt heavy as the truth rushed over my skin. "Dad would cut him."

She gave me a sad smile. "Max seems to have a lot on the line. Is your relationship strong enough to survive that?"

That question made my blood go cold. Max loved hockey more than life itself. Perhaps a year ago, it wouldn't have mattered. Back then he had been one of the league's hottest commodities, but after his incident with Joseph, he'd been lucky to even get a contract.

Would another NHL team give him a home if he got cut from the Wolves? Maybe they would in a year after he had a chance to shine on our team without incident, but right now he was too vulnerable. That fight with Joseph had blacklisted him. If he got cut from Vancouver, his career would be over. This wasn't news. I had known that from the moment I saw him on the ice. And he knew it too.

As much as it destroyed me to say it, we needed to end this. The kissing. The flirting. All of it.

It had to stop.

"I'm going to end it," I promised Mom. "I couldn't bear to watch Max lose hockey."

She paused. "Whatever you do, don't tell him the reason."

I pulled my hand from hers. "Why?"

"Don't make him resent hockey or this team. You want him to turn to hockey, not against it."

She made sense. But the whole thing made me feel sick. I needed to crawl into bed and not come out until this year was over. "I'm going to bed."

She leaned forward and kissed my forehead. "It will be okay."

CHAPTER 36

THE PLAYERS MEETING DRONED ON. I sat at the back and stifled a yawn. The team had been on the road for 3 games and we only had tomorrow night's game before we headed into a five-day break for Christmas.

I felt someone staring at me. I lifted my head from my page and my gaze clashed with Max's intense blue stare. I ducked my head over my book, feeling heat wash over my face.

Mom had lied. Nothing was okay.

After my talk with Mom, I had spent a fitful night debating how to handle this situation with Max. Mom was right. If Max got cut from our team, the odds of him being picked up from another team would be slim. He needed a full year, proving himself on and off the ice, to ensure the longevity of his career. And if Dad got a hint of anything between us, he would get rid of Max. Max was a rebel at heart, and being told that he couldn't be with me, might make him want to be with me just to thumb his nose at authority.

Did I need to say anything? Besides our hotel time together after the crash, we had only kissed twice. So why did it feel like there was so much more between us?

It was all the other stuff. The way he held my hand under the blanket whenever the plane took off. How he'd come to my room to check up on me after Minnesota. The way he stared at me from across the room. It was all the little ways he acted that made this so difficult.

I needed to protect him, but I needed to do so without letting him know what I was protecting him from.

So, I took the cowards way out. For the last week, I returned to avoiding him like my life depended on it. I didn't talk to him. I didn't flirt. Hell, I didn't even look at him. If we spent no alone time together, he'd be safe. It felt like a rotten thing to do, since he'd done nothing wrong, but I needed to keep him safe.

The only problem was that Max didn't seem to get the hint. Anyone else would react to being so obviously blown off and would back off. Not Max. He never approached me, but he watched me every chance he got.

I peered up at him through my eyelashes. His unblinking gaze stared back.

I dropped my head forward, letting my hair curtain in front of my face. He was making this so difficult. All I wanted to do was be near him. Pushing him away was my version of torture.

The meeting broke up. I gathered my stuff and moved out of the hotel conference room. I almost made it to the elevator when a strong hand grabbed my arm and steered me around the corner.

"What are you doing?" I anxiously peeked around Max's shoulder, scared that someone would see us talking.

"Why are you avoiding me?"

I met his gaze and lied my ass off. "I'm not."

"Bullshit."

"Just... don't."

"What happened? You've been weird ever since the Christmas party."

"I'm not weird."

"Tell me what is going on."

I felt emotionally exhausted. I knew this was the right thing for him, but his anger-laced hurt was gutting me. My only move was to step around him towards the elevator, punching the button several times. He didn't follow, and I made my escape to my room.

For the hundredth time, I reminded myself that I was doing this for him. To *protect* him.

I missed the shared team lunch, and in an act of rebellion, decided I'd skip the afternoon practice too. I answered only necessary emails before collapsing on my hotel bed for a nap.

I WOKE up with a dry mouth and noticed that I had also slept through the team dinner. I did not care. I took a hot bath, shrugged on the robe over my naked body and then ordered room service. I needed to get through one more night, one more flight and then I'd have five days off, away from this team, and away from Max.

A knock sounded on my door.

I swung it open. Max stood there, a dark expression on his face.

His presence bewildered me. "What's going on?"

"Can I come in?"

That was a bad idea. But having him standing in the hallway was an even worse idea. I opened the door wider, and he walked in. He moved to lean against the desk, his arms crossed. Max was in a mood.

"I'm not leaving here until you tell me the truth."

"What truth?"

"The truth about why you did a 180 and fucked off."

Oh. *That* truth. "I've been busy."

"Bullshit." His eyes narrowed on my face. "What did your mom say about me?"

"What makes you think she said anything?"

"She busted us at the party and next thing I know, you can't even look at me."

"That's not what happened."

"What did she say about me?" The tendons of Max's muscles stood out and his jaw clenched.

I realized Max thought I was avoiding him because of something Mom had said about him. Something bad or unsavory. Which made me feel terrible.

"Nothing. She said nothing about you," my voice wavered.

His eyes narrowed. "She wants you to be with Calder. Someone with a pedigree, is that right?"

I shook my head.

"Tell me you're not dating that Baby Boy."

It was in that moment I knew Max meant what he said. He wouldn't leave the room until he wrangled the truth out of me. A truth I couldn't afford to share.

So, I implied a lie. "Calder's a family friend."

"He's a drugged up punk who doesn't deserve you."

I avoided his gaze and shrugged.

Painful and cold silence ticked between us. Matching the beat of my bruised and sore heart.

"Answer this one question and then I'll leave."

My eyes met his outraged expression.

"Have you slept with him yet?"

I'd rather be celibate for the rest of my life before I slept with Calder. "Not yet."

Max's nostrils flared as he worked to get his emotions under control.

With my arms crossed, I watched him. I felt horrible for how this was ending. I hated that I was hurting him and I hated that whatever was between us, I was killing with my lies. But I was doing this for him. As pissed off as he was, losing hockey would be a million times worse. We'd never be able to survive that. And then he'd have nothing.

He pushed off the desk, and his eyes, dark and stormy, pierced mine when he passed me towards the door.

I took a deep shuddery breath and followed him to lock the door behind him. I tried to think of something, anything to say that would make him feel better, but redemption was impossible after this conversation. Max had shown me nothing but kindness and now I was throwing his friendship in his face so I could allegedly choose Calder over him.

He reached to open the door, but his hand paused on the handle. I faltered behind him, unsure of what verbal scorn he'd unleash on me. Whatever he had to say, I deserved it and more.

He stared down at me. His eyes were like blue diamonds, glittering like hot ice. He took a step towards me.

I stepped back.

He kept coming until my back was flat against the wall. He towered over me, staring down at me, with those angry hot eyes. He planted the palm of his hand against the wall beside my head. A total dominant move. A thrill shot into my gut.

"This is complete fucking bullshit."

My lips parted as my brain tried to think of some words.

"Don't," his lip curled. "I don't want to hear it."

He traced a finger down my lips, pausing so that one finger pressed against my mouth as if to hush me. Our eyes met.

He reminded me of a wolf. Big. Hungry. Aggressive. And such a fucking turn on.

His eyes were on my mouth. "Do you think your drugged up Baby Boy can satisfy you the way I can?"

Not a chance in hell. I didn't answer but my wide eyes remained on his face.

"Drop your robe," he growled.

"Why?" I whispered over the furious pounding of my heart.

"Because I'm going to give you something to remember when he tries to make you come."

I swallowed. I was naked beneath my robe. This was madness. I should tell him to leave. I tried to remember why I had been pushing him away in the first place.

"Now," he commanded.

My hands fumbled with the robe belt. The robe fell slightly open. Delicious tension quivered in my stomach. I hesitated.

I shouldn't be doing this. I should ask him to leave. This can't happen.

I glanced up at his beautiful, hard-to-read face and then shrugged my shoulders, letting the robe slide off my naked body and puddle at my feet.

Two huge warm hands grabbed me around the waist and spun me around, pushing me against the wall. I gasped as I felt him step in closer. The heat of his warm chest through his t-shirt pressed against my naked back. With infinite gentleness he brushed my long hair away from my back, over my shoulder.

His voice was low in my ear. "God, you're so fucking beautiful."

My body tightened in response.

"Now I'm going to show you what it means to get properly fucked."

A shiver wracked my body.

His fingertips trailed down my arms. And he captured my wrists in his grasp. I inhaled sharply as he brought my hands up, and placed them above my head, flat against the wall.

"Spread your legs for me."

It took two breaths before I had the guts to move my legs apart.

"That's it," his lips were on my back, trailing kisses across my shoulder.

I arched, quivering when I felt his teeth graze the skin of my shoulder.

"Tonight, I'm going to control every inch of you." He sucked my earlobe into his mouth. "After tonight, no matter who you're with, you'll only think of me."

One big hand slid around my neck, and I felt his hand gently squeeze my neck. I could feel the pulse of my heartbeat under the pressure of his thumb. It was a move designed to dominate, to let me know he was in charge. My entire body trembled with responding lust.

I whimpered when I felt him kick out one of my legs, forcing me to spread my legs open wider. I felt so vulnerable. So exposed.

"I usually like to draw things out, torture a bit, but right now I feel impatient. I want to feel you come all over my fingers. Hard and fast."

"What?" I blinked, my eyes opening wide.

I cried out when I felt his hand slide between my legs. He didn't give me a chance to process. He buried his fingers into me. His fingers plundered me the way I imagined he would fuck me. Primal, greedy and demanding.

Oh my god.

My entire body reacted. I was on my tippy toes, arching back, my head against his chest, and his fingers were relentless, rough and wild; pushing me into a frenzy. He was driving me to the point of madness.

"That's it," his stubble rasped against my neck. "You're so hungry for it, aren't you? You want it so bad from someone who knows how to actually fuck."

My legs were shaking and my head pressed hard against his chest as my body tightened like a bow. I couldn't contain my need. I was moaning, my hands curling against the wall, and still his magnificent fingers impaled me, moving at an impossible speed.

"Do you like it when I fuck you like this? I can feel you clenching around my fingers. So hot, so tight, so wet," he murmured in my ear.

I responded with a choked noise. I was so close. So close.

"Come for me. Come all over my fingers," he commanded as his hand tightened around my neck.

A half scream escaped my lips as I felt my universe fly apart. I exploded. My body shuddered and quaked as my orgasm rolled through me.

I clung to that wall, panting like I had run a marathon, while my body twitched and trembled.

"That was just to get you warmed up, so you're hot and ready for my cock," his voice was hoarse.

CHAPTER 37

I MOANED as he torturously pulled his fingers from me. I almost stumbled when he hustled me over to the dresser. His hand pressed on the back of my neck, so I was bent over. My ass was in the air. Our eyes met in the mirror. He radiated dangerous male and it made me so hot.

I needed him inside me now.

I stepped my legs apart, opening myself to him. Blatant, like a dog in heat, so desperate and hot for him. Without taking his eyes off my face, he stepped behind me. He unbuttoned his jeans and pushed his pants down. I could feel the long length of him press between my buttocks. He messed with my hair. It took me a moment to realize that he was gathering my hair into a long ponytail. My head pulled back as he tested tugging my hair.

Our gazes held in the mirror. So much heat passed between us, the air almost crackled with it.

Max was finally going to fuck me. From hate or anger, I didn't care. I needed him inside me more than I needed to breathe.

I held my breath as he poised himself at my entrance and then thrust hard inside. The pleasure was so intense, my eyes almost rolled back into my head.

He was so big that it took three hard thrusts before he was buried inside me.

"Your body doesn't lie. You want me. Only me." He still sounded so angry.

I pulsed around his length.

Nothing in my life had ever felt better.

He moved, with long, glorious thrusts. I pushed against the dresser, bracing myself against the speed and strength in which he drove into me. I could feel myself tighten and clench around him. He fucked like he played hockey. With a single-minded intensity.

I groaned when he yanked at my hair, pulled my head hard enough that my entire back arched. Every time he slammed into me, he drove me closer and harder towards my orgasm that was barreling towards me. My throbbing core welcoming every pummeling drive. I might not walk after this, but it'd be worth it.

"You think your little boyfriend can fuck you like this?"

"More," I gritted my teeth. "Give me more."

His eyes never left my face. His lip curled with exertion and he slammed into me with such a ferocity, he was forcing me onto my tippy toes. I was off balance, shameless as I chased my release.

"When he's trying to keep his whiskey dick hard, you will only think of my hard cock fucking you."

"Come on," I panted. "Harder."

He leaned over me, wrapping a huge arm around my waist, and braced his other muscular arm against the dresser.

Holy fuck.

He pounded me like a savage. And my body couldn't get enough. I felt wasted. Volatile. Insane with need. Yet I couldn't stop goading him.

"Is that all you got?" The words strangled out of my throat. "Are you sure you're not a Baby Man?"

Reckless words, considering my position, but I wanted him to lose control. I wanted him as mad with lust as I felt. I needed to bring him to the same insatiable need that was coursing through my blood.

"You're such a hot little bitch," he breathed hard.

"Shut up and fuck me like you mean it."

He responded by ramming me with intensity. My body responded by clenching around him. We were raw. Relentless. Exquisitely primal.

I fought my orgasm. Tried to slow it down, but it was like trying to stop a train with a feather.

"Come on my cock," he breathed hard. "Come all over my hot cock."

My body stiffened and arched back against him.

His big hand covered my mouth muffling the scream that ripped out of my throat.

I bucked against his imprisoning embrace as my world shattered around me. I writhed hard, swimming in sensation. Wave after wave of wicked lust threatened to drown me.

"I'm coming," he gritted his teeth, and then he crushed me to him. He buried himself high into me. My core pulsed, milking him as he jerked again and again against me. I could feel his release as it streamed, hot and deep inside of me.

———

WE DIDN'T MOVE. Except for our hard breathing. I felt him twitch inside me. My body responded by tightening around his girth. Not wanting to let go of him. Not wanting him to leave my body.

Our eyes met in the mirror. His face was still a mask of savage desire. He winced as he pulled out of me. I straightened up to stand on shaking legs. My entire body trembled like a leaf. It surprised me that I could still stand. My bones had melted. My world was slowly spinning backwards on its axis.

He stepped back from me. I spun around, clutched the dresser behind me and watched as he tucked his still hard cock back into his jeans. He was dressed, shoes and all and I was naked, a hot mess, with his hot cum dripping down my thighs.

If he walked out after this, I would not survive.

"Are you okay?" his voice was low, his eyes avoiding my face.

I nodded.

I watched as he moved to pick my robe up off the floor. He held it up for me, so I could slide my arms in. Then he tied it around my waist.

Our eyes met. His gaze full of lust, shame and regret.

I started to speak, but the shrill ring of his phone interrupted me. He glanced down at his phone. "It's Baxter."

"Answer it."

With reluctance he took the call. "Logan....yup....was out for a walk. On my way upstairs now."

He clicked his phone off. "Crew check."

The Wolves had a loosely upheld curfew for players when they were on the road. Apparently, tonight, Baxter was holding the players to their curfew. Typical bastard move on Baxter's part.

"You need to go."

"We have to talk."

"The fine you'd get is not worth it. Go."

I could see him internally debate.

"Go," I stepped forward and pushed on his chest. "Do not give Baxter any ammunition."

With reluctance, he took a step backwards. "This conversation isn't over."

"You've got three minutes. Don't give him reason to fine you."

With one last, hard-to-read look, he left.

⬜

I STAGGERED to bed and lay curled up on my side. MY entire body hummed with post-orgasmic pleasure. My mind was going in circles.

That had been, hands down, the best, most insane sex of my life. Max exceeded all my expectations. What had I thought the first time I saw him?

He was built to fuck.

That was the understatement of my life. But that didn't matter. Our actions had put Max in jeopardy. Even though that had been the best sex a girl could ever dream of, it could never happen again. Max's career depended on that.

I needed to think about what was best for Max. Sleeping together was a terrible risk to his future.

My phone pinged.

Max: Can I call you?

His text surprised me.

Me: Okay

Wait! I knew Max was sharing a hotel room with another player. It happened every Christmas holiday season when room vacancy was at a premium. He couldn't have this conversation in front of anyone else.

My phone rang.

My question blurted out, "Where are you?

"Why?"

"Don't you have a roommate?"

"I'm hiding in the bathroom."

I relaxed against my pillows. "Oh. Okay."

Neither of us spoke.

Max cleared his throat, breaking his silence. "It wasn't supposed to be like that."

"What wasn't supposed to be like that?"

"Our first time."

My heart flipped. "What was it supposed to be like?"

He paused so long, I wasn't sure he would answer. "I wanted to savor you."

I curled up tighter in bed, clasping the phone to my ear. Why was

I supposed to stay away from Max? I decided that only the truth could salvage this situation. "I'm not seeing Calder."

"You're not?"

"No."

He took his time. "So, why were you avoiding me?"

"Your career."

"What about my career?"

"I don't want you to jeopardize it. If my dad ever found out about this, he'd find a reason to terminate your contract. I don't want to be the reason you lose hockey."

"That's the reason you were avoiding me?"

"Hockey is your life, Max."

"Now I feel like a complete asshole."

"Why?"

"Because you were looking out for me and I was..."

"What?"

"The idea of you and Calder pissed me off."

"Calder's sleeping with Katrina."

"What!?"

"And she's sleeping with Baxter."

I guess tonight, I was blurting out all my secrets.

Disbelief laced Max's voice. "Katrina!? Media Katrina is screwing Baxter?"

"Tell no one."

"Who am I going to tell?"

"I don't know. My point is you don't need to be pissed about Calder."

He took a deep breath and shifted the conversation back to us. "I didn't use a condom, but I'm clean."

I knew that. All players have to go through a medical when they started each season.

"I'm good there, too."

He cleared his throat. "I've never not used a condom before. I don't even want to think about why I didn't, but if something happens, I want you to know I will man up."

It took me a few moments to realize that he was talking about me accidentally getting pregnant. My stomach pitched wildly at the idea of being pregnant with Max's baby. *Do not go there.* "I'm on the pill."

"You are?"

"Yeah."

"Well. I guess that's good."

I guess that's good!? I bite my lip. "We can't do that again."

"Why not?"

"I told you. My dad..."

"I give everything to this team. But I will let no one fucking dictate who I date in my personal life."

My eyes widened at the word *date.* "Max."

"We need to sit down and talk about that, but not while I'm whispering on the phone in some fucking hotel bathroom."

I tried to keep my heart from dancing in my chest. I tried to remember why we needed to stay away from each other. "Let's talk in the new year when we come back from break."

The time apart would be good for both of us. I needed to think. Max also needed to process how much was on the line here.

"Yeah, okay."

Neither of us seemed to want to hang up.

"Rory."

"Yeah?"

"That was the best fucking sex of my life. So, if you think I'm going to let you walk away from me, you can think again."

My stomach quivered and my ovaries did backflips. "Okay."

He sounded satisfied. "See you tomorrow."

"Night."

I wasn't sure how we'd moved from me crushing on Max from afar to him kicking down doors and demanding that he would not let me go, but here we were. And I liked it. Way too much.

CHAPTER 38
TWEET

Hockey Gurl @hockeygurl

I heard that Rory is the team diva. She complains about everything. The flight, the food, the hours. No one is sure why she bothers showing up for work when she does nothing. #SOS

CHAPTER 39

AN HOUR after my plane landed, my parents and I headed up to Whistler. Calder's parents had rented a deluxe five-bedroom log cabin that came with two stone fireplaces, an outdoor hot tub, and antler chandeliers. Someone had gone to a lot of work, to decorate the place with three Christmas trees and a variety of other decorations.

The only thing I wanted to do was lie down but I forced myself to head downstairs, where Betty and Mom visited over a bottle of wine.

"Where are the guys?"

Mom's lips twitched. "I think they headed to town to get last minute Christmas gifts."

"Calder too?"

Betty smiled. "He hasn't arrived yet. He said he'd drive up here himself. After dinner."

That bastard. Why hadn't I thought of doing that? "Okay."

Betty studied me. "Are you dating anyone?"

Avoiding eye contact with Mom, I shook my head. "I'm way too busy for a relationship."

Betty smiled at me with hearts in her eyes. "You know, Calder is single."

God help me.

"You know, I have some lovely single girlfriends."

Her expression fell. "I hoped that you and Calder would learn to enjoy each other's company."

I worked to not let my smile slip. "Calder isn't interested in me. He's made that clear."

Mom hid her smile behind her wineglass.

"I had no idea."

I gave her another smile. "It's okay. I got over it."

———

DECEMBER 24TH, Calder and I sat together on the couch. He was sipping a bottle of water. Our parents were singing Christmas carols in the kitchen while they prepared lunch.

"Thanks for telling my mom that I was the one not interested in you." Calder narrowed his eyes on my face.

"You weren't around."

He sipped his water while his leg bounced up and down. "I'm heading into Vancouver after lunch."

"Shut up."

"Wanna come?"

My parents were in their own world. "What are you going to tell your parents?"

"Don't worry, I have that covered."

My eyes dropped to his water glass. "Is that why you're drinking water?"

"You think I'd remain sober in this antler infested candy land for any reason other than to negotiate my escape?"

"What are you doing in Vancouver?"

"Kat's all alone because her bastard prick of a boyfriend is spending Christmas with his family."

"I'm not sure I've ever seen you care about anyone but yourself."

He snorted.

"No, it's a good look on you."

"Whatever, Roar. Want a 24 hour escape from this horror house, or should I leave you with the raisins?"

I glanced back to my parents. Dad finished telling a funny story and Betty snorted red wine out of her nose. I could nap in peace without someone telling me to come help them decorate cookies or head out for yet another brisk and refreshing walk.

I turned back to Calder. "Count me in."

———

CALDER WAS brilliant at not quite lying. He spun a masterful story about how a mutual friend had been left alone by her heartless boyfriend, and she had no family close. Calder had begged her to join our festivities, but she didn't want to impose. So, now, in a short trip, Calder and I wanted to head back to Vancouver to spend time with her.

Betty had tears in her eyes. "I'm so proud of my baby boy. You've become so wonderful."

I somehow managed to not roll my eyes.

"I get my heart from you, mama."

With promises that we'd be back in time for Christmas dinner, we got in Calder's racy black sports model and headed back to the city.

"What are you going to do?" Calder pulled into my driveway.

"I'm going to sleep my ass off and watch a lot of Netflix."

"You should get out more. I'll be back tomorrow to pick you up at 4 PM."

"See you then."

———

THE HOUSE WAS QUIET. I toyed with my phone. I wanted to text Max, but I still struggled knowing that this relationship could come at great risk to him. I really liked him, more than I should, but the outcome if we ever got caught terrified me. I wanted to see him so bad, it took all my effort to not get into a cab and head to his apartment. He had told me he was spending Christmas in Vancouver. What was he doing? Was he spending his time with friends?

I heated a frozen pizza and resisted turning on my laptop to work. This was my downtime. I would relax if it killed me.

I will not text him.

I. Will. Not. Text. Him.

My phone rang. A smile crossed over my face when I realized it was Max.

"Hello?"

His voice was low, reverberating in my ear. "Merry Christmas."

"Same to you."

"How is Whistler?"

"I'm in Vancouver."

"What happened?"

"Calder and I headed to Vancouver."

His voice changed. "You're with Calder."

"Calder is with Katrina."

His voice relaxed. "So, what are you doing?"

"I'm hanging out with Netflix."

"By yourself?"

"All by myself."

"I don't like it."

I shut my eyes and smiled again, not wanting to admit how much I enjoyed talking to Max.

"It's fine. We're heading back to Whistler tomorrow for a big dinner."

"I wish I was in town. I'd invite you over."

Wait. *What?* Max wasn't in town? I thought he had told me that he was staying in Vancouver over the holidays. "So, did you end up going home for Christmas after all?"

"Not exactly."

"Oh."

"I'm in Idaho."

"Oh!"

I don't know if it was his tone, or something in his voice, but it made me sit up straighter.

He cleared his throat. "Someone here needed my help."

My questions burned in my chest. "I hope everything is okay."

He didn't respond.

I felt hurt that he didn't want to talk about it, but damn if I would force the issue. "So, what else is new?"

"I'm almost done with my book."

"Harry Potter?"

"Yup."

"Well, what do you think?"

"If you tell anyone, I will deny it..."

"You like it."

I could hear the smile in his voice. "I like it. In fact, I can't stop reading it."

My toes curled as I remember the rest of the series that I had individually wrapped up and packaged up into a gift bag, along with a box of chocolates. Now that gift didn't seem that stupid. "I knew it."

"So, do I still get my bonus?"

My stomach pitched. I knew what I wanted to give him for his bonus. "Oh yeah."

"What is it?"

"Finish your book and I'll tell you."

"Is it good?"

"I think you'll like it."

His voice dropped a level. "I know I will."

"You don't even know what it is."

"I can fantasize, can't I?"

I liked the idea of him fantasizing about me. I heard a woman's voice in his background. I strained my ears to listen.

"Max, dinner's ready and my parents have arrived."

Max answered her. "Okay. I'll be right out."

Something cold and terrible washed over me. Who was that? He never mentioned that the friend who needed help was a woman! Did he even call them a friend? He just said *someone*. Which wasn't the most reassuring thing in the world.

Trying not to jump to conclusions, I worked to even my breath.

An awkward pause settled between us before he spoke. "I should go."

I would not be that girl. The one that came across as clingy and insecure. Was it any of my business? It wasn't. And I needed to keep my mouth shut.

"Who was that?" The question came out of me, burning hot and edgy.

"Lolita."

No explanation from him. Just one word. One name.

"Enjoy your dinner."

"Rory."

Hot tears stung my eyes. I had wrapped up a fucking Christmas gift for him and meanwhile, he left to spend the holidays with someone named Lolita and her parents.

I was the fool.

I felt vulnerable which I covered with indifference. "You don't have to explain."

"I want to."

"I don't need you to."

"Can you let me explain?"

"Fine."

Silence creaked between us.

My tone sounded brittle. "Thanks for clearing that up."

"Lolita is only a friend. Who needs my support."

What did that even mean? A friend. Is that how Max would describe me? As just a friend?

"That's nice for her."

"It's not what you think."

"You don't know what I think."

"I have a good idea."

"And what is that?"

"Nothing good."

This conversation was destroying me. "Enjoy your dinner."

"Rory."

"Good night, Max."

I hung up and threw my phone down. I pressed the palms of my hands into my eyes, willing myself not to cry. I didn't even know what to think. Max had told me that he wanted to date me, but the guy was a notorious player. Should I be shocked that he left to spend time with the mysterious Lolita? What did she need help with? And why wasn't he more open about it with me?

If this situation was as innocent as he professed why hadn't he shared with me who Lolita was? If she was an old friend, like he said she was, why did it feel like he was keeping her a secret?

I forced myself to finish watching the movie and then climbed into bed. I felt exhausted, but sleep refused to claim me.

My phone vibrated on the nightstand. It was Max calling again.

"Hello?"

"How are you doing?"

I sighed. "Fine."

"You don't seem fine."

"You don't have to explain anything to me."

"Rory. Can you trust me?"

"About what?"

"There's nothing between Lolita and me, nothing more than a friendship, but I can't tell you more than that. I can't talk about her and what's going on with her."

In a very nice way, he was telling me it wasn't any of my business. "Okay."

"This has nothing to do with us."

"What is us?"

"What do you mean?"

I tried to formulate my answer. "I don't know what is happening between us."

"Do you want to have this conversation on the phone?"

No, I wanted to talk to him in person. This was an intimate conversation and it would benefit me to look into his eyes and watch his body language while we talked. On the other hand, it killed me to not know what was going on between us. I vacillated between wildly fantasizing about dating him and reminding myself that he was off limits. Somehow, it felt like if I knew where he was coming from and what he wanted, it would help prevent me from going off course.

"We probably should."

"I suck at this."

"What?"

"This."

"Max, I have no hold over you, or what you do."

"First of all, you have a huge hold over me. And secondly, I should have told you."

My stomach was zooming all over the place. "You didn't need to."

"I wanted to. I still want to. But I can't. And I'm trying to protect Lolita's privacy and it was easier to not even bring it up."

"Oh." I took an uneven breath. "Max?"

"Yeah."

"I feel better."

"Yeah?"

"Totally."

"What did I say? Tell me so the next time I fuck up, I can say it again."

My laugh was breathless. "You said all the right things."

"You're not going to enlighten me?"

"Nope."

"I hate that you're alone."

"I'm good."

"I don't get back until late Friday night. Saturday morning we head out of town for our next game."

"I know."

"Promise me we'll find time to talk."

"I promise."

"I'll see you on Saturday."

That seemed like a lifetime away. "See you then."

CHAPTER 40

CALDER WAS AN HOUR LATE. He showed up with a couple hickeys on his neck and appeared hung over.

"You're late," I grumped as I got into the car.

He squinted over his sunglasses at me. "Can you drive?"

"What! Why?"

"I think I'm still drunk."

I rolled my eyes. "Fine."

We switched seats, and I ground through his gears a few times before I got the hang of his touchy clutch.

"Did you get out, Roar?"

I ignored him. "You going to put on a turtleneck to cover up Katrina's bite marks?"

He flipped his visor down. "Damn, my lady has a set of teeth."

I shook my head. "Please don't gross me out."

He laughed and leaned his head back, with his eyes shut. "I found out some juicy gossip about you."

"Have you ever watched Gossip Girls?"

"Why?"

"You remind me of Chuck Bass."

"Please, I'm way better looking than him."

"You also like to stir the shit as much as he did."

"Baxter was lined up to be the new Assistant GM."

The car swerved. I recovered, gripping the wheel with sweaty palms. "Excuse me?"

"Your dad and Baxter were in serious talks about him moving to be your dad's right-hand man."

"When?"

"Last year."

I swallowed. "What happened?"

"Apparently, they got into it over your boy toy."

"Max?"

"You have any other boy toys?"

I gritted my teeth. "What about him?"

"Your Dad insisted on bringing him onto the team. Baxter wanted the dude he beat up."

"Joseph Flanynk?"

"Is that his name?"

"Then what happened."

I waited with impatience while Calder lit up a joint. He inhaled. "You happened."

"Excuse me?"

"School ended. Your dad had you lined up to work with Katrina in media, beneath some web designer but then he sideswiped Baxter without warning by announcing in a general meeting you'd be taking over as the new assistant GM."

I almost felt lightheaded. "Are you telling me this year I was supposed to be in media working with a web designer?"

"Yup. But you got Baxter's promotion and then to add insult to injury, your dad gave Max a contract but kept Baxter out of the loop."

"Holy shit."

Calder blew smoke towards me. "Pieces fitting together more?"

"How did I not know this?"

"Your father told Baxter that if he ever told you about this, he'd fire Baxter."

"What?!"

"So, Baxter hates you and your lover."

Well, I knew that. I just never knew why. "That makes sense."

"Katrina is getting sick of his bullshit."

"Baxter's?"

"Yup, but she doesn't want to make it official with me."

"Why not?"

"She said I'm a bad risk."

My mind raced. Baxter was supposed to take over as assistant GM and he lost his chance over a fight with Dad about Max? That explained why the guy was such a complete dick and why he hated Max so much. It didn't explain why Dad seemed intent on acting like Max was always on his shit list.

"Do you think I'm a bad risk?"

I glanced over at Calder. "Yes. Totally."

His eyes opened wide. "Why?"

"Calder!"

He sat up straight. "Tell me."

"You're an unemployed guy who still lives with his parents and you have one, possibly two substance abuse issues."

"Bullshit."

"What part of that wasn't true?"

"You can't get addicted to pot."

"You're high all the time."

"Doesn't mean I'm addicted."

"Do you live with your parents and are you unemployed?"

"Yes and yes."

"You're a bad risk."

"Baxter is married."

"He also has a reason to get out of bed in the morning."

"Well, what am I supposed to do with this information?"

"If you want Katrina, get your shit together."

"Meaning?"

"Find a job and move out."

Our eyes met. He reacted with horror. "You're serious."

"Or not."

CHAPTER 41

EVEN THOUGH I only had 5 days off, my body already adjusted to sleeping in. It hurt when my alarm woke me at 6 AM.

At the airport, players milled around. I didn't see Max until I was standing in line to board the plane. I glanced over my shoulder, taking in his angular features, height and muscular frame. The man was drool-worthy. He winked at me when he busted me checking him out.

We arrived in San Jose, and we headed to the rink for a practice. Afterwards, we had a team meeting lunch and then everyone parted ways with some downtime.

I spent the rest of my afternoon in my room, working through the endless number of emails. I was debating going out to find some dinner when there was a slight knock on my door.

I opened it to find Max standing there with a large brown paper bag.

"Hi," I sounded breathless and too eager.

"I finished the book."

I opened the door wider, and he stepped into my room. "You know there is going to be a verbal quiz."

"Just a verbal quiz?"

"What were you thinking?"

"I was hoping we could play a game of Quidditch."

"You think you'd be good at that?"

"I think I could catch the golden snitch."

"You seem confident for someone who has never flown on a broom before."

"I'm confident I could catch on."

I could feel the goofy grin on my face but I couldn't stop smiling if I tried. "What's in the bag?"

"I might have stolen something."

"You stole something?" my eyes were wide. "What?"

"An idea."

"I'm confused."

"I stole a page out of the Baby Boys' book."

"Now I'm intrigued."

"Do me a favor and climb on the bed?"

"With or without my clothes."

"You dirty girl," he teased, but his eyes darkened as they focused on my mouth. "Clothes for this stage."

I climbed on the bed. He set the box down and put his hands on his hips. "I've never done this before."

"Done what?"

He stared at me for a moment. "I brought you dinner."

"What?"

"It's a picnic." He dug into the box. "Here is the wine." He pulled out a bottle of white.

"You brought me a picnic?"

"Yes."

That day on the plane, I had told Max that the Baby Men brought me picnics. And he had scoffed. Now he was here, looking slightly unsure of himself.

"I thought you didn't do this kind of stuff?"

"I don't."

Which made this even more meaningful. I sat on my knees and the smile on my face was huge. "Show me."

"Fruit." He pulled out a plastic tray of cut fruit.

"I love fruit."

"Veggies." Another plastic tray followed.

"I adore veggies."

He studied a box. "Some saltine crackers."

"How did you know those are my favorite crackers?"

"Cheese?" He held up a block of cheese. Not a Camembert or a delicately wrapped Emmental, he had bought a block of plastic wrapped marble cheese. It might be the most adorable thing anyone had ever done for me.

"My mouth is watering."

He took a deep breath. "And I bought dessert." He held up a bag of brownie bites.

"I thought I was your dessert?"

"You are. This is for you."

I smiled at the food on my bed. The Baby Men used to bring over handmade pasta, homemade appetizers and gourmet pastries from the finest bakeries, but this gesture meant the most to me. "This looks amazing."

"I couldn't find candles."

I reached out to grab his hand. "Come here."

I pulled his face down so his mouth was on mine. "This is better than any meal anyone has ever brought me."

Our kiss was so hot, so intense, I debated ravishing him, but I didn't want to spoil his gift. I pulled back from him and stared into his eyes. "Thank you."

"You like it?"

"I love it."

"You hungry?"

"You have no idea. Now get on this bed so we can eat."

He poured me a glass of wine and cracked open a beer for himself. We clinked glasses and then began to eat.

"This is so good," my mouth was full. It was, but it wasn't the food. It was that the man I adored, had gone out of his comfort zone to do something he thought I'd like. And now he was lying across the foot of the bed, looking relaxed and happy. My happiness made everything taste better, including my saltine crackers and marble cheese.

"You sure they fed you over Christmas?"

I laughed. "I ate for five days straight."

Blue eyes met mine. "Did you have a good vacation?"

"I got caught up on my sleep. When did you get back?"

"About 3 AM last night."

"Oh no."

"My flight was delayed."

"You must be tired."

"I had a nap this afternoon."

I wanted to, but didn't ask him about Lolita. "I found out some interesting news."

"Oh yeah?"

"Baxter was supposed to be promoted to assistant GM."

Max's eyes went wide. "Isn't that your job?"

"It is."

"What happened?"

"Baxter wanted to contract Joseph Flanynk."

Max went still. "Oh yeah?"

"But my dad wanted you instead."

Our eyes met.

I could see the surprise in his eyes. "Really?"

I nodded. "Baxter pushed back too hard and I guess my dad decided he didn't want to promote Baxter."

"Wow."

"I was supposed to be working in media, but my dad decided at the last minute to put me in this role. The thing is, my dad has never talked about this with me. Katina told Calder, and he told me. My dad has always pretended that this was his dream for me."

"Are you going to ask him?"

I shook my head. "Nope."

He nodded. "I get that."

"Don't take Baxter personally."

Blue eyes met mine again. "You worry about me."

I shrugged, not wanting to talk about my feelings. "So how come you didn't want to go home for Christmas?"

"My family doesn't celebrate Christmas."

"Why not?"

"It's just my mom and my uncle and usually my mom insists on working the Christmas shift."

"Even if you come home?"

He studied his beer can. "Especially when I come home."

"You don't get along?"

His honest blues held mine. "It's a work in progress, but my mom and I had a falling out years ago and she's never gotten over it."

"Do you talk to her?"

"I want to have a relationship with her, but she's never forgiven me."

"Max."

He gave me an enigmatic smile. "It's fine, but if I head home for the holidays, she stays at work. And then she doesn't have any time off."

"So, you stay away."

"I stay away."

My heart couldn't even process what he had shared with me. All I knew is it made me sad. "I'm sorry."

"It is what it is." He sat up. "You finished with all this?"

"This was the best picnic ever." It was the truth. This meal would make it into the top five of all meals in my life.

He leaned over and planted another kiss on my lips. "I'm glad you liked it."

I helped him pack everything back into the bag. When we were done, I grabbed his hand and pulled him back onto the bed to lie down beside me. "Want to watch some TV?"

Amusement crossed his features. "Just like old times?"

He was referencing that first night in North Dakota. "Just like old times."

"I'd love to."

We picked a movie, only this time, I settled up against his chest, curling my body against his. I sighed into him. I wanted to tell him how much it meant that he had opened up, but I didn't want to ruin the moment. So, instead I snuggled closer. His arm wrapped around me, pulling me close.

"This is nice."

"Yeah, I think cuddling is underrated."

We watched the movie, and I soaked up every moment with him. We still hadn't talked about us. We still had so much to say, but I didn't want to talk. I only wanted to absorb this moment.

When the movie ended, I lifted my head so I could study his beautiful face. Max glanced down at me with a content smile.

"You ready for your bonus?"

He laughed. "You serious?"

I moved to straddle him, my hands on his chest. "Do you think you can handle it?"

"I sure as hell will try."

I pushed my hands up beneath his t-shirt, marveling at the feel of the smooth, hard expanse of his abdominal muscles. Our eyes met. His gaze was dark.

"Put your hands behind your head."

Curiosity reflected in his expression, but he tucked his hands behind his head.

I took my time enjoying the feel of his body before my hands slid down to the button on his jeans.

"What are you doing?" He lifted his head.

"Shh," I soothed, as I focused on undoing his pants. His cock was hard and straining up against the black cotton of his underwear. "What do we have here?"

He laughed as his head fell back on the bed. "Oh boy."

I peeled his underwear down and licked my lips when I saw the sheer size of him. I grasped his cock by the base and lifted it up so it was free from the confines of his clothing. It was thick, long and rock hard. My fingers traced over the wide head. I bent down and licked the tip, loving the taste of the salty pre-cum on my tongue. He tasted like clean living and hot male.

Max groaned as he lifted his head to watch. "Oh shit."

"What do you think I should do now?"

I blinked at him with a pretend wide-eyed innocence.

"I think you should slide that gorgeous mouth around my cock."

I moved my head down. Without breaking eye contact, I opened my mouth and sucked his hard length into my mouth.

"Oh yeah, fuck, just like that. Take me into your mouth. As far as you can go."

I dropped my jaw open and brought more of him in. I swirled my tongue along the ridged veiny length of him. I felt his hips jerk.

I loved his guttural groan.

I stretched my lips over his length and my tongue was going crazy along the bottom, teasing him. Using my fist on the base of his cock, I bobbed my head, sliding him in and out of my mouth.

Two big hands pushed my hair off my face. Every so often I would pull my mouth to the tip and suck and swirl my tongue over the thick tip of his dick. My eyes never left his face. He was breathing hard. His beautiful lip curled as he stared down at me. His face was a mask of concentration.

I wanted more than anything to please him. To make him feel as good as he made me feel. I wanted to know what made him tick, what he liked and didn't like. I also wanted to watch him lose control, like he always made me lose control.

"Jesus," he tipped his head back.

I sucked harder, wanting him to come.

He yanked me up the bed, flipped me onto my back.

I gave a breathless laugh when he reached down and pushed my yoga pants and panties down off my legs.

"Are you going to tell me where you learned to do that?"

"I don't remember," I breathed, excited beyond belief.

"Good answer."

He shifted, so he hovered above me. I spread my legs, and he reached between our legs, and I could feel the head of his cock tease my opening.

"You have no idea how many times I've thought of you like this."

I wrapped my arms around his thick neck. "What is this?"

"Hot, wet and about to get fucked."

His mouth claimed mine, and I moaned as his kiss deepened.

"Ready for me?"

"Oh yes."

He lifted his head and blue eyes watched me make a soundless cry as he slowly pushed his cock deep into me. It felt intimate, intense and so perfect, my eyes almost rolled back in my head.

"Max."

His corded arms strained as he looked between our bodies where we joined. "Fuck you feel so good."

I wrapped my legs around his back. "Are you going to move?"

A smile played on his lips. "You want me to move?"

"Do you want to?"

He laughed. "I'm trying to restrain myself so I can do this nice and slow."

"What if I don't want it slow?"

He bent down and pressed his lips to mine. "Tell me what you want."

"I want you to lose control."

"Well you're in luck because I'm barely hanging on here."

His thrusts began slow. Long and hard. I moaned and moved with him. He increased his speed. I moaned. He grunted. And then we were riding wild. Fast, furious. Intense.

Noises, wild uninhibited noises, were coming out of me.

"Come for me gorgeous, before I embarrass myself."

"I'm so close."

"I'm about to lose control."

I tightened my legs around his waist, loving how fast and hard he was thrusting into me.

He yanked at my hair, pulling my head back. "Your pussy is so fucking hot and tight, I've never felt anything so perfect in my life."

I clawed my nails down his back.

"I want my face between your legs. I love the way you taste."

I moaned.

"I've been thinking about being inside you all day."

I could feel my body tighten as my climax shivered at the base of my spine.

"I want to feel that sweet little pussy clenching around my cock when you come."

I felt myself spasm and then my entire body stiffened as my orgasm rushed over me.

"Oh fuck," he grimaced and then he pulsed his release into me.

We lay there, both panting. He lifted his head and pushed the damp hair off my face. "My girlfriend likes dirty talk."

My eyes widened at the term *girlfriend*. "I do."

He rolled off me and yanked my body against his. "Damn I think you're going to ruin me."

I smiled and rested my chin on his chest. "I knew you'd be good at that."

"Oh yeah?"

"I knew it the moment I laid eyes on you."

He kissed me. "I wish I could spend the night. I have about four thousand other positions I've fantasized with you."

I checked the clock. "Oh shit. You're past curfew."

"Doesn't matter."

I sat up and shoved at him. "It does. You should go."

He sat up and kissed me again on the lips. "You using me and losing me?"

"Never."

"You going to come to my next game and cheer for me?"

I laughed. "I'm at every game."

"But are you going to cheer for me?"

I lifted my hand to his cheek. "I always cheer for you."

CHAPTER 42

I LOVED it when our team traveled, because that meant Max and I could spend time alone together. When Max came anywhere near me, it felt like I would combust.

We had sex. Lots and lots of sex. Max was a masterful lover, and he wasn't satisfied until he made me come until I couldn't speak. He took me on the bed, against the desk, up against the wall, in the shower. None of that surprised me. I had known from the moment I had seen Max that he'd be gifted in the bedroom. What surprised me about Max, was his sensitive side.

Any chance he got, he loved to touch me, hold me, wrap his body around me.

"Did you know when two people cuddle, your body releases a chemical called oxytocin?"

"No, what's that?"

"They call it the feel-good chemical."

"This feels good."

"Right?"

HE ALSO LOVED to leave me little surprises. I'd find stupid little jokes in my make-up bag, scrawled in his messy print.

What's the difference between a hockey game and a boxing match? In a hockey game, the fights are real.

WHY IS *the hockey rink hot after the game? Because all the fans have left.*

I loved them and I kept every single scrap of paper. They were love notes I savored when I was alone.

———

ANOTHER THING that surprised me was how much Max loved to laugh. When we were alone together, he became an easy-going guy who liked to tease and joke around. Yes, I loved the sex. It was hot and intense, and hands down the best sex of my life, but I loved the after sex too. We did stupid things, goofy things. Like when Max put on my t-shirt, which was more of a tiny midriff on him, and we had a Britney Spears dance off. He won, by the way, because I laughed so hard, I couldn't even dance.

———

I DIDN'T EVEN MIND his pensive side. The quiet side, when he disappeared into his head, shutting everyone, including me, out. I'd snuggle up to him, and he'd let me. He'd wrap his arm around me. He rarely shared what troubled him, but I knew when he rolled over, sighed and buried his face into my neck, that my closeness eased his troubles.

"You want to talk?"

I didn't expect he did, but I always asked.

"My mom called me."

My fingers in his hair stilled. "How did that go?" I knew his relationship with his mom was strained.

"It was a tough call."

"Are you okay?"

He rolled me over so he could stare me in the eyes. "Rory."

"Yeah?"

He fought with his words, but failed. I could see him struggle, wanting to tell me, but he resorted to kissing me instead. A deep, emotional kiss that left me breathless. He lifted his head and the look he gave me made me swoon.

"Rory."

"Yeah?"

I could see the debate in his eyes. He was fighting something, dealing with something. Something bigger than us, but also involved the two of us.

He rolled to the edge of the bed and sat up.

"I should go."

Shock passed through me. "What? Why?"

He glanced back at me. "I'm not great company tonight."

"Oh, okay," I sat up disoriented.

He couldn't get his shoes on fast enough.

"See you tomorrow?"

"Yeah, okay."

He didn't even give me another kiss goodbye.

I worried that night. Scary feelings of doubt crept in, replacing my joy.

It will be okay. Don't worry. It will be okay.

CHAPTER 43

TWO DAYS LATER, I sat in the stands near the ice with my notes, watching a practice. I waited for Dad, who had texted me to tell me that he was at a doctor's appointment. We had two defense men who wanted to retire after this season. I would have no part in the decision about who we'd contract to replace those positions, but Dad expected me to present him with my ideas as if I was.

There was a break in practice. I felt concerned that Dad hadn't made it back yet.

Me: Everything okay?

Dad: Had a couple routine tests. Pulling up to the stadium now

Me: I'm still at practice

Dad: Wait for me near the ice

I studied my notes.

"You're cute sitting there."

I smiled and lifted my head.

Max, dripping wet with sweat, leaned against his stick. Something inside me eased up. Sunny Max was back. Whatever internal debate he had been fighting, my side had won. For now.

I gave him a saucy smile, "How's it going?"

"Better now that I'm talking to you."

"Your fancy skating moves impressed me."

His smile made my toes curl. "So, you want to go on a date?"

"With whom?" I pretended to look around for a suitable candidate.

"Smart ass."

"Does it involve sex?"

"It could."

"Sold. When and where?"

Baxter skated up and glanced between the two of us.

"What's going on?"

I shook my head. "Nothing."

He glared up at me. "You have no business coming here and distracting the players."

"Excuse me?"

Max interjected. "Baxter, we're all on break."

Baxter ignored Max and glared up at me. "If you can't contribute anything, at least refrain from bothering the players."

Max moved closer to Baxter, staring him down. "I came over to talk to her, not the other way around. And I was discussing business."

Baxter glared up at me, and as he turned to skate away, he spoke in a low voice. "Slut."

Too stunned to respond, I sat frozen.

Max moved his stick, caught Baxter's skate and yanked. Baxter tripped hard and landed on his chest. Without equipment on, I knew that fall had hurt.

"You okay, coach?" Max skated to his side and stopped short, spraying his face with ice.

"Fuck you."

"What?" Max asked with an innocent expression.

"You tripped me," Baxter rolled over and climbed to his feet to face Max. "Fuck you."

"You're mistaken."

Baxter faced Max with a murderous expression.

"You're going to pay for that."

Everyone on the ice stopped to turn and watch.

Baxter swung for Max's face. Max didn't even bother to move and he let Baxter's fist connect with his chin.

My hand covered my mouth when Max tossed off his gloves and dropped his stick.

Max wanted to fight.

Max pushed Baxter against his chest. Baxter flailed back, nearly losing his balance, but he stayed upright.

Baxter swung again, but this time, Max ducked back, avoiding getting hit.

Dad appeared beside me. "What the hell's going on?"

Max pulled Baxter's jacket over his head, and he got in three hard right shots on Baxter's face.

"Enough!" Dad barked.

Max let go of Baxter. He picked up his gloves and stick, circling. Staring up at Dad with a hard to read expression.

Baxter pulled his jacket off his face. Blood spurted out of his nose. He froze when he spotted Dad. He pointed at Max, "This fucker has to go."

"Both of you. In my office. Now!"

Dad turned and walked up the steps. Eyes wide, I threw a worried glance towards Max, before I scrambled after Dad.

Dad seethed. "Want to tell me what is going on?"

I could barely keep up with Dad. "Players were on break and Logan skated up. We hadn't spoken two sentences when Baxter came up and told me I had no business being in practice because I was distracting his players. As he skated away, he called me a derogatory name and Max tripped him. Baxter got up and hit him in the face."

"I saw that part." He stopped walking. "Why is Max always in the middle of your shit?"

"He's not, but you can't deny that Baxter hates me and he hates Max."

"That's an excuse."

"That's the truth, Dad. You want to tell me why Baxter has hated me from day one?"

"I don't know what you're talking about."

"I know."

"Excuse me?"

"I know that Baxter wanted to be assistant GM. I also know you fought Baxter for Max instead of Joseph."

"Joseph Flanynk is about two drinks away from being an alcoholic."

"You keep blaming Max or me for all the shit that happens with Baxter, but have you ever considered that Baxter might instigate this stuff because he doesn't like us?"

"Max should have never tripped him."

"He was protecting me."

"Are you saying I'm not?"

"Dad!" I grabbed his hand. "No. I'm trying to prevent you from blaming the wrong person in this situation."

"Who should I blame?"

"Baxter!"

Dad stared down at me. "I don't want you in this meeting."

"What?"

"I will give Logan a fine."

"What about Baxter?"

"I'll deal with him."

I could not understand the blind spot Dad had for Baxter. Without responding, I turned on my heel and walked away.

⸺

THAT NIGHT, my phone rang. It was Max.

"Hello?"

"Hey."

Worry laced my voice. "Are you okay? What happened?"

"Nothing, I only got a fine."

"Max! I'm so sorry."

He laughed. "Baxter got a bigger one."

"Really?"

"All good."

"Thanks for standing up for me." I meant it. I appreciated how protective he was.

"I would have done a lot more to that asshole if we hadn't been in practice."

That I believed. "Be careful, okay?"

"Can you do me a favor?"

"Yes."

"My uncle is coming to town this weekend to watch one of my games."

"Yes!"

I could hear the smile in his voice. "You don't even know what I'm going to ask."

"Doesn't matter. I'm in."

"I'd like to get him a decent seat for the game."

"I can take him out for dinner first."

"You'd do that?"

"I'd love to."

"Thanks, babe."

My heart squeezed at the term of endearment.

CHAPTER 44

UNCLE RONNY WAS the exact opposite of what I expected. I expected a big strong man that resembled an older version of Max. Instead, he was short and slight in stature, with a handlebar mustache and a military crew cut. He shared Max's blue eyes. They twinkled when he smiled, and he smiled often.

We enjoyed dinner at the restaurant in the arena, and then we made our way down to our seats, which were right behind our bench.

Ronny was an avid hockey fan. He stood up and screamed when Max had a breakaway and scored a goal. It sounded like he was the only one in the entire stadium cheering.

He turned towards me, his eyes baffled.

"What the fuck is going on?"

I chewed on my lip. "It's a long story."

He sat down heavily beside me. "They don't like him here."

"They are warming up to him."

"Come on, little lady, that's bullshit and you know it."

I rubbed my eye. "The fans are skeptical about Max because of his past including his fight with Flanynk."

Ronny scratched the side of his face. "Well, that sucks."

"I know."

"Did he ever tell you what happened there?"

I shook my head. "No, you?"

"Nope, but Max has his reasons. Just because he doesn't talk about them doesn't make them wrong."

"I know."

The game continued. We cheered, ate popcorn, drank beer and made it our mission to scream for Max.

When the second intermission started, we sat back in our chairs and watched as the Zamboni circled the ice.

Ronny turned. "So how does someone as young and pretty as you get to be in a role that is so important?"

"Who says I'm important?"

"Everyone in that restaurant treated us like royalty. People were either nervous around you or desperate to impress you."

"It's not me they want to impress, it's my dad."

"He a big man around here?"

"He owns the team. And this building."

His eyebrows shot up. "Your father is Mark Ashford?"

"The one and only."

His whistle was low and long. "You ever dated a hockey player before?"

My eyes widened. "I... we're... my dad."

He nodded. "It's a secret."

"Kinda. I don't know what's going on."

He nodded and stared out over the ice. "How much has Max told you about his past?"

"Not much."

'Did you know his mom, my sister, used to live in Vancouver?"

"No."

He sighed and rubbed his chest. "Sharon moved to Vancouver, bright and fresh, so full of life. My parents were dead set against her coming out here."

I did but didn't want to hear what he was about to tell me. I knew it would be bad. "What happened?"

"Max happened. My parents wanted her to give up the baby. And when she refused, they disowned her."

"Oh no."

"She was unprepared for motherhood. I moved her to Ontario so that I could help her. She worked her fingers to the bone as a waitress. I helped where I could, but I was still in school."

Our eyes met.

He gave a sad smile. "Damn, Max was one cute kid. I loved him more than life itself, but his mom didn't bond with him. She gave him the basics, but she didn't fall in love with him like I did."

My heart cracked for Max. I couldn't imagine having a baby and not loving it.

He continued. "When Max was five, he came apart. Big temper tantrums. Acting out. No one could handle him. One day Sharon showed up with Max and his stuff. She disappeared for seven years."

Holy shit.

"Where did she go?"

He squinted. "Not sure. Max was beside himself. So, I stuck him in every sport I could think of. I figured he needed to channel his emotions somewhere."

Poor Max. I sat in silence, trying to imagine a cute blue-eyed boy whose mom had abandoned him. The thought broke my heart.

Ronny stared at me with familiar eyes. "The sport that stuck was hockey. Kid looked like he was born on skates. We never looked back. Only problem was Sharon hates hockey."

"Why?"

He turned to study me as if to see if I could handle the truth. "That's Max's story to tell you."

Which meant it was bad.

"Okay."

"Sharon despised hockey, and she fought against him playing

every step of the way. She never forgave Max when he pursued hockey."

I tried to process this. I couldn't even imagine what Max's life had been like. I always thought Max was averse to commitment because he wanted to play the field. It never crossed my mind he might not know how to commit.

"I don't know what to say." I didn't. This conversation was leaving me speechless.

"Max has come a long way."

I felt like this was too personal, too intimate to be sharing with me.

I cleared my throat. "Why are you telling me this?"

"You're the first girl he's ever introduced me to."

"I don't know if you'd qualify this as him introducing us."

"He's been in front of the media acting like a total jackass for the entire world to see, but I've never met a single girlfriend. When I'd get tickets for his games I'd pick them up at the front gate. Tonight, he warned me no less than six times to be on my best behavior."

I could feel myself blush. "I care about him."

"I can see that." He cleared his throat. "Max is bad at talking about himself, but I think this is stuff you should know."

The words blurted out of me. "I don't know what is going on with us."

He turned and studied my expression. "Max is crazy about you."

My mouth dropped open. "What? Did he tell you that?"

He winked at me. "He didn't have to."

I stared at the ice. The third period was about to start and the players were streaming back onto the ice. Max, as if he could sense my gaze, looked up at me. His smile was beautiful.

I smiled back, losing myself in his gaze. Was he crazy about me? Was that even possible? That seemed like leaps and bounds from where I thought we were.

Ronny nudged me with his shoulder. "One request."

"Anything."

"Please be gentle with his heart. His mom was the first and last woman he ever loved and she broke his heart. He's kept that thing tucked away so long, I'm not sure he knows how to use it, but I see a shift in him. He feels things. And it scares him."

I put my hand on my chest. "I can't even express how I feel about Max. But there's something you should know. My father would not approve."

"You're worried about his career."

"Hockey is his life."

He smiled, his blue eyes crinkling. "That's where you are wrong. Hockey is his job and there are far more important things in this world than our jobs."

My eyes blurred with emotions. "I don't want him to have to choose."

He patted my hand. "Let Max make that decision. The only thing you need to decide is how you really feel about him."

"Is it that easy?"

"It is if you let it be."

CHAPTER 45

AFTER THE GAME, I left Max's uncle in the green room so he could meet up with Max. I didn't want to bring any more attention to Max or myself, so I slipped away before Max showed up. I knew it'd be a couple hours before Dad finished partying with his friends, so I made myself a drink and used that time to think.

I had been born to two loving parents who did everything they could to give me a stable and loving environment. No matter what happened in my life, no matter how big my screw-ups, I always knew they were standing strong behind me, protecting me.

As much sympathy as I had for Max's mom, I still couldn't forgive her for abandoning Max.

I moved to my computer. Feeling like a stalker, I went online, and searched him as far back as I could, studying social media pictures, trying to get a glimpse of his social life. Had he ever had a serious relationship? I found an embarrassing amount of photos of him with puck bunnies and scantily clad women, but there was no evidence he had dated anyone. The only bonds he seemed to make were with his teammates. They were his family.

My feelings for Max were getting so big, so strong, they scared me, but it seemed impossible that Max might feel the same way. I vowed that no matter what happened, I'd do anything to protect his heart.

My phone buzzed.

Max: Why didn't you stick around?

Me: Trying to be incognito

Max: My uncle can't stop talking about you and that T-Bone steak he ate

Me: Ha! Really?

Max: Yup. Thanks for that.

Me: It was my pleasure - honest

Max: You still want to go on a date?

Me: Yes! When?

Max: We have a home game on Friday. How about after the game?

Me: That works

Max: Any chance you could spend the night?

I squeaked. I could ask Ola to cover for me. I could tell my parents I was spending the night with her to avoid questions.

Me: I think I could make that happen

Max: The dirty things I'm going to do to you

Me: Promise?

Max: What are you wearing?

Me: WHERE is your uncle?

Max: Sitting next to me on my couch

Me: GOOD NIGHT

Max: LOL

Me: I'm looking forward to Friday

Max: Me too. What are you doing?

Me: Lying on my couch in my office, trying not to fall asleep

Max: WHY are you there?

Me: Waiting for a ride home

Max: You want me to come and drive you home?

I stared at my phone in disbelief.

Me: You'd do that?

Max: Yup

Me: Wow - thanks! But my dad will probably be ready soon

Max: We could do dirty things in my vehicle...

Me: Stop temping me. You should spend time with your uncle

Max: He doesn't mind

Me: Tempted. So tempted. But I'll see you on Friday

Max: ;-)

Me: XOXO

Only when I hung up, did I realize that on Friday, we had our first home game against Minnesota.

———

FRIDAY BEFORE THE GAME, I slipped into the back of the room where the players and the coaches gathered to discuss game tactics. I looked around for Dad, but he wasn't in the meeting.

Me: Dad. Player meeting started. Where are you?

Baxter stood up in front of the room. "Tonight, we are playing our old Minnesota friends. We all know what happened the last time we played them. The game was dirty. Tonight, we will change that. I want this game to be clean."

The players looked at each other in disbelief. My eyes found Max. He was leaning against the wall with his arms crossed. His eyes were down and he didn't react to the news.

One guy spoke up. "They're going to come after us."

Baxter pointed at him. "Doesn't matter. We are a professional club and we will not fight back. We are hockey players, not fighters. We will not stoop to their level."

"With all due respect," another player spoke up, "But if we don't rise to the occasion, Logan will take a pounding. You know they will come after him."

"Clean game," Baxter repeated, his voice harsh. "Anyone who goes against that will answer to me."

"That's bullshit," someone muttered.

I turned and left the meeting, with one intention. I needed to find Dad.

———

I FOUND Dad sitting in his office. "Dad, where were you?"

"I had to take care of some stuff."

"It's not like you to miss the player meeting. This is a big game."

"Well, why don't you tell me what happened," he opened a desk drawer looking for something.

"Baxter wants the players to play a clean game."

Dad froze for a moment. Then he pulled something out of his desk. A bottle of anti-acids. "Well, you know we stay out of coaching decisions."

"Dad, you know what the last game against Minnesota was like. No one likes to fight, but if we don't defend ourselves, our players will get hurt."

"Baxter has his reasons."

"His reason is he wants Max to be a sitting duck in that game."

Dad popped two pills into his mouth and chewed. "Why are you always so concerned about Logan?"

"I'm the monkey on his back, remember? Besides, he's our star player. If he gets hurt, we will all suffer."

"Rory, you need to learn to step back. Everyone has their role and Baxter's role is to call the shots on how we play the game so we win."

"You can't tell me Baxter is making this decision to win. He's making this decision because he wants Max out of the game."

"You don't know that."

"How do you not know that?"

Dad sighed. "Logan has brought nothing but issues to this team since he arrived."

I scoffed. "He's the sole reason we're ranked number two in our division."

"Let it be, okay? Some things are out of our hands."

I resisted the urge to scream. "Fine."

My phone buzzed. It was Calder.

Calder: At the front gate. Tickets?

I stomped to the front gate. Dad's attitude was both baffling and confounding. Why was he giving Baxter so much power to make such bad decisions? Tonight terrified me. If we played a clean game and let Minnesota take as many hits as they could, Max would not make it through the game. What was going on with Dad? He seemed so distant and distracted. This wasn't like him.

Calder and six of his buddies were waiting at the gate. I handed him the tickets.

"Thanks, Roar," Calder grinned at me.

"You're different," I studied him. "You're sober!"

He shrugged. "Seeing Kat after the game. She hates it when I'm drunk."

"You know your relationship with her freaks me out."

He slung his arm around me. "So how bloody do you think this game will be?"

I shuddered. "I'm dreading this game."

"You doing okay?"

"Fine."

"You look pissed."

"I'm fine. What's going on with you?"

"I got a job."

"Bullshit."

"Yup. Parents are so proud they bought me a condo."

"You're joking. Where are you working?"

"Dad pulled some strings. I'm working as a junior analyst at a trading firm."

"Tell me which one, so I call pull my money."

He laughed and looked over his shoulders. "Come on, boys. I'm taking you to the bar. Drinks on me tonight."

——

DAD and I sat alone in the box, waiting for the game to start.

"Where's Mom?"

"Told her to stay home. She hates fighting."

"So, you know this game is going to be brutal."

He shook his head and didn't answer.

I fumed. I wanted to ask him why he brought Max to Vancouver if he would not protect him and treat him like a member of the team, but I didn't want to fight.

So, we sat silently together, watching the warm up.

CHAPTER 46

THE GAME WAS BRUTAL. It was like watching a Game of Thrones fight scene. Minnesota was out for more than blood. They were out to maim and disable. Every time Max got onto the ice, I held my breath.

Two minutes into the second period someone illegally hit Max from behind after the whistle blew. He went flying and hit the boards.

The entire stadium went silent when he crumpled to the ice, his hands over his face. Trainers skated over to him and when they helped him up to his feet, blood gushed from his eyebrow. The entire stadium watched in silence as the trainers helped him off the ice.

The moment he disappeared to the dressing room, Minnesota became a different team. They weren't there to fight; they were there to play hockey and to win.

Dad looked at his phone. "Logan doesn't have a concussion but required 3 stitches."

"Tell them to keep him off the ice for this period."

Dad looked at me. "Why?"

"Because I want to see if Minnesota is changing their tune."

"You want me to go over Baxter's head?"

I steeled Dad with a look. "Why don't we give Baxter a taste of what life is like without Max?"

Dad studied me for a moment. "Your call."

He typed something on his phone. "Logan's not happy."

I stood up.

"Where are you going?" Dad looked at me.

"To talk to my project."

I COULD HEAR Max arguing with the trainers. I rounded the corner of the dressing room. Max loomed over the two trainers, who were doing their best to get him to stay.

"I'm fine. Let me get out there."

"Max, sit down for a moment."

"Is it Baxter? That prick doesn't want me to play?"

One trainer looked puny compared to Max, but he tried to block him from leaving. "We're not cleared to get you back on the ice."

"Get out of my way."

I stepped forward and spoke above them. "It was me. I ordered you to remain off-ice for the rest of the period."

Max froze and lifted his eyes. "What the fuck?"

I glanced at the two trainers. "Can you give us a moment?"

With relieved expressions they walked out of the room.

Max seethed. "Why would you do that?"

"This club will survive 13 minutes without you."

"You have no business making these kinds of calls."

"The moment you stepped off the ice, Minnesota began to play hockey."

"Excuse me?"

"Not one illegal hit, not one penalty."

"What's your point?"

"They're skating circles around our team."

Max's nostrils flared. "Even more reason for me to get out there."

"Do you trust me?"

"Yes."

"Then let me do this."

"For what purpose?"

I stuck my hands on my hips. "No one appreciates you. Not the fans, not Baxter, not even my father. Let them get a taste of what life is like without you."

Max stared me down. "No."

"Yes."

"We're going to lose the game. I know that team."

"Max, we're ranked second in our division. What will happen to our rank if you get injured and are out for several games?"

"I'll be fine."

"You got lucky that you didn't break your neck with that hit against the boards or get knocked out with a concussion."

"I want to play."

I locked eyes with him. "And I want you to trust me."

"Fuck." He tossed his gloves across the dressing room.

"Listen to my reasons. The fans need to love you. When they do, the media will back off. When that happens, you become a commodity, not a liability. It means, you will have your pick of clubs after this season."

He turned and I could see the emotion in his eyes. "You think I don't know that?"

"Everyone uses you. They all expected you to show up and perform and they treat you like shit."

"How does not playing help with that?"

"They need to realize how much they need you. Let them sweat out there."

"Why does that matter so much to you?"

I shut my eyes and took a deep breath. This was my moment. To be real with him. To be honest. "Because if we get found out, I don't want your career to be over."

His head reared back like I had slapped him.

I dropped one more bomb. "I don't know what you want but I want whatever this is, to continue. And I don't want you to have to choose between hockey and me."

He moved across the dressing room in four steps and then his mouth was on mine. His hands pushed into my hair. I moaned, opening my mouth to the kiss.

He lifted his head. "You want more?"

I moaned. "I can never get enough of you."

He lifted his head and his eyes studied my face, looking for my truth and my honesty. "You know how I feel, right?"

I winced. "Not really."

He stroked my hair back from my forehead. "If you were a sport, you'd be hockey."

But you love hockey!

I reached up on my tippy toes. "Kiss me."

He bent his head down. "Why are you so short?"

I laughed, "You're wearing your skates."

He yanked me over to the bench, sat down and pulled me over his lap so I straddled him.

"Max," I felt nervous, "Anyone could come in."

"Kiss me."

I wrapped my arms around his neck and put everything I had in my kiss. We kissed until my head swooned. He pulled back and winced.

"What?"

He shifted under me. "My protective gear doesn't go well with a hard-on."

I laughed again. Max had that effect on me. I felt happy when I was with him. "I can get off."

He held me in place. "Did you mean that?"

"Mean what?"

"That you want this to continue?"

I stared into those blue eyes I had grown to love. My voice was soft. "Yes. Every word."

He responded by kissing me breathless. He rested his forehead against mine. "Still on for tonight?"

"Wouldn't miss it."

His eyes dropped to my mouth. "I can't stop thinking about your mouth."

"You're dirty."

He laughed. "You don't know the half of it."

I traced my fingers over the butterfly bandage on his brow. "Are you okay?"

He shrugged, indifferent. "I have a hard head."

"Please be careful out there."

"You going to let me play the last period?"

"You promise not to get hurt?"

"I can handle them."

"Make it to our date in one piece, please."

The siren sounded, signaling the end of the second period. I scrambled off his lap, bending down to kiss him hard on the lips. "See you later."

I could feel his blue eyes follow my ass as I walked out of the room.

———

I STOOD in the box and looked down at the Zamboni cleaning the ice. We were down 4-1, which was an impossible score to come back from. Dad moved to stand beside me.

"How was Logan?"

"Resistant."

"We're down 3 points," he sounded sour.

"Well, perhaps we should protect the one person on the ice who actually can beat these assholes instead of making him a sitting duck."

"I told you..."

"Dad," I stopped and turned to look at him. "Sometimes you're wrong."

His eyes widened, but to his credit, he didn't speak.

—▭—

THE THIRD PERIOD was a different game. Instead of being on the defense, our team worked together like a swarm of soldiers, cross-checking and hitting anything and everything that moved on the ice. It was violent and brutal and three fights broke out. Our players didn't stand around watching. When one of their own got into an altercation, all the players got involved.

We were bleeding and bruised. But Minnesota bled more.

We fought our way back to a tie and when Max got a breakaway, it felt like the entire stadium held its breath. When he shot the puck, in what seemed like an impossible shot, and scored, the entire stadium went berserk.

Dad stood beside me, his arms crossed.

"You hear that?" I asked him.

"What?"

"That's the sound of long overdue appreciation."

Max circled the net, and for the first time since I had seen him play for the Wolves, he lifted his head and smiled up at the crowd. The roar of the crowd heightened.

"Thirteen minutes," I shook my head.

"What?"

"That's how long it took this crowd to realize they needed him."

CHAPTER 47
TWEET

Hockey Gurl @hockeygurl

Last night I heard that Rory offered four different Wolves players a blow job, but no one wanted that filthy mouth anywhere near them. She threatened to fire each and every one of them. #NastyGirl

---

CHAPTER 48

I STOOD in the shadows and watched as the players came out of the locker room. When Max came out, I stepped forward but paused when a flock of women swarmed him. I narrowed my eyes. They were all holding something.

He signed copies, and it took me a moment to realize that he was signing a calendar. When he was done, he lifted his eyes up, looking for me. I walked towards the staff parking lot. I sensed him fall in behind me. We got into the vehicle and didn't speak. It was only when we pulled out of the parking lot, away from potential eyes and witnesses, did I breathe a sigh of relief.

When we arrived at his place, he yanked at his tie. "I'm going to change. Make yourself at home. Grab a drink."

I poured myself a glass of wine.

"What did you think of the rest of the game?" he called from the bedroom.

"I think you're winning over the crowd." I wandered around his kitchen. He had some bills on the counter. A big canister of protein shake powder sat next to a blender. "I also noticed that you had some new fans outside the dressing room."

"Yeah," he sounded less enthused.

"What did they want you to sign?"

"Nothing."

"Liar!" I laughed. "Where is it?"

"You don't want to see it."

"Tell me."

"In one of the kitchen drawers."

I pulled open drawers, noting that most of them were empty. There it was. The NHL calendar. I eagerly flipped it to the month of December.

Oh my god.

Max's photo was stunning. He stood in his skates and stared at the camera. His sexual charisma smoldered off the page. This man, on this page, was in the next room. And tonight, he was all mine.

"I want an autograph," I called out, unable to tear my eyes off his naked, huge muscles. And that bulge. In those black boxers. Totally not photoshopped.

"You did not just say that."

Something dropped on the floor. I bent down to pick it up. It was a card. Something fluttered out of the card. I flipped it over.

It was an ultrasound.

My heart pounded.

"It's not what you think." Max's voice from the doorway was emphatic.

I lifted my eyes to his. "I wasn't snooping, it fell out of the calendar."

I put everything onto the counter and then wiped my hands on my jeans.

Max stepped closer, his eyes were on my face. "Lolita's pregnant."

No. No. No. No.

"Okay." My throat almost closed as I swallowed. "Is the baby yours?"

"No. I'm not the father."

Oxygen filled the room and I could breathe again. "Oh. Okay."

"She's had it tough."

"Is the dad in the picture?"

"Can I trust you with the truth, Rory?"

"Yes."

"Lolita was sexually assaulted and her baby results from that."

Holy shit.

He took my hand. "Come sit with me."

I followed him to the couch. We sat looking at each other.

He broke the silence. "Did you mean that?"

"Mean what?"

"That you want this to keep going?"

Why was he asking me this again? Wasn't it obvious? "Yes."

He picked up my hand. "The same thing happened to my mom."

"What happened?"

"My mom, like Lolita, was raped, and I resulted from that assault."

Oh Max!

I squeezed his hand. "I'm sorry."

He sat so quiet before he spoke. "When I was five, she dropped me off to live with Ronny."

"Ronny told me that."

"I was a terrible kid."

"Max, you were five."

He shrugged. "She couldn't handle me."

"She was the mom."

His serious eyes held mine. "She came back when I was 12. Things were going well. I had friends, I was doing good in school, and I excelled at hockey. I lived for hockey. But she wasn't back two days before she demanded I quit playing. In the heat of a huge fight, she told me about her assault."

My eyes filled with tears.

"Our relationship wasn't good. I wanted to be a good son, but I couldn't give up hockey for her."

"Max, no one should ask you to give up hockey."

"When I was 15, I got offered a scholarship to go to hockey school. She told me that if I went, she'd never forgive me."

I could hear the emotion in his voice and it made me want to weep.

"I'm glad you went," my voice sounded fierce.

He leaned over and wiped a tear off my cheek. "Are you crying for me?"

"Yes."

He pulled me over so I straddled his lap. His two thumbs wiped the tears off my face. "I never want you to worry about Lolita, okay?"

"Okay."

"She's only a friend."

I stared into his concerned eyes. "That's why you're helping her, because she's like your mom."

"In part. And because no one deserves what happened to her."

I touched the butterfly bandage on his forehead and then traced my fingers over his lips. "You are an amazing man, Max Logan."

His kiss covered my mouth. I moaned and then I felt him lift me up. He carried me through the kitchen and then lay me down on the bed.

"I want it to be different this time," he lay down beside me.

I rolled over to face him. "How so?"

"I want to savor you."

"Okay, but let's hurry to the good parts."

His smile spread over his face. "The good parts?"

"You know what I mean."

His lips found the pulse on my neck. "This is a good part."

My neck arched. The man knew how to kiss my neck. I tried to bring his head back up so I could kiss him. I knew when I opened my mouth to his and moaned, it sent him into overdrive, but tonight he was having none of that.

He pinned my hands above my head and continued to kiss my neck until I was almost whimpering.

When his hand pushed up beneath my blouse, I sighed because when the clothes came off, this is where things got a lot more heated, but Max had other plans. He undressed me with care.

He lifted his head to study my breasts. Breasts that were heaving with desire.

"Max."

His blue eyes met mine as he lowered his mouth to one puckered nipple.

"Let me enjoy your body, Rory."

His idea of enjoying my body, had me quivering like a bow with so much heat and desire, I thought I might burst into flames and we hadn't even gotten past second base.

When he pulled off my jeans, I thought we were getting somewhere, but he left my panties on. And the man, who knew no patience during sex, suddenly had the willpower of a saint.

"Max," I panted. "Please touch me. Please touch me."

He ran tickling fingers up and down my thighs while his lips nibbled on my inner knee. "I'm touching you."

"You know what I mean."

He traced light fingertips over my apex, a sensation that drove my hips off the bed. Fighting for more. Needing more.

"Someone's turned on," his eyes were dark.

"Don't torture me."

But torture me he did. Magic fingers, wicked tongue. He'd bring me to the edge and then slide me back.

By the time he took off his pants and pressed the tip of his hot cock against my clit, I wasn't even making coherent sounds any more.

"What do you want? Tell me?"

"You," my head tossed back and forth. "Only you."

He pinned my hands above my head as he pushed inside me, his blue eyes on my face.

I worked to focus my eyes on his face. His expression made my heart want to burst. His expression was a mixture of tenderness and lust, heat and emotion.

"Max," I couldn't tear my eyes off his face. I wanted to stay in this moment forever. Commit it to memory. Never forget the tiny details.

The length of his eyelashes.

The emotion in his eyes.

The taste of his lips.

The sensations of him filling me up.

He shifted his hips and his eyes never left my face when I came apart. I cried out, as my body bowed and arched beneath his, but my cry wasn't for my physical release. It was for an emotional release I didn't quite understand. He watched me as every cell in my body flew apart and then came back together.

Only I didn't quite come back the same person.

Something had shifted.

Something had cracked open in me and it felt like a million butterflies were pouring out of my chest.

"You're so fucking beautiful," he breathed, watching me.

"Please join me," I begged, not sure what I meant.

He buried his face in my neck and I held onto him while he moved. He gathered me into his arms, and each thrust felt like commitment. Each time he drove up into me, it felt like he was becoming a part of me.

I clung to him, wishing I could fuse myself to him. Not his body, but the essence of what made Max.

When he came, he came with a carnal groan against my neck and as his big body thrust up into mine, I held onto him, overwhelmed by the intensity of it all.

"Rory," he lifted his head and looked into my eyes, while he remained buried inside me.

"I know," I breathed.

CHAPTER 49

I SNUGGLED my back harder against Max's chest, loving the way his heat and strength enveloped me.

"Remember when we were in North Dakota?"

"I'll never forget."

"I asked why you worked so hard on the plane to calm me down and make my last few moments good even when you didn't believe we'd live."

"I remember."

"Do you remember what your answer was?"

"Tell me."

"You told me it was for atonement. Do you remember that?"

"Yup."

"What did you mean?"

He took his time answering. "I guess I'm looking for redemption."

I twisted in his arms, so my face was inches from his. "For what?"

He held my gaze but didn't answer.

I placed the palm of my hand flat on his cheek. "Tell me."

"For being born? For ruining my mom's life? For not giving up hockey for her? For being selfish?"

"Max." I sounded anguished. "You're not responsible."

He dropped his gaze, avoiding my eyes. "I'm starving. Want to order dinner?"

I lay there, feeling helpless, as he rolled over and got out of bed. Did he know? Did he understand that what happened to his mom wasn't his fault? So much emotion rolled through me, I thought my chest would burst. It took all my effort not to blurt out the words, *I love you.*

I sat up. *I loved Max.* My heart pounded in my chest. It wasn't supposed to happen like this. Max and I had only started to date. Love wasn't supposed to happen this fast. But I loved him with my entire heart and I knew I would do anything for this man. Did he want the same thing? Or would my heart get crushed in this situation?

"Are you okay?"

I raised my eyes to Max, who watched me as he pulled on his pants. "What?"

"You look like you saw a ghost."

"I'm okay."

I realized that I'm head over heels in love with you. No biggie.

"Come on, let's order food. I'm starving."

I flopped back onto the bed. "I'll be out in a minute."

I knew one thing. This would be complicated.

▭

MAX HEAPED his third helping of pasta onto his plate. I had long finished eating and now I sat, watching him eat. Every movement he made, the color of his eyes, the size of his hands, the way he sighed when he was enjoying his meal—all of it. I loved. There was nothing about this man I didn't adore.

Why hadn't I seen this coming? I worked to contain my feelings. I needed to act normal. I never wanted him to suspect how I felt about him.

He smirked at me. "You've been staring at me for this entire meal. What's up?"

My skin flushed. "Have I been staring?"

"You know you have."

"It's that calendar," I lied. "It gives me dirty thoughts."

His fork hovered between his plate and his lips. "Really?"

"Oh yeah. Really dirty."

The fork hit the plate, and he moved around the island with remarkable speed. He grabbed my hands and walked backwards towards the bedroom.

"What about your dinner?"

"I can heat it up."

━━━

THE NEXT MORNING, I was heading home after a shower with Max that would be burned in my memory for the rest of my life.

"You sure you don't need a ride?" Max hovered over me in the doorway.

"I'm sure. You need to get to practice, and we don't want my dad to see who is dropping me off."

His mouth covered mine. He tasted like minty Max. I moaned. "I love this."

He pulled back and his blue eyes pinned mine. "Thanks for the date."

"I'll see you later."

Halfway to the elevator, his voice sounded behind me. "Hey girlfriend."

I spun around. "You talking to me?"

"See any other hotties around here?"

My cheeks hurt from how hard I smiled. "What?"

"See you later."

Oh yup. This was going to get really complicated.

ON MY WAY HOME, I stopped off at the shops to pick up a few things. My phone rang as I climbed back into a cab.

Brian (lawyer) calling.

"Hello?"

"Rory, the police have arrested one of our players for sexual assault."

"Excuse me?"

"I'm on the way to the central police station downtown. Your dad will meet us there. Can you join us?"

I leaned forward and gave the cab driver instructions. "When did it happen?"

"The assault happened last night, but they recently picked up the player and are bringing him downtown to the station."

"What about the media?"

"They're all over this. They got a tip off before the arrest and have footage of him being led to the police car."

"Oh shit. How's the victim?"

"She's at the hospital. Talking to the police. She is refusing a rape kit."

"What? Why?"

"She is traumatized and refusing treatment but the doctors say they have up to 96 hours to collect evidence."

"Okay. I'm five minutes out, where are you?"

"Approaching the station. The media is going ballistic. Try coming in through one of the side doors. I'll meet you inside."

"Okay. See you soon."

"Yup."

"Wait," I asked before he disconnected. "Which player?"

"Max Logan." He disconnected.

CHAPTER 50

I STARED at my phone in disbelief. What the actual fuck. This was a horrible mistake. There is no way that Max had assaulted anyone. Brian must have gotten the player's name mixed up, because I had been with Max all night.

I called Max's cell, but it went to his answering service.

Shit.

"Lady, we're at your destination."

"Sorry," I apologized, handing the driver a fifty-dollar bill for an $18 ride. I got out.

"Your change, Miss."

"Keep it."

I braced myself heading into the building. Using the side door, I avoided the media. I worked my way through the maze of hallways until I found Dad pacing near the front entrance.

"Where's Brian?"

Dad shook his head and pointed at some offices. "He's in there."

"Who's the player."

"Max Logan." Dad spit out the words at me.

"What? That's impossible."

"No, it's not. And now we've got a shit storm on our hands."

My breath felt erratic, as if someone had sucked all the oxygen out of the room.

"Where's Max? Is he okay?"

"Who gives a shit? He assaulted a woman. I knew he was trouble. I never should have brought him on. Look at this mess he's put us in!" Dad's voice escalated to a near shout.

"Dad, calm down." I stepped closer and rubbed his arm. Sweat beaded on his forehead. "This is a big misunderstanding."

Brian walked towards us. "I found us a room to talk in."

Dad and I followed him into a small room.

I tried to keep the panic out of my voice. "Where's Max? Is he okay?"

"They're processing him. Haven't started the interviews yet but they're not allowed to talk to him without me in the room."

"Let him rot!" Dad slammed his fist into the table.

Ignoring Dad, I held Brian's gaze. "What are they charging him with?"

"A level 1 sexual assault. He met a woman, left the bar with her last night and she is asserting that she said no and he forced her."

"That's impossible."

"The police say otherwise."

"Brian," I licked my lips. "Can I talk to you for a moment?"

"Whatever you have to say, you can say in front of me." Dad's voice filled the room.

"Dad. Trust me."

"Rory, spit it out!"

I swallowed in fear. Dad looked apocalyptic. "There is no way that Max Logan could have assaulted anyone, since I was with him last night."

Brain's eyebrows went up.

"No! Rory no! I will not have you protect that animal."

I turned to Dad. "He's not an animal, Dad. He's the man I love."

"Okay, okay." Brian soothed. "Why don't you tell me what happened last night."

"Max and I left the stadium together after the game. We drove back to his place. We ordered some food around 1 AM. I left around 9 AM."

Brian nodded. "Did he leave the apartment?"

"No. We arrived there together and neither of us left."

"This is bullshit, Rory," Dad blustered. "You will not protect Garrett, okay? He's an animal and you don't need to sacrifice yourself to protect him."

"Who is Garrett?" I turned to Dad. "I was with Max."

Dad's breathing sounded labored. "You don't have to cover for him. Our team can do without him."

"Dad! I'm telling the truth."

"Did anyone else see you together?" Brian interrupted.

"I don't know. I can't remember if the doorman was there. I didn't see the delivery guy, Max paid for the food."

"This is not happening!" Dad slammed his fists on the table. "This is not happening!"

Brian pinched his nose. "Rory. If you're trying to cover for him."

"I'm not. I'm dating Max Logan and I spent the night with my boyfriend. Trust me. He assaulted no one."

"Okay, this is good. You're a credible alibi."

"You will *not* cover for him!" Dad's voice trebled.

Brian held my gaze. "The police will need to interview you. Can you do that?"

"Yes."

"I won't have it. Garrett will no longer ruin this team and this family."

I turned towards Dad. His face was white, and he was yanking at his tie. Beads of sweat poured down his face.

"Dad, are you okay?"

"It's hot in here."

"No, it's not."

"I'm fine," he wheezed. "I need some air."

"Dad, you don't look fine." I moved to his side.

He held his left arm against his chest. "I need some air."

I grabbed him as he slid to his knees.

"Dad!"

Then his eyes rolled back, and he fell against me.

"Brian, call an ambulance."

I worked to lower Dad to the floor. "Dad, dad! Talk to me. Are you okay? What's happening?"

I heard Brian shouting. Then two officers rushing into the room. One pushed me out the way while the other touched Dad on the neck.

"This man is having a heart attack."

"What?"

"Go get the AED machine!"

The other officer took off.

"Medics are 5 minutes out," Brian spoke.

Hand over my mouth, I watched as the officer ripped open Dad's shirt and started compressions.

"Oh no. Oh no."

The other officer returned to Dad's side. He attached wires to Dad's chest.

"Charging."

"Clear."

"Set, go."

Dad's body jerked.

Brian pulled me up to my feet, but I couldn't take my eyes of Dad's lifeless body. "Rory."

Please wake up, Dad. Please wake up.

"Rory!" Brian's face loomed in front of mine.

"What?" I felt dazed, like I was in a bad dream. This wasn't happening.

"Rory," Brian snapped his fingers in front of my face. "You need to call your mom."

"What?"

"She needs to meet you at the hospital."

"Okay, good idea." I stumbled to the table, dug through my purse and dialed.

"Hello, darling. How was your night last night?"

I squeezed my eyes tight. "Mom. Something's happened. I need you to stay calm."

"Rory, you're scaring me."

"Is the car there?"

"No, your father took it."

I heard shouting and behind me, two paramedics pushed a stretcher into the room. I got distracted by their conversation.

"What do we have?"

"A 56-year-old man, unresponsive. No pulse. One AED charge."

"Okay let's try again."

"Charging."

"Clear."

"Set, go."

Dad's body jerked.

"No pulse."

"Okay, resuming CPR."

"I'm bagging him."

"I'm starting a line."

"Rory!" Mom's voice commanded in my ear. "What is going on?"

My voice sounded thready and weak. "Mom, I need you to call a cab and then go to the hospital."

"What? Why?"

"It's Dad."

"Rory. What is going on?"

"He collapsed. And the paramedics are here. They are working on him."

"What? What is going on? Rory, talk to me."

"I don't know, Mom. He was yelling and so upset and then he dropped to his knees."

"What's happening?"

"They are putting him on the stretcher and they are doing CPR."

"Oh my God!" Mom cried.

Brian stood beside me. "I called her a cab."

I spoke into the receiver. "Brian called you a cab, okay? So, get your purse and your shoes and go outside to wait for it. We will meet you at the hospital."

"Which hospital?"

"What hospital are you taking him to?"

"VGH."

"Mom, tell the driver to take you to the VGH."

"I don't know where that is," she sounded so panicked.

"The driver knows, Mom. Do you have your purse?"

"Rory, don't let him die. You can't let him die."

Brian put his arm around me. "Come on. You can ride in the ambulance."

"Mom, I have to go. I'm going with Dad."

"Rory," she was crying, "Don't let him die."

"Mom, I'll take care of him. I'll see you soon."

I followed the stretcher down the hallway. I looked at Brian. "Are you coming?"

"I'll stay with Max."

Oh shit. Max.

The panic must have shown on my face.

"Go with your Dad. I'll handle this."

———

THE RIDE to the hospital was a nightmare. I sat in the front with the driver while the sirens screamed and we swerved and weaved around traffic. The paramedic in the back continued to perform CPR on Dad.

At the hospital, they took Dad away, and a nurse stopped me, asking me questions I didn't have answers to.

Did Dad have a history of heart disease?
Had he had an EKG in the last 6 months?
Was he on any medication?
Did our family have a history of heart disease?
What was his cholesterol count?
"I don't know," I repeated.

CHAPTER 51

THAT DAY IN THE HOSPITAL, was the worst day of my life. Dad went in for quadruple by-pass surgery. Mom showed up, half-hysterical. The nurse called his GP, who reported that he had diagnosed Dad with advanced blocked heart valves and he had recommended to Dad that he should take immediate action, but for reasons only Dad could answer, he ignored his doctor's advice.

Dad survived surgery. Now he lay, in critical condition, in the intensive care unit. Mom was beside herself. Barely functioning and not speaking.

After hours of tending to her, I went home to retrieve some items for her, some clothes, a book, her toothbrush. I booked her a room in the hotel across the street, in case she wanted to go lie down for an hour, or take a shower, but she refused.

The media stalked the front of the hospital. Dozens of well-meaning friends called Mom's cell, all of which I fielded.

At ten PM, I watched in disbelief as Baxter showed up and hugged Mom.

"How's he doing?"

Mom fought tears. "They don't know. They said that the next 48 hours are touch and go."

Baxter gave Mom a sympathetic smile that made my stomach roll. "What can I do to help?"

She shook her head. "Nothing."

"The timing is terrible, Helena, but we've got February trade deadlines looming."

"I don't care about hockey."

"Your husband does." He rubbed her shoulder. "Let me handle this for you."

She lifted her tear-stained face. "Would you do that?"

"Mom," I cut in. "I can handle that."

"Rory, your place is here with your father."

"Mom."

"Enough!" She silenced me with her steely eyes.

Baxter pressed his lips together. "I'd need you to give me legal proxy."

"Whatever you need."

He patted her hand. "I hoped you'd say that. I've already asked our lawyer to draw up some paperwork."

I crossed my arms. "I'd like to talk to my mom alone for a moment please."

He hesitated.

"Now," I commanded.

His smile made me sick. "I'll wait outside."

I shut the door after him. "Mom. You're making a big mistake."

"Your father trusts Baxter."

"And that trust is misplaced."

"Stop! Your father is hanging onto his life and you are worried about hockey?"

"I'm asking you to not put Baxter in charge. He could cause reprehensible damage."

"He's a good man, and he's trying to help."

"I can handle it."

She stood up. "I think your judgement is skewed."

"Excuse me?"

"I'm giving Baxter the power to handle the team until your father is on his feet."

A tap sounded on the door. Brian poked his head in. "Baxter called me a couple hours ago to draw up paperwork to give him the power of proxy?"

"Well, that vulture didn't take long to get his claws in," tears clogged my throat.

Mom ignored me. "Thank you, Brian. I want to sign those papers."

Brian sat next to her. "Are you sure this is what you want to do? You will be giving Baxter complete legal authority over the team."

She raised her eyes to my face. "I'm sure."

I WALKED Brian down to the main lobby of the hospital. There were so many bad things happening today, I couldn't even focus.

"How's Max?"

"Bail hearing has been set for tomorrow morning."

"I'll be there."

"I can handle it."

"I need to be there, Brian."

He nodded. "Okay."

"How's he doing?"

"He refused to tell anyone you were with him."

That shocked me. "Why would he do that?"

"I don't know. I told him you were vouching for him, but I don't think the cops are buying your story."

"When are the cops going to interview me?"

"They will send someone down to the hospital tonight."

I couldn't believe this was happening. "I'm not suggesting the woman wasn't assaulted, but she is mistaken. She's blaming the wrong man. Max is innocent."

"She's sticking to her story. She's adamant it's Max. She even picked him up out of a lineup."

"Why would she do this? She knows this isn't true. I was with him. This is a complete fabrication."

"She isn't aware that Max has an alibi. And the prosecutor can't drop the charges until they are certain he is innocent."

"Has she provided any physical evidence?"

"She is refusing to give up her clothes or let anyone examine her."

"Why would she do this? Why would someone try to set Max up?"

"Money? Publicity?"

I thought about that. "Even if they drop the charges, this is going to devastate his career."

His lips thinned with regret. "Do you want me to hire a private investigator?"

"Yes."

"I'll take care of it."

"What happens next?"

"Well, based on the fact that they don't have any physical evidence, I'm hoping that the charges will get dropped."

"How did they arrest him with no evidence?"

Brian ran his hands through his hair. "Sometimes you get a trigger happy cop, who makes the arrest and then the defense attorney has to decide on whether they will follow through. They might drop the charges if they can't make it stick, but now they are stuck with the arrest."

"This is bullshit!"

He put a hand on my shoulder. "Stay with your dad. Two officers will come down in about an hour."

"My Mom made a big mistake handing over proxy to Baxter."

"Hockey can wait. We can sort that out later."

I nodded, fighting tears. "Yeah, okay."

THE INTERVIEW with the cops left me exhausted. They repeated the same questions over and over, with a disbelieving tone. I could tell they doubted me, doubted that I was with Max. They suggested that I was only trying to cover up for the team, to ensure that our star player didn't get arrested. By the time the interview was over, I was in tears.

They wouldn't answer any of my questions or tell me what was going on with Max.

Finally, I made my way back to the waiting room where Mom was curled up in a chair.

"How's Dad?"

"He hasn't woken up yet."

I dropped into a chair, exhausted. "Have the doctors come by?"

"The nurses are pleased with his vitals."

"Okay."

"Where were you?"

"They arrested Max Logan. I am his alibi, so the police came by to interview me."

"Is that why your father had a heart attack?"

I didn't understand or like the accusation in her voice. "Max Logan is innocent. I know because I was with him at the time of the alleged incident. So, he's not to blame for this."

She shook her head and rested it on her fist. "You told me Dad was upset."

"Dad ignored sound medical advice about his blocked arteries. That is the reason he is here."

She turned her face away from me. "Don't blame your Dad for this."

"I'm not blaming anyone."

We sat while angry silence swirled around us.

I scrubbed my face with my hands. I wasn't being fair to Mom. "I'm sorry."

"What was he so upset about?"

My voice sounded weary, "I spent the night with Max Logan. Which is when this alleged attack took place."

"Rory!"

"Dad was upset. He screamed and kept calling Max by the name of Garrett."

Mom's head shot up, her eyes ~~were~~ wide. "Leave that alone."

"Leave what alone?"

She refused to answer.

"Who is Garrett?"

"No one."

"Mom!"

"Someone from your father's past."

"Is that who Max reminds him of? Is it this Garrett person?"

"I don't know."

I could tell she was lying. "What's with the secrets?"

"Leave that alone."

To prevent myself from making things worse, I excused myself and locked myself in a bathroom stall. I sat down on the toilet lid, covered my face with my hoodie and wept. Big, heaving sobs. Would Dad be okay? What would happen to Max? The two men I loved the most were in the worst trouble of their lives. Dad lay in a hospital bed surrounded by tubes and in a cement cell at the mercy of the legal system, Max was locked up.

I felt helpless. I was doing everything in my power to make sure they were okay, but nothing I did was enough.

When I couldn't cry anymore, I washed my face and went in search for a cup of tea. Mom needed taking care of, and that was my job tonight.

CHAPTER 52

THE COURT SET Max's bail for one hundred thousand dollars which I offered to post. Brian helped me prove my assets to the justice of the peace.

I stood in the side room waiting. "What's taking so long?"

"They're processing his release."

"What did the police say after they interviewed me? Why aren't they dropping the charges?"

"It's your word against the victim's. She has no known motivation for making these allegations against Max, but you are motivated to lie on his behalf."

"I'm not lying."

"Police are doing their diligence to legitimize your claims, but this takes time. They have to subpoena a warrant for the cameras in Max's building, but there are no cameras in the stairwell, and the defense is claiming that they can't prove that he didn't leave."

I pushed my fingers into my hair. "This is insane. He's innocent."

"I know that, but they need to be sure before they drop the charges."

"They shouldn't have pressed those charges in the first place."

"The media isn't helping."

"What are you talking about?"

"Your new GM is making a bunch of unholy claims in front of the media."

"Like hell he is."

I walked over to the television in the corner and I turned to the local sports channel. Dozens of reporters surrounded Baxter, who stood on the front steps of the arena.

"We report with deep shame and sadness, that two nights ago, one of our players, Max Logan, was arrested for the violent and disgusting sexual assault on an innocent woman. She remains in the hospital. We do not stand behind this player or his reprehensible act. We do not condone violence against women. As I am now acting on behalf of Mark Ashford and the Vancouver Wolves, I will do everything in my power to manage this situation."

"Will you trade Logan?" A reporter shouted.

Baxter stared into the camera. "I'll be doing everything I can to ensure that animal never plays hockey again."

Holy fuck!

I turned to Brian. "Can he do this?"

"If your mother gave him full proxy, he can do whatever he wants."

A knock sounded on the door.

I turned to see a bailiff open the door. Max stepped in. He looked tired, and he wore the same clothes I last saw him in, but he appeared unharmed.

I rushed to him, throwing my arms around him. "Are you okay?"

He unwrapped my arms from his waist. "Can we talk? Alone?"

Without speaking, Brian stepped out of the room and shut the door.

Something cold and ugly walked across my chest. "Are you okay?"

"How's your Dad?"

"Doctors believe he will make a full recovery."

"Good."

"This is insane. I'm sorry this happened."

"Why did you tell them about us?"

My head snapped up at his harsh tone. "What?"

"I was trying to protect you. Why did you give me an alibi?"

Why did he look so pissed?

"Because I was your alibi. I was with you."

"I didn't want you to get involved."

"Too late. I already am."

He rubbed his face. "I should have known nothing could ever change."

"Max," I stepped closer. "We're going to get these charges cleared. This is bullshit."

"My career as a hockey player is over. My reputation is ruined."

"This is a smear campaign, but once the truth comes out everything will be fine."

"It's over Rory. All of it," he stepped back from me.

"What?" Panic seized me. "Where are you going? We have to talk, plan our strategy."

He shook his head. "You're better off without me. This will never go away. And nothing good can come of this. You need to let me go."

"Don't talk like that. We're going to get the charges dropped."

"Even if you do, it's too late."

"Max," I took a step towards him. "I understand that you're upset, but you have to work with us on this."

"It's over, Rory. Between us. I don't want to see you again."

Air sucked out of my lungs.

"Max! No!"

"Go be with your Dad. Forget about me. I'm done with all of this. With you, with hockey, with Vancouver. Nothing will ever change."

"Don't do this," I begged.

"Goodbye, Rory."

I stood still as he exited the room. Too numb to cry, I could only lift my eyes when Brian stepped back in.

"Max left."

"I know."

"He said it's over."

"He's upset."

"I don't know what to do."

"Go back to the hospital. Take care of your mom."

"You have to help Max."

"I'm doing everything I can."

▭

BACK AT THE HOSPITAL, I sat with Mom for hours. She was a mess and didn't talk. I was a mess, and I spent my time fetching her coffee, buying her food and trying to persuade her to rest.

Every time I thought of Max, I wanted to cry, so I forced myself to focus only on Mom and Dad. If I started to cry, I was sure I wouldn't stop.

Dad woke up. The color in his face was better and the nurses teased a smile out of him. Mom stood by, holding his hand and fighting tears.

I felt like progress was being made when they moved Dad out of the ICU and onto a regular ward. Only when he went back to sleep, did Mom agree to go across the street to the hotel for a shower and a rest.

I sat with Dad for hours, watching him sleep. When Mom returned, she instructed me to go home for the night.

When I argued she told me she wanted to be alone with Dad.

Defeated, I took the car home.

I couldn't even process how bad I felt. I tried calling Max a few times but each time, my calls went to voicemail. The numbness in my body, made it impossible to cry. I operated on rote, unsure what to do next.

When the car pulled up in my driveway, I saw a familiar sports car.

I got out and scowled at Calder and Katrina.

"This is a shit time," I walked towards the front door, not caring about how rude I was being.

"I need to talk to you," Katrina spoke. "It's about Max."

My eyes found Calder.

He shrugged. "You should hear what she has to say. She can help."

Katrina rushed forward. "I know that Max was set up."

It felt like my blood turned to ice. "I guess you two should come inside."

WE SAT in the living room. I sat across from them.

"Okay, talk."

Katrina licked her lips. "I've been sleeping with Baxter."

"Old news."

"Baxter planned the entire thing."

"What did he plan?"

"He told me he would set Max up. With a fake assault."

"He said this?"

"Yes. He was hiring someone to lie about the whole thing."

"What was his plan?"

"He said that even if they found out Max was not guilty, it'd be enough to take down his career."

I rubbed my face with both hands. "Okay. Do you have any proof of this?"

She shook her head.

"Are you willing to testify to this?"

She stole a glance at Calder who reached out and took her hand. "Yes. I'm done with that asshole."

"Well, that asshole has proxy over the team. He is running the show."

"I also have one other thing to confess."

I sighed. "What?"

"Baxter has been using me to take down Max."

"How?"

Her voice faltered. "He wanted us to put Max in front of the media. He knows how much your Dad values a wholesome image for the team, so he wanted Max to be front and center with his scandal."

"Anything else?"

"When that reporter attacked him? That was a set up too."

Anger ticked in my heart. "What was your involvement?"

"It was my job to get Max to that restaurant."

I sat quiet, thinking. "Why is Baxter so against Max?"

Her voice wobbled. "Your Dad promised Baxter the assistant GM position. Baxter wanted to bring Joseph Flanynk onto the team, but your Dad and him butted heads over that. Baxter couldn't let it go when your Dad brought Max on. They fought hard over that and then your Dad withdrew his offer to make Baxter an assistant GM."

I knew this already. What I didn't know is why he hated Max so much. "Why take it out on Max?"

"Baxter can't admit when he is wrong. He blamed Max for everything that happened. He thinks he can have the perfect team if he brings Joseph Flanynk in."

"He has the perfect team already. We're second in our division."

"He doesn't see it like that. He's obsessed with putting together the team he envisioned and that includes making Joseph Flanynk part of the team."

"Oh shit." I shook my head. The worst part about this whole thing was how blind both my parents were to Baxter's manipulations. "This is bad."

"I'm sorry. I was only thinking about myself. I thought if Baxter got that position, he'd leave his wife and we could be together."

Her eyes met mine.

"Katrina, you can do a lot a better than that prick."

Her laughter was watery. "I know that." She glanced at Calder. "I figured that out."

I rubbed my face. "I appreciate you coming and talking to me. That goes a long way in my books."

Calder rubbed Katrina's back. "Is your Dad okay?"

"He will make a full recovery but he's weeks away from returning to work."

Katrina wiped tears from her eyes. "Is there anything I can do to help?"

"Would you be willing to share what you told me with our lawyer?"

"Of course."

Calder stood up. "We'll get out of your hair."

I sat slumped in the living room. This mess with Baxter was out of control. If we didn't get Max reinstated before the trade deadlines, it would screw Max. Possibly for the rest of his career.

I called Brian and left him a detailed message.

I called Max and left him yet another message.

I took a hot shower and collapsed in bed. Despite my exhaustion, sleep eluded me. I thought about Max. The sadness and defeat I saw in him today made big rolling tears erupt from within me. Why had he pushed me away? Why had he ended it? Did he blame me for this?

The only thing I knew was no matter what, I would not stop fighting until I got his name cleared and reassigned him back on the team.

How I would manage that, I did not know yet. But I would make it happen.

Me: Can't stop thinking about you. I hope you are okay

CHAPTER 53

THE NEXT MORNING, I took a cab to the hospital. I dialed Max's number but there was no answer.

I called Brian again. He answered.

"Hey Brian. Did you get my message?"

"Yes. I've talked to Katrina, and she is meeting me at the police station to be interviewed."

"Thank god. Do you think it will help?"

"I don't know. The police don't seem that interested."

"Why not?"

"They made their big arrest. They act like heroes in the news. If it breaks they arrested the wrong guy, they have egg on their face."

"So, they don't want the truth."

"They do. But this whole thing is a big process."

"Have you heard from Max?"

"No."

I rested my head against the window of the cab. "Okay. If you hear from him, will you let me know?

"Yes."

"Thanks Brian."

AT THE HOSPITAL, I found Dad sitting up in his bed, eating breakfast, while Mom and a nurse chatted with him.

"There's my girl," Dad opened his arms so I could give him a kiss on the cheek.

"How are you feeling?"

"Well, I've almost got a new ticker, so I feel like I could waltz out of here. You want to go dancing, beautiful girl? Maybe I could take both of you for a night of dancing."

I studied him. His cheeks were pink and rosy. "You're color is better."

"What are you doing here?"

"Checking up on you."

"Oh, come now, your old man is fine. You should be at work. Haven't I taught you better?"

"Dad!"

"Just because I'm here on vacation, hanging out with the cute nurses and my gorgeous wife, doesn't mean you get paid time off too."

"You almost died."

"I'm more than alive. I feel fantastic. I feel like I have a new lease of life. I've never felt better. When I get out of here, I want to learn how to sail. In fact, I think the whole family should learn so we can take some fun family vacations together."

What the hell? Dad didn't sound himself. "You sure are chipper."

"Your mom told me how Baxter stepped up and took over. I should have let him do that years ago so that your mom and I could take time off together." He kissed her hand.

It felt like an alien had taken over Dad's body. Who was this man?

"Dad, about that."

Mom stepped forward and took over. "We're so pleased that Baxter is helping us out. It gives us so much peace of mind knowing that Baxter is there for our family, right Rory?"

I paused, knowing she wanted me to shut up. "Yes, but we are also glad it's only temporary."

Dad laughed. "He'll do great. Baxter is one of the most trusted men I know. I'd trust him with my life."

I wanted to tell Dad what was going on, but I was sure it'd only upset him.

"Dad, maybe I'll stay here for the morning."

"What? No! Go on! You're not doing any good sitting here staring at me. Go to work. Baxter will need someone to show him the ropes."

My eyes lifted to Mom. Did she not see that this was not my father in this bed?

She lifted her chin. "Your father's right. Let's get back to normal."

This whole situation made me want to scream. "Okay well, don't eat too much Jello."

Dad laughed harder than if I was a late-night comedian. "You're so funny. Come back tonight and tell me all about it."

With a lingering gaze back at my parents, I headed off the ward. I ran into the doctor at the nurses' station.

"Miss Ashford, how is your father doing? I'm on my way to see him."

I debated. "He doesn't seem himself."

He frowned. "How so?"

"That's not my dad. The guy in that bed doesn't care about his job and he's talking about dancing and vacations and he seems indifferent about things he used to be obsessed about."

The doctor patted my hand. "Your father is heavily medicated. That's the drugs talking."

"Really?"

"Really. Did he seem euphoric?"

"Yes!"

"We'll be weaning him off most of the pain meds in the next couple days and he will seem more like himself."

I let out a sigh of relief. "Okay. That sounds good."

He studied me. "Are you okay?"

His concern made tears claw up my throat which I had to work to swallow back down. "I'm fine. I'm heading to work."

"Your father has made a remarkable recovery so far. We're confident he'll be himself in short order."

"Thank you."

———

ON MY WAY to the stadium, I tried calling Max again, but his voicemail was so full, I wasn't able to leave a message.

Me: Max. Please call me

Me: It will be okay. I'm handling everything

Me: Even if you don't want to date me, I'm going to fix your career. I have your back

Me: I miss you. I hope you are okay

I waited impatiently, but he never responded.

When the car pulled up to the stadium, I sat stunned, taking in the huge crowd gathered on the front steps. Standing in front of a podium, stood Baxter. He wore a suit and a flashy tie and he was giving a speech like he was running for mayor. He was holding a press conference, like he owned the place.

I approached, but no one paid me any attention. They only had eyes and ears for Baxter.

"We will make some significant changes to our lineups. As you know, I terminated Max Logan's contract this morning, for breach of contract. We do not stand behind players who break the law. In his place, we are in talks with Minnesota's left winger, Joseph Flanynk. We know that the deadline for trades is looming, but everyone wants this, so we will make this happen and we will make this team the success it deserves to be."

I rolled my eyes and walked around the side to another door.

Fuck Baxter.

I made my way up to my office, but someone had already moved into my space.

"Julie," I yelled.

She appeared at the doorway. "Yes?"

"Want to tell me what is going on with my office."

"Baxter asked me to move your stuff out and he moved his stuff in."

"Excuse me?"

"I have your belongings in boxes at my desk." She sounded scared. "I didn't know what to do."

I didn't give a fuck about my office. "Don't worry about it. You did the right thing."

"None of the staff know what to do. He's making all these demands."

"Tell no one to stick their necks out. Right now, Baxter is in charge, so everyone should do what he says and keep your head down."

Her eyes filled with tears. "Is your Dad okay? Is he going to come back soon?"

"He's fine. But he will be out of commission for a while."

"The whole staff signed a card. And I want to send a basket."

I reached out and touched her shoulder. "That's a lovely idea."

"What the hell are you doing in my office?" Baxter strode in, almost shoving Julie into me.

I nodded my head to her, indicating that she should leave.

"Didn't take you long to make yourself comfortable."

"I'm busy. What do you want?"

"You can't terminate Max Logan's contract."

"We already did."

"Joseph Flanynk? You know my dad opposed bringing him in."

Baxter gave me a smile. "Your father isn't here, is he?"

"This is insane."

"By the time your Dad is back on his feet, Joseph and I will show the world that he was the right hire."

"You had the perfect player with Max."

"Well, that ship has sailed, hasn't it?"

I couldn't contain my frustration. "Why are you doing this?"

He came around my desk and stood nose to nose with me. "One more thing."

"What is that?"

"You're fired."

I scoffed. "You can't fire me."

"Yes, I can. And I just did. I want your ass out of my sight."

"My family owns this building and this team."

"But legally, I'm in charge."

"Career limiting move, Baxter," I spun on my heels.

"You're a fucking little bitch. I'll be canceling your access to the building. Just stay the fuck away."

I gave him the finger as I walked out.

———

I HIT BRIAN'S NUMBER.

"Rory."

"Baxter fired me and had me banned from the building."

"What?"

"Tell me he can't do that."

His pause was so long my heart sank. "Technically he can."

"Has the entire world gone insane?"

"Until your father takes back over, Baxter is in control."

"Have you heard from Max?"

"No."

I wanted to toss my phone across the parking lot. "Okay. If you hear from him, let me know."

"Will do."

———

I ORDERED the car to go by Max's building, but the concierge said that Max had left with some bags and hadn't been back since. No, he didn't know when he would return. Yes, he'd leave a message for me.

Disheartened, I walked out of the building.

Someone grabbed my arm. "Rory?"

She was cute and blonde and she was pregnant. "Yes?"

"I'm Lolita, Max's friend? Can we talk?"

CHAPTER 54
TWEET

Hockey Gurl @hockeygurl
   Rory Ashford is a bully and a tyrant. She uses her position with the Wolves to literally torture the rest of the staff. No one can stand her. No one likes her. Not even her Dad. #SpoiledHeiress #DaddysBrat

---

CHAPTER 55

LOLITA! I studied her. Damn but she was cute. Behind her, I could see reporters watching us talk.

"We should get out of here. Would you like to come with me?"

We got into the car. I didn't know where to go, so I told the driver to take us home.

We remained quiet as the car moved through traffic. I smiled at her. She smiled back.

"When did you arrive in Vancouver?"

"This morning."

"Were you able to get in touch with Max?"

She shook her head. "I saw the news, and I didn't think. I found a flight and came straight here, but now I don't know what to do."

That made two of us.

"We'll sort it out," I promised. I was great at making a bunch of promises I wasn't sure I could keep.

When we pulled up to my family home, she stood in the driveway and stared with a slack jaw up at the house. "You live here?"

"I live with my parents, but no one's home."

She followed me into the house, her eyes wandering over the elaborate staircase. I led her into the kitchen.

"Would you like something to eat or drink?"

"Maybe some fruit?"

"Take a seat," I instructed her. I pulled some strawberries out of the fridge and sliced them onto a plate.

"You're as pretty as Max said you were."

My knife paused. "He talked about me?"

"All the time."

That took me off guard. I didn't even know where to begin this conversation.

Her voice sounded soft. "Do you know where he is?"

I bit my lip. "He's upset about being fired from the team and getting arrested. He's not talking right now."

"He always told me that Vancouver was his last chance to be a hockey player."

Our eyes met. I placed the plate in front of her and walked around the island to sit next to her.

"You said you wanted to talk?"

She ignored the fruit, and her big eyes searched my face. "I used to live in Minnesota."

I figured as much.

"I was a waitress at a popular bar that all the hockey players came into. They came in like a pack and whatever they wanted they got. Girls flocked. There was lots of booze. Those guys knew how to party."

I knew what she was describing. "Go on."

"As a waitress, I flirted with the players. It was part of the scene. Everyone knows the more you flirt, the more money you make. One night, my shift ended early, and I walked into the back parking lot to get to my car."

I didn't want to hear this. I really didn't.

"He came out of nowhere. He told me I was a tease, and that I wanted it. I fought him off, but he was too big and too strong."

I reached out and grabbed her hand.

Tears fell down her cheeks. "When he was done, I threatened to go to the police and he told me that if I told anyone he'd find me and kill me. Then he hit me so hard he knocked me out. He left me lying there, on the pavement, with my skirt up around my waist. When I came to, Max was bending over me."

Holy shit.

"Max was gentle. I was scared of him, but he talked in such a quiet voice. He asked if he could help and then he carried me to his car and took me to the hospital. The doctors ran tests and confirmed that someone had raped me and they also did a DNA test. I was too frightened to reveal who did that to me."

"Oh Lolita."

"I didn't know Max other than from seeing him in the bar, but he sat with me all night. He didn't pressure me to tell him who it was. He sat with me. I was a mess. A complete mess. I wanted to run away."

"What happened?"

"Max happened. I didn't have enough money to move back home to Idaho, but Max bought me a flight. A week later, a professional moving van delivered all my stuff to my parent's home."

"Oh wow."

"I couldn't work. I couldn't leave the house, but Max phoned me every night. He felt like my lifeline. That summer, when I found out I was pregnant, he flew to my parent's place and spent the weekend holding my hand while I cried. And he told me about his mom and his story and it made me realize that this baby is innocent and now I want to be a good mom to my baby," she rubbed her belly.

Tears clouded my voice. "You're going to be a great mom."

"Max set me up with a counselor and he paid for everything. He's been here for me every step of the way."

This story about Max didn't surprise me. That sounded like the Max I knew. "I'm glad he was there for you."

"I felt so bad when he got into a fight over this. That caused so much trouble for him. It's the reason he had to leave his team. I know that helping me has cost him so much."

I froze. "What do you mean?"

"When he found out who raped me, he beat him up."

Time didn't slow down, it fucking stopped. "Are you talking about the fight with him and Joseph Flanynk?"

She flinched. "Yes. Did you hear about it?"

The entire world heard about it. "Yes."

"I guess Joseph was bragging about it, about how I begged him to give it to me real hard and Max lost it."

We stared at each other. Here it was. The real reason Max had beat up Joseph Flanynk. "No one else knows who did this to you?"

"Up until now, it's just been Max, but he said you were a trustworthy person. He told me you're the only one he trusts in Vancouver."

"You can trust me."

She stared at her hands in her lap. "I want to help."

That she wanted to help Max made me love her. "I'm not sure what you can do."

"I can't stand how they are talking about him in the media. I heard how he is getting kicked off the team and being replaced by Joseph, so I decided that I'm ready."

I held my breath. "For what?"

"I'm ready to tell my side about how Max helped me."

Holy shit. This was already a media circus, but if Lolita went public with this, the media would melt down.

"Are you sure?" I touched her with concern. "This will get a lot of attention."

"I want to help Max. I want to tell the world how Max helped me, but I also want Joseph to pay for his crime."

I worked to keep the shock off my face.

"I'm ready," she took a deep breath. "The detective says they have enough evidence to make an arrest and that I only need to give them a name. Do you think if he gets arrested that might prevent him from coming to Vancouver?"

Holy fuck. "The Vancouver Wolves would not hire Joseph if he got arrested."

"Well then maybe they would hire Max back?"

I kept it to myself that fuckhead Baxter was calling the shots right now.

"You'd do this for Max?"

She tilted her head. "I think I'm doing this for me."

"Are you sure you're ready for this?"

"I am," she squared her shoulders. Will you help me do this?"

I paused. Max reassured me that there was nothing more than friendship between him and Lolita, but I worried that this single, pretty mom had more than friendship feelings for Max.

"Lolita. Are you and Max just friends?"

She studied her hands. "Max was really good to me, and I had hoped that he would become interested in me. At one point, I thought he might feel the same way. We never kissed or anything, but he spent a lot of time with me that summer, but when he moved to Vancouver, everything changed. He's been there for me, every step of the way, but when he moved here, he backed off."

"Oh."

"I knew that he had met someone." She gave me a sad smile. "He always told me he didn't do commitment, but when he told me about you, he said you were different."

My heart ached. Why did everyone else seem to know how Max felt and I had no clue? "He did?"

"He loves you."

"He does?"

"Of course," she frowned. "He's so crazy about you. So, when I realized that, I accepted it. I want him to be happy and you make him so happy."

Max loved me? I couldn't get past that point.

She rushed, "Don't worry. I'm okay with that."

"I know how important you are to him."

"So, what happens now?"

I rubbed my forehead in shock. "Now I make some phone calls."

⸺

"HELLO?"

"Katrina?"

"Rory?"

"Remember when you asked me if there was anything you could help with?"

"Yes, anything."

"I have a huge favor."

"Are you in your office?"

"You don't know?"

"Know what?"

"Baxter fired me and had me banned from the stadium."

"What? He can't do that!"

"Legally he can."

"Is he insane? Where are you?"

"I'm at my house."

"I'm on my way."

CHAPTER 56

FOUR HOURS LATER, Lolita sat in my living room, being interviewed by one of Vancouver's biggest sports reporters in an exclusive interview.

Katrina and I stood in the kitchen, watching from the doorway.

I chewed my bottom lip. "Can we trust this guy?"

"He's the most trusted guy in the business."

Brian walked into the kitchen from the deck. "How's the interview going?"

Katrina smiled over her shoulder. "She's killing it."

"Did you talk to the Minnesota police?"

He nodded. "I did. They are eager to arrest the bastard responsible for Lolita's assault. The DA said they have an airtight case as long as they can match the DNA to a perp. They will question Joseph Flanynk and will subpoena his DNA, but there is one hitch."

"What?"

"He's on the road with his team. They can arrest him on the road, but with crossing state lines it could get complicated. So, their preference is to wait until he gets back to Minnesota."

"When will that be?"

Brian winced. "Late tomorrow afternoon."

"The trade deadline is two days from now."

He held up his hands. "I know but that is what we are working with."

I turned to Katrina. "Will your reporter sit on this until they take him into custody for questioning?"

She crossed her arms. "He promised."

I rubbed my temples. My headache felt like a tight band around my head. "I need to find Max."

Me: PLEASE call me. I need to talk to you

<hr>

KATRINA LEFT with the reporter and Brian left after that. Then it was just Lolita and me. I found her curled up in a chair in the living room.

"I ordered dinner, if you're hungry."

She gave me a sad smile. "Thanks. I should get back to my hotel."

"Are you okay?"

She shrugged. "That was harder than I thought it'd be."

I sat down beside her. "I think you were brave."

Her eyes searched mine. "Will it help Max?"

I nodded. "I hope so."

She began to cry. "I want to go home."

I put my arm around her. "Okay. I get it."

"My flight isn't for three more days."

I pulled back and smiled into her eyes. "Here's what we're going to do. I'm going to feed you some dinner and tuck you back into your hotel room for the night. And tomorrow, I will pick you up and take you to the airport. And there will be a flight waiting for you."

"Really?"

"Unless you want to fly back tonight, but I think you could use some rest."

She nodded and continued to cry. "I'm sorry. I always cry. It's the hormones."

I pulled her into a hug. "Thank you for doing this for Max."

"I hope it helps him."

Me too. God, me too.

———

AFTER DINNER, I ensured Lolita got back to her hotel room. I booked a new flight for her and then stopped by the hospital. I felt so exhausted, I almost couldn't cope.

I found Mom in the waiting room.

"How's Dad?"

"He's sleeping."

"Has he heard the news?"

"What news?"

"Baxter fired Max and is bringing in Joseph Flanynk."

"Rory, do you think I care about this?"

"Dad would care."

"We've moved the TV out of his room. Anything to do with hockey right now upsets him. We wanted him to avoid all the news about Max."

I rubbed at my head. My head felt like it was about to explode. "Baxter fired me."

"What?"

"He fired me. He banned me from the stadium."

"Rory, come on. Stop being so dramatic."

Mom's level of denial made this conversation impossible. "What do you want me to do?"

She sounded baffled. "Well, I don't know."

"You have to get me reinstated."

"Maybe it's better if you're not involved."

"What?"

"With that horrible business with Max. Rory, we taught you better."

I wanted to scream. "Mom."

"Do not tell your father."

"You're not going to do anything?"

She crossed her arms. "I have one priority right now and that is your father. I want nothing to upset him."

I hated that she was right. Right now, the only priority should be Dad's health. And the one way I could help him was to shelter him from the shit storm that was blowing up around us. I prayed I wasn't too late. I wanted to help Max. It felt like my entire future depended on that.

"Rory, you look exhausted. Why don't you go home and take a hot bath?"

I realized that Mom was incapable of dealing with anything but Dad. The shit storm would hit and we'd deal with it when it happened.

"What about you?"

"I will head back to the hotel in a few minutes."

"Why don't I leave the car for you."

The hotel was only across the street, but I hated that she'd need to walk across the street in the dark. "That'd be nice."

I kissed her forehead. "I'll be by tomorrow."

━━━

IN THE CAB RIDE HOME, I dialed a number I had hoped I'd never had to call.

"Ronny here."

"It's Rory."

A long pause. "I was expecting your call."

The sound of his warm voice made me want to burst into tears. "Things are shitty here."

"I've seen the news."

"I can't find Max. He's not taking my calls."

"I know."

"Have you talked to him?"

"I talked to him this morning."

Tears blurred my voice. "How's he doing?"

"He's been better."

"I'm trying to help him, but he won't talk to me."

"It's not you, darlin'. Max's demons are raising their ugly heads."

"I'm so worried about him."

"Give him time. He'll come around."

"Do you know where he is?"

"He's tucked away at some hotel."

"In Vancouver?"

"Yup."

I breathed a sigh of relief. At least he was still in the city. "I have a team of people working to help him."

"I know."

"I'm going to do everything to get his life back."

"You're his life."

"He ended it with me."

"I know. Just... be patient with him. He's going through some stuff."

I started to cry. "I want to be there for him."

"He knows that. When he comes back, be open to what he has to say."

"What if he doesn't come back to me?"

"He'll be back. Try and be patient."

I prayed to God he was right.

"How are you holding up? I hear your Dad's in the hospital."

"He's rallying. He will make a full recovery."

"Seems like Baxter Nicols is trying real hard to take over."

"He's more than trying. He's succeeded."

"It'll all work out."

"I hope so."

"You sound tired."

Exhaustion washed over me. I felt so beaten down, I wasn't sure I would ever get up. "I'm okay."

"Get some sleep. You may have lost a few fights, but the big battle hasn't been decided."

Talking to Ronny made me miss Max. "Thanks, Ronny."

"If I talk to Max again, I'll let him know you called."

"Thanks."

We disconnected, and I spent the rest of the trip home working to not bawl. I knew how much Max was hurting and it killed me that I couldn't help him.

Once I got home, I sent one last text to Max.

Me: I know you're hurting and this situation sucks. But I love you. And I'm doing everything to fix this mess we're in. Please don't give up on me

I stared at my phone for an entire hour, but no responding text came back.

CHAPTER 57

EARLY AFTERNOON, I picked up Lolita at her hotel and then drove her to the airport. At security, she gave me a sweet hug.

"I hope my interview helps Max."

"I think what you did will help."

"The detective called and said they will pick up Joseph today for questioning."

"Will you be okay?"

"My mom is meeting me at the airport. She said she's proud of me."

"Max will be proud of you."

"Will you give him a hug for me?"

"If I find him."

"He'll come back."

It seemed like everyone believed he would. I wasn't so sure. "You need anything for your flight?"

"I'm good."

"Are you scared?"

She smiled the most serene smile. "The funny thing is, I've been scared since this has happened, but today, for the first time, I woke up without fear. It's like I'm being set free."

"You're an amazing woman."

"Will you come and see me when the baby is born?"

"You can count on it."

She hugged me again. "Take care of Max, okay?"

"I'm trying."

FROM THE AIRPORT I headed straight to the hospital. Dad wasn't in his room. The nurse said they had taken him down for some tests and my mom had gone with him.

Max: Where are you?

My heart pounded as I stared down at that text.

Me: At the hospital. Where are you?

But no responding text came back. I slumped in the waiting room, willing my phone to beep. Hours passed while I flipped through old health magazines. My stomach growled. I debated going down to the cafeteria to get something to eat, but I didn't want to miss my Dad coming back so I remained seated.

My heart jumped when my phone rang, but it sank again when I realized it was Brian.

"Talk to me."

"The private investigator found a correlating payment between Baxter and the alleged victim."

"I knew it. That fucker set Max up. Did you hand that over to the police?"

"It wasn't legally obtained."

"Dammit."

"But she is still refusing to allow them to do a physical exam and refuses to hand over her clothes."

"Because there was no assault."

"Right? I'm going into court today to make a motion for the

charges against Max to be dropped."

"Do you think it will work?"

"I'm going to damn well try."

"What about Flanynk?"

"His flight is scheduled to land any minute. The Minnesota DA is standing by at the airport to take him in for questioning."

"What time did Katrina say they would release the interview?"

"As soon as they apprehend him."

"Holy shit."

"Can you convince your mom to reverse the proxy that gives Baxter power?"

"I will try. She doesn't want to think about hockey right now."

"Keep trying. I drew up the paperwork. We only need a signature. But you need to work fast. If Max's contract doesn't get reinstated by tomorrow, he won't play the rest of the season."

"I'll make it happen."

I hung up, wondering how I would get that done. Mom was in denial. And right now, she didn't give a rat's ass about hockey.

"Rory?"

I lifted my head. Max stood in the doorway. He wore a baseball hat low over his eyes.

I sat frozen, staring up at him. "Max."

He shoved his hands in his pockets. The expression on his face was inscrutable.

I stood up and moved towards him, approaching him with caution, terrified that he'd leave. "Are you okay?"

He shrugged. "I've been better."

"Things will come together, okay? I've been working around the clock and I'm trying to get you reinstated."

"I don't give a fuck about hockey."

I froze. "What?"

"Did you mean it?"

"Mean what?"

"You said you loved me. Did you mean it?"

Everything rushed up over me. All the anxiety and fear over Max pushing me away. Tears blurred my eyes. "Yes. I meant it."

"Say it."

"I love you."

"My life's a fucking mess."

"I don't care about that."

"I may never play hockey again."

I swallowed the tears that wobbled my voice. "That would break my heart because I know how much you love the game, but it doesn't change how I feel about you."

"I suck at this."

"At what?"

"Showing you how much you mean."

"I mean something to you?"

He stared past me for a moment before his eyes returned to my face. "Rory, you mean everything to me. I've spent my entire life working toward being a professional hockey player, but none of that matters if you're not in my life."

So much emotion coursed through my body, my lips trembled. "I was scared you would leave me."

"I needed to clear my head. I didn't want you to see me like that."

"Like what?"

"I was low, Rory, and I said some shitty things to you at the police station."

"You told me it was over."

"I didn't mean it. I don't want this to end between us."

I stepped forward and then his mouth was on mine. His big hands were in my hair and my entire world righted itself again. We spoke between kisses, our lips mashed against each other.

"Max, I was so scared."

"I know."

"I've thought you hated me."

"I could never hate you."

"I'm trying to fix things, so you'd want to give me another chance."

"I don't need things fixed to want you in my life."

"Please tell me you're not giving up on me."

He pressed his forehead to mine, his gaze burning me. "I never gave up on you. I gave up on myself."

"I never gave up on you."

"All your texts. They kept me going."

I pulled him tight against me. "Where did you go?"

"I booked into a hotel to lie low."

My phone buzzed. I stepped back.

Brian: Turn on the TV

Max gave me a questioning glance as I moved to the TV and flipped the channels until I found a sports channel. Max moved to stand beside me. There on the TV was footage of Joseph being led out of the airport in handcuffs.

"Police have taken Joseph Flanynk into custody for questioning at the Saint Paul airport. Although no one has confirmed the charges, we believe it has something to do with allegations made against him in the exclusive interview we have with Lolita Patterson. Stay tuned."

"What the fuck?" Max breathed.

"Listen, I can explain."

"What are you doing here?" Mom's voice sounded shrill from behind us.

"Mom, wait."

"You," she pointed a finger at Max. "You stay away from my daughter."

I stepped in front of Max. "Mom, stop."

"No, you listen here."

"Mom!" I almost yelled. "Watch this interview and then we can talk, okay?"

She crossed her arms. I turned my back on her and focused on the television.

"You okay?" Max's voice was only for me.

"I will be."

Lolita's interview started. They had edited it to create a succinct story about how she was brutally assaulted by Joseph and how Max stepped in to care for her.

The reporter lifted his head. "Is this the reason Max Logan beat up Joseph Flanynk?"

She nodded, her big eyes staring straight into the camera. "In the locker room, Joseph was bragging about how I wanted it and he called me a slut. Max knew the truth. He knew what had happened had been against my will. Max held my hand that night in the hospital when I couldn't stop crying. I think he lost his cool when Joseph was making it sound like I had a choice in that matter."

"Lolita, tell me why you are doing this interview."

Her voice sounded clear. "Max Logan is a compassionate, caring friend and I think the media and the world have unfairly judged him. Now with those false charges against him, I want the world to know who he really is as a person. Max protected my secret at great cost to himself, but now I want the world to know the truth of what happened."

"Lolita, why do you think the charges pending against Max are false?"

She smiled. "Because he spent that night with his girlfriend. His alibi is airtight. The truth will come out soon enough."

The television cut to the reporter who stood outside the stadium. "Well, folks, as you have heard, that interview, coupled with Joseph being taken in for questioning, has left the Vancouver Wolves fans reeling. That Baxter Nicols stood yesterday on these steps, announcing the Wolves' intention of buying out Flanynk's contract leaves everything in flux. We don't know where Max is or if he will return to the team, but we know now we have a lot more questions than answers."

I stepped forward and shut the television off. Max wore a shocked expression. Mom's hands covered her mouth.

My phone buzzed.

Brian: Alleged victim has reversed her story. She confessed that Baxter paid her to falsely accuse Max. They have dismissed all charges

I read the text out loud. Max dropped his head, and a sigh escaped him.

Mom shook her head. "I don't know what to say."

I stepped forward. "Mom, everyone has made mistakes here, but Baxter has unfairly canceled Max's contract. If we don't get that reversed by tomorrow, then that's on us."

Her eyes were big. "I didn't know."

"Please reverse the proxy. Put me in charge so I can reinstate Max back on the team."

Her face was white. "I'll call Brian."

"I can text him and he can bring the paperwork here."

"Okay," her voice sounded small.

Me: Brian can you bring the paperwork to the hospital?

Brian: Already on my way

I looked behind me at Max. He was sitting, with a confused expression on his face. His face lifted to mine. "You did that?"

"Lolita showed up here on her own. It was her idea."

"Is she okay?"

I nodded. "She wanted to do this. Brian has been working with the detectives in Minnesota. They're confident they have enough to arrest Joseph."

He swallowed a lot of emotion. "I wanted to tell you."

"You were protecting Lolita."

"She showed up here?"

"Looking for you. I ran into her and this whole thing was her idea."

"I need to call her."

"She'd love that."

He stood up and disappeared out of the waiting room.

CHAPTER 58

MOM and I stared at each other.

"I'm sorry, Rory."

"Mom, don't apologize. It's been a trying few days."

"Why would Baxter try and set up Max?"

"Dad and Baxter got into a fight. Dad wanted to bring Max onto the team, Baxter wanted Joseph. Their difference of opinion cost Baxter his promotion to assistant GM."

"Baxter came here and asked me to put him in charge."

"You didn't know."

"I signed the paperwork that put him in charge."

"Brian is on his way here with the paperwork to reverse that."

"Rory, I'm sorry I misjudged Max."

I stood there, feeling helpless. "What's the truth, mom? Dad has taken a dislike to him since he got here. And so have you."

Her face became more pale. "It's a long story. From the past."

"Does it have to do with someone named Garrett?"

She flinched. "Yes."

"Can you tell me?"

She sat down on the seat with a heavy sigh. "It was the first year we owned the team. Garrett Walter's was our star player."

I sat down beside her. "He played for the Wolves?"

"Yes, and he was a total cowboy. Things were different back them. The NHL was like the wild west. He was handsome and a star on the ice. But he was also wild with his partying."

"What happened?"

"Rumor was that he wasn't a gentleman with the ladies, but he was such a gifted hockey player, your father turned a blind eye to his antics. We didn't have the media reporting things like they do today. It was a different time back then."

A sickening feeling grew in my stomach. "But something else happened."

Her lips trembled. "I was waiting for your father one night after the game. He was in meetings with the coaches. He was much more involved back then. And Garrett found me waiting. We were alone, and no one was around."

"Mom, what happened?"

"He tried to assault me, but your father interrupted him. It was terrible. Your father didn't want that negativity to impact the team, so we didn't go to the police. Your Dad kicked Garrett off the team. We would have won the cup that year but with Garrett gone, we didn't even make the playoffs. Garrett died a few years later in a drinking and driving accident."

Holy shit.

"Oh Mom."

She swallowed. "Max is a dead ringer for Garrett. I didn't see it at first until that night at the ball when you mentioned Garrett. And it all came rushing back."

"Mom, Max is not Garrett."

"I know," she breathed. "But he reminded me so much of him, and I was scared for you. We let that cloud our vision. Then with everything going on, it was easy to believe the worst of him."

"I think he was my father," Max stood in the doorway.

"What?" We both spoke at the same time.

Max came over and sat down across from us. Trouble clouded his eyes. "When I was 15, my coach told me that my playing style reminded him of Garrett Walters. I became obsessed and did everything I could to research him. My mom walked in on me watching footage of him and she became hysterical. I put two and two together after that."

"Garrett Walter's didn't have any children," Mom managed to speak.

"My mom waitressed in the restaurant at your stadium at the same time Garrett played for Vancouver."

Holy shit.

"Hey guys, I got here as quick as I could." Brian stood in the doorway, wearing the same clothes he was wearing yesterday. His gaze skittered between the three of us. "What? What's wrong?"

"Nothing," Mom recovered. "Do you have papers for me to sign?"

"Right here."

Max stood up and moved out of the waiting room. With anxiety, I followed him.

"Wait, Max."

He turned. Pain etched his expression. "So, now you know."

"Know what?"

"The entire truth about who I am."

I touched his arm. "That's not who you are."

"My father was not a good person."

"What does that have to do with anything?"

"You just heard that my father tried to assault your mom. Doesn't that scare you?"

"The only thing that scares me about you is that you're about to leave again."

"Maybe I should."

"Please don't talk like that."

"Everything that happened this week makes me think of my Dad. I feel like I'm paying for his sins. What if I'm like him?"

"Max, you are nothing like your dad. You are a kind, incredible man."

His blue gaze, so vulnerable and troubled held mine. "Why do you believe I'm good?"

Emotion choked me, halting my words. "How could I not believe in your goodness? From that first fateful flight, when we thought we were dying, you took care of me. You drove across town in the middle of the night to make sure I got home from my non-existent date. When I was attacked at that Minnesota game you fought off half a dozen men to save me. You came to my defense with Baxter. You've encouraged me and believed in me every step of the way. You fought for Lolita and she told me what you did for her, how you supported her and helped her. I've listened to how you've tried to help your mom. You're such a good man, Max. Better than I deserve."

He took a deep breath. "I never want to be like him."

"You're nothing like him. You're your own person. And you make me so proud."

He wrapped his arms around me and pulled me tight against him. "Rory."

I snuggled against him, mashing my face against his chest, breathing in his clean scent. "I need you."

Brian cleared his throat. "Sorry to interrupt but Rory I need you to sign the papers. And I have the other thing too."

He meant the paperwork, reinstating Max onto the team.

I lifted my gaze to Max's. "So, do you want to play hockey?"

He blinked. Thinking.

I repeated the question from that first fateful meeting. "The question, number 33, is do you give enough of a fuck to play for this team?"

His face broke into the most beautiful smile. "My name's Max."

"Okay, Logan. Do you want to play? Because we have a lot of money with your name on it, if you're willing."

"What about the fans?"

"Fuck the fans."

"And your dad?"

"He's the one who fought for you from the start."

"I think we can win."

"Only if you come back."

"Will you be my girlfriend still?"

I couldn't keep the stupid grin off my face. "Yes."

"What about Baxter?"

"We'll deal with him."

"Hell yeah."

I whooped so loud, the two nurses at the station lifted their head and gave me dirty looks.

We moved back to the waiting room.

"Where's my mom?"

"She went to check on your dad." Brian handed me a pen. "Sign here, sign here, sign here."

When I finished, he handed Max some papers to sign.

"Congratulations, you've been reinstated as a member of the Wolves hockey team."

Max shook his hand. "Thanks, man. For everything."

"My pleasure."

I handed the papers back to Brian. "Thanks for all your help."

"Congratulations, you're the new temporary GM of an NHL hockey team."

Oh boy. "What happens with Baxter? Do I have to fire him tomorrow?"

"Your mom already took care of that."

"She did?"

"She called him and gave him a rather feisty piece of her mind."

"Way to go, mom."

"We've suspended his contract as a coach and have terminated his access to the building. You can sort out the rest tomorrow."

I must have had a stunned expression on my face because Max put his arm around me and squeezed. "You got this."

"Take care, guys," Brian put the papers in his portfolio. "I'm going home for a hot shower and the biggest drink imaginable."

I pulled Brian into a quick hug. "I won't ever forget what you did for my family."

He grinned. "It might have been the most exciting legal week of my life."

"Thanks, Brian," Max shook his head. "I owe you."

Brian laughed. "Can you both stay out of trouble at least until I get home and change my clothes?"

"No more trouble," I promised. This promise I was certain I could keep.

"I'll see you at work tomorrow," he winked at me, before he walked out of the room.

Max studied me. "You okay?"

"I've never been in charge of anything in my life."

He smirked. "You've been running circles around all of us since day one."

"Now what?"

He shoved his hands in his pockets. "Would you think less of me if I suggested we head back to my place for some cuddles?"

I laughed. My chest felt so light and free. "You don't do cuddles."

"I don't mind them."

"Are you saying that we cuddle just for my benefit?"

"Pretty much."

"That's big of you."

"I do what I can."

"I'd love to."

Hand in hand, we walked out. Tonight was my time. I would come back and deal with my parents in the morning.

Max squeezed my hand. "I need to go check out of my hotel and grab my stuff."

"And I need to swing by my place and grab some clothes for work. Apparently, I've been unfired."

"Baxter actually fired you?"

"He banned me from the building."

"He banned you from the building that has your name on it?"

"I told him it was a career limiting move."

Max laughed, and it sounded like music to my ears. My heart zinged with so much happiness, I thought it'd burst.

In the elevator, Max pressed me against the wall for some mind reeling kisses. "We might do more than cuddle."

"I could get on board with that."

"Let me drive you to your place."

I pushed him away from me when the door slid open. "It'll be faster if we meet at your place. Maximize our cuddle time."

He reluctantly let go of my hand. "See you soon."

CHAPTER 59

MY PHONE RANG as my cab pulled up to the house. I paid the driver as I answered.

"Hello?"

"Roar."

"Calder."

"So, we saw the news and the interview."

"Yeah, things are looking up."

I unlocked the front door and unset the alarm.

"They drop the charges against Max?"

I headed upstairs to my room. "The police have dropped the charges, we have reinstated Max, and I was made temporary GM."

"Look at you, climbing that corporate ladder."

I pulled a duffle bag from out of my closet. "So, what's up?"

"Kat's worried."

I paused. "About what?"

"She thinks you hate her."

I laughed. "Past tense."

"Really? Because she's been stressing all evening about how things will go for her at her job."

"Calder, be serious."

"I am. And when she's stressed, she's not in the mood for anything fun."

I pulled clothes out of my walk-in closet. "Stop. My ears are burning."

"Help a guy out."

"With what?"

"Is she going to get fired?"

I bent down to find my black heels. "Katrina and I have had our differences, but she's great at her job."

"So, you're not going to fire her?"

"No one is getting fired."

"So, she's good."

"Unless she tries to burn the place down, her career with the Wolves is safe. She did some horrible things to Max but she was under the influence of Stockholm Syndrome with Baxter, so all is forgiven."

"You're all right, you know that, right?"

I moved to my bathroom and dumped toiletries into a bag. "Tell her to kill Hockey Gurl."

"What do you mean?"

"The tweets? About me?"

He cleared his throat. "That wasn't her."

I frowned. "Are you sure?"

"A hundred percent. I thought it was Kat at first, but she showed me her phone to prove it."

I tossed my toiletries into my duffle bag. "Okay, I believe you."

"You're not going to hold that against her, because I swear, Roar, it wasn't her."

I swung the duffle bag over my shoulder. "I promise, I won't hold it against her."

"You believe me?"

I jogged down the stairs. "I believe you."

"So, are you and your boy toy going to celebrate tonight?"

"He's my boyfriend now." My inner thirteen-year-old bragged.

"Oh, yeah. You making it official?"

"We are no longer hiding our relationship."

I needed water. I dropped my duffle bag and headed for the kitchen.

"You want to double date?"

I gave a little snort of laughter, but stopped short when I saw Baxter, standing in the kitchen. He held a large, shiny black gun. Baxter motioned for me to put my phone down.

"I need to go."

A beat from Calder. "Yeah, okay."

"Talk soon?"

"Sure."

I hung up the phone.

"Put it on the island," Baxter motioned with the gun. I set the phone on the large marble island.

"Slide it over."

I pushed it and watched as my only chance of a lifeline slid across the island towards him.

"What are you doing, Baxter?"

"Shut up and sit down." He pulled a chair close.

I tried to even my breath. I moved towards the chair. His hand shoved my shoulder, pushing me to sit.

He tossed me two cable ties. "Put them on your ankles. And don't try any funny shit. If they are too loose, you will experience what a pistol whip feels like."

I bent down and secured each ankle to a chair leg.

"Hands behind your back."

I winced when he yanked my hands together and secured me to one of the back rungs of the chair. I tested my bondage. I couldn't move any of my limbs.

"What are you doing, Baxter?"

"Shut the fuck up," he raised the gun, in a threat to hit me. "God,

I'm so fucking tired of your voice. Grating on my nerves. Talking back to me."

My entire body trembled, but I worked to keep my breath even and my spine straight. I was a fucking Ashford. We *don't do* fear.

I watched him as he paced the length of the kitchen.

One.

Two.

Three.

Four.

Back and forth he moved, like some deranged manic who had taken himself off his meds. His eyes lifted to mine and then he strode towards me.

I winced when he cocked the gun and butted it against my forehead. The metal felt cold against my skin.

Would you rather be on a burning plane that is crashing or have a lunatic point a gun at your head?

Max was on the plane, so my choice is definitely plane crash.

"You ruined everything, you know that?"

I forced my voice to stay strong. Insolent even. "What is your end game, Baxter? Are you going to kill me? Is that your big plan?"

"Shut up!' His scream reverberated through the house.

He pressed the gun harder to my head and for one horrible moment, I thought I might piss myself.

People talk about being so scared they piss their pants, but this is the first time I understand that statement.

He uncocked the gun and returned to pacing.

"I tried to scare you off, you know? With my tweets, but you're so fucking stubborn."

"You're hockey gurl?"

This time, when he looked at me, I dropped my gaze.

He laughed a scary, messed up laugh that made my blood run cold. "You learn fast, don't you?"

I kept my eyes down.

"You know, you remind me of my wife. When I first met her, she was so feisty. God, she had a temper and a backbone."

I couldn't reconcile the sad sack woman in the baggy cardigans with anyone that had ever had a backbone. "What happened to her?"

He leaned down so close that his stinky breath blew in my face. "I broke her."

Our eyes met. He smiled, and for a moment, he reminded me of the Baxter I knew. "I enjoyed it. Just like I would enjoy breaking you."

Keep him talking. When he runs out of stuff to say, bad things will happen.

"How did you do that?"

"How did I do what?"

"How did you break your wife?"

He smiled again. "When I first dated her, she was a bossy bitch. I let her think that she was in charge. I bought her flowers and treated her like a queen. Until she agreed to marry me."

Our eyes met. I could smell my fear. It was a mixture of sweat and something sour.

"So, she married you, what happened?"

He crossed his arms, indifferent to the fact that he held a 9 mm in one hand. "I waited until she made the slightest infraction against me. It was nothing. She tipped the doorman of our hotel room. And I slapped her so hard for that, for disrespecting me, she hit the floor. She spent the night in the bathroom crying. In the morning, I pretended nothing had happened."

He leaned down so his face was in front of mine. "And you know what?"

"What?"

"So did she. She wanted to pretend that it hadn't happened at all."

I nodded. "Yeah."

"She was wary at first. Watching me. Careful around me. But I made sure she got comfortable again before I hit her a second time."

"What happened?"

"She cried and threatened to leave me. She went through all the motions, but I knew she wouldn't leave."

How long could I keep him talking? How long before Max realized I wasn't coming? How long before he called?

"How did you know that?"

He scratched his head with the butt of the gun. "Because she stayed the first time."

"That's how you knew?"

He shrugged, bored with the conversation. "I thought she had more moxie in her. I thought she'd run."

"But she stayed."

"Yup, and it was more of the same."

"What about Katrina?"

His eyes sharpened. "What about her?"

"I heard you were dating?"

He rolled his eyes. "Hardly. She was a dumb piece of ass that waited around for me to come and bone her."

"She left her marriage for you."

"Yeah," he shrugged. "I don't give a fuck."

"Weren't you planning on leaving your wife for her?"

"Fuck that."

"Oh."

"She was just someone to fuck, you know? Don't you ever just want to fuck? Without strings?"

Don't answer that.

My phone vibrated on the island. We both turned towards it.

"Where were you going anyway?"

"To see a friend."

"Which friend?"

"You don't know him."

My phone buzzed, moving of its own accord across the island.

"Someone wants to talk real bad."

"It might be my mom."

"Or it might be your friend."

I remained silent.

The phone began again. This time Baxter picked it up. "Well this is interesting. It's our friend, Mr. Logan."

I swallowed.

He brought the phone to me. "Get rid of him."

I watched as he swiped the phone and then he bent down so he could also hear while he pressed the phone to my ear. With his other hand, he pressed the nozzle of the gun against the back of my head.

"Hey, Max."

"Where you at?" his sexy drawl brought tears to my eyes.

"You know, I'm not feeling good. I think it's a lack of sleep and food. I think I'm going to stay in tonight. Can I take a raincheck?"

Please fucking understand. Please don't come here.

"Are you sure? I'm good at nursing cuties back to health."

I forced a laugh. "I'm so sure. I'm half asleep already. I'm going to crawl into bed. Is that okay?"

There was a long pause. *Please say yes. Please say yes.* "Sure, gorgeous. I'll see you tomorrow."

"Brilliant. Maybe we can get lunch after practice."

"Yeah, sure."

"Okay, night!"

"Night."

Tears leaked down my cheeks as Baxter swiped my phone off.

"I'm impressed, Rory. You're quite the little actress."

I didn't raise my head. That might be the last time I ever talked to Max. Defeat made my shoulders slump.

"What are you going to do with me?"

Baxter's smile sent chills down my spine. "I can think of a few things."

"Will I live?"

He drew the butt of the gun down my cheek. "Doubtful."

"You think you're going to get your job back?"

He laughed. "You're so naïve."

"What?"

"This isn't about getting anything back. This is old testament."

"What does that mean?"

"Eye for an eye. Your Dad and Max stole something from me. Now I will steal something away from them that will make them regret those decisions every day of their lives."

The doorbell rang.

We both turned towards the hall as the chimes rang through the house.

"Are you expecting someone?"

I shook my head. "No."

He put the gun against my cheek. "Don't lie to me."

"I swear to god."

He walked to the island and opened and shut drawers. He pulled out a knife. I whimpered, but he only used the knife to slice the cables.

My shoulders were so numb I almost couldn't use my hands. He yanked me to my feet.

"You're going to get rid of them."

He pushed me towards the front door. "And if you don't, they will die and it'll be your fault."

The door chimed again.

He pushed the gun up against my chin. "I'll be right here behind you. So play this smart."

I wiped the tears off my cheeks and then Baxter, who hid himself behind the door, opened it.

A guy stood there with a pizza box. "Got your delivery."

"There must be a mistake. I didn't order a pizza."

"Is this 2435 Beach Road?"

I swallowed. "That is my address, but I didn't order a pizza."

The man frowned. "Damn, that is the second time they've gotten the address mixed up. We have a new girl working the phones and I swear she's dyslexic."

"That's okay," I stepped back to shut the door. "Have a good night."

"Wait, could you do me a favor? My cell phone died. Could you call them and confirm where this pizza is supposed to go?"

"I'm busy right now."

"It won't take a minute. Please? Could you do me a solid?"

Baxter stepped into view. "My wife said she's busy. So, piss off before I call your shop and make a complaint to the owner."

"Well, do you guys want a pizza?" The guy smiled with a shrug. "By the time I get back it'll be cold and they'll just toss it. So, you can have it for free."

Baxter stared at the box. "What kind is it?"

The guy lifted the box lid and pulled out a gun which he pointed at Baxter's forehead. "It's called get the fuck on your knees, motherfucker."

"What the hell?" Baxter staggered back, letting go of me.

Complete pandemonium broke out. Men in black SWAT uniforms came from all directions of the house. From the kitchen, the living room, down the stairs. They screamed and pointed huge guns at Baxter. More men in black ducked in and out of rooms, pointing their big guns, shouting back and forth to each other.

"Clear."

"Clear."

"Clear."

I watched as they flipped Baxter over onto his stomach. The pizza guy knelt on his back and patted him down, removing the gun from his waistband.

"I didn't do nothing," Baxter screamed. "She begged me for a date. She's been begging me to fuck her since the day she met me."

"Shut up, asshole," one of the scary guys in black kicked him.

Baxter yelped with pain. "This is police brutality. I didn't do nothing."

Pizza guy stood up. "Get this piece of garbage out of here."

Only when they had hauled Baxter to his feet and shoved him out the front door did anyone pay attention to me.

"Ma'am," the pizza dude spoke. "Are you Rory Ashford?"

I nodded, fighting tears.

I heard a different voice shouting from outside. "Let me inside. Let me see her."

Max!

Pizza guy smiled. "There's some big as fuck hockey player claiming to be your boyfriend. You want me to let him in?"

I nodded again, working overtime to keep my shit together.

I hung on until he pushed through the front door, looking wildly around until he saw me. Big strong arms came around me. Protecting me. Holding me. I clung to him and at that moment I felt safe enough to cry. Except I didn't. With his arms around me, and his big hand stroking my hair, I no longer felt like crying.

I stared up at his face, unable to speak.

"Rory." He crushed me in his arms. "Rory."

———

FOR THREE HOURS, Max didn't let go of me.

His arm was around me while the two detectives interviewed me.

He held my hand when I walked through the house, explaining what happened.

His hand was on the back of my neck when I phoned my mom to assure her I was all right. Promising that I'd explain everything tomorrow.

And he pulled me into his lap and wrapped his arms around me when the forensic team worked in the kitchen to dust for prints. They lit up the kitchen with their high density flashes.

"How did the police know to come?" I buried my face in Max's warm neck.

He rubbed my back. "Calder called me."

I lifted my head. "He did?"

"He told me that something was wrong. I arrived here the same time Calder got here. He recognized Baxter's car down the street."

"What did you do?"

He grimaced. "I climbed up to your deck."

"You did what?"

"I saw Baxter with the gun and I lost my mind. We called the police."

"Oh my god. If he had seen you, he'd have killed you."

"The police and the SWAT team arrived within minutes. They had a sniper on your neighbor's roof, but they couldn't get a clear shot."

"Holy shit."

"So, they entered the house from upstairs and the garage and then they sent in the guy with the pizza box."

"You saved my life."

"Calder saved your life."

I wrapped my arms around his neck. "Can you get me out of here, please?"

CHAPTER 60

THE NEXT TEN days passed in a blur. The police arrested Baxter on multiple charges and they denied him bail. The police interviewed everyone multiple times. Max, Joseph Flanynk, Lolita and the Vancouver Wolves were on the front page for a week straight.

The media frenzy was out of control. I spent every night at Max's place. By unspoken agreement, we didn't go on social media and we didn't read the newspapers. We didn't want to listen to what the media was saying about us. Other than the times we needed to be at practice or at work, the rest of the time we cocooned together, blocking out all the noise. We watched movies, cooked, joked around and had a copious amount of sex. We didn't talk about what had happened. We didn't want to know what others thought. All I cared about was that Max was safe and happy. Everyone else could go fuck themselves.

Dad came home from the hospital. My parents didn't talk about Max and I didn't bring him up. They didn't breathe a word when I left every day to go to his place. It felt like everyone was working overtime to not rock the boat.

With Dad's guidance, I temporarily promoted one of the assistant coaches to take over as head coach. When Dad was back on his feet, we'd work to hire a new head coach, but so far, based on the number of wins we had to date, he was doing great and would be a candidate for the job.

Despite everything, the Wolves would make it to the playoffs.

The first time Max and the team left to go on the road, they left without me. As acting GM, my place was in Vancouver, but I still cried when he left.

⸺

TONIGHT WAS our first home game since the police had arrested Max. Dad and Mom opted to stay home for the game. I sat in the executive box alone. When the players streamed onto the ice for their warmup, I waited and waited, but Max didn't come onto the ice. My phone buzzed.

Dad: Where is Logan?

Trainer: Can you come to the dressing room?

I ignored Dad's text and rushed down to the locker room. When I strode into the room, the two trainers stood up and walked out. Max sat, fully dressed in his uniform, in front of his locker. He didn't lift his head.

Something was wrong.

"Are you okay?" I sat on the bench in front of him, leaning my elbows on my knees, my eyes on his face.

His eyes remained down. "I'm not sure I can do it."

"Do what, Max?"

"I'm not sure I can go out there."

"Are you worried about the fans reaction?"

His eyes met mine again. "I haven't played a home game since they arrested me."

"Falsely arrested you."

He glanced around the dressing room. "If you tell me to go out there and play, I will, Rory. I'll do anything for you."

I shook my head. "No. I'd never tell you to do something you don't want to do. If you go out there, you do it on your terms."

He sighed. "Fuck."

"Max, do you still love to play hockey?"

"More than anything."

"Tell me what you are thinking?"

"I don't need to be loved by this city, but I can't take the hate anymore."

"What if they don't hate you anymore?"

"What if they do?"

"Then those assholes can go fuck themselves. Then I'll finish out my year here with my Dad and we'll move somewhere better."

Blue eyes held mine. "You'd do that?"

"In a heartbeat."

"Why?"

The vulnerable expression on his face broke my heart. It reminded me of his mom, and how she had let him down. Interesting, that Max had needed her to let him play hockey. And now, Max was asking my permission to quit the game. I would not make the same mistake she made. The only thing that mattered was Max's happiness. "Because I love you and I can't imagine my life without you in it. And I want you to be happy."

His smile was wistful. "You make me happy."

I balanced between being Max's girlfriend and his GM, but in this moment, I think he needed a GM. "Even if you decide not to play out the rest of the year, we'll honor your contract."

"That's not fair."

"The Wolves haven't been fair to you. Baxter, my dad, these fans, the media. You've endured enough to warrant your contract being honored."

"Do you think the Wolves will go all the way this year, if I quit?"

I shrugged. "Probably not."

His eyes dropped. "I can't let the team down. Or you. I'll play out the rest of the year."

I crossed my arms. "This isn't about anyone else, Max. This is about you."

"I'm not an asshole. I don't want to let anyone down."

"You don't have to go out there."

He winced. "I think I do."

Worry scratched my heart. "You have my permission to leave the game at any time, without consequence, if something bad happens out there."

"No, I'm good." He swallowed. "I think I needed you to give me a choice."

"What choice was that?"

"I needed to know your feelings weren't based on whether or not I play."

"It never has been and it never will be."

He stood up. "Will you cheer for me?"

"I always do."

He bent down and dropped a hard kiss on my lips. "Thanks."

I clutched his arm. "Have fun. I want you to love this."

"Why?"

"Because when you're happy, I'm happy."

He dropped a second kiss on my lips, this time more lingering. "You will get a big reward for saying that later tonight."

My stomach whooped in anticipation. "I'm counting on it."

He nodded, grabbed his helmet, and walked towards the door. I followed behind him to the gate that led onto the ice.

The players were done warming up and now stood beside the benches, drinking water and waiting while the officials rolled out the red carpet for the anthem singer.

Max stepped on the ice and skated around our half of the ice. It took the crowd four seconds to recognize him. The entire place fell silent, so quiet, you could hear the blade of his skates scrape the ice.

My hands covered my mouth, and I held my breath.

Dear God, please let them be kind.

Then, one lone voice screamed from the blue section. "We love you, Logan!"

A heartbeat later, the entire stadium erupted. Screaming, clapping, wild cheering. It was so loud, I couldn't hear myself think.

Max kept his head down as he circled the ice.

Homemade signs lifted in the air.

WE LOVE YOU, LOGAN.

I'M 33's BIGGEST FAN

MAX LOGAN, YOU'RE OUR HERO

The wild cheering erupted into a chant. Together, 19,000 fans chanted his name.

"*Logan. Logan. Logan. Logan.*"

He lifted his face to the crowd, and a smile started on his face. The frenzy only heightened when he acknowledged them with a beautiful smile.

And in that moment, I knew everything would be okay.

―――

TWO WEEKS LATER, Max and I stood on the walkway of my parents' house.

"How are you doing?" I squeezed his hand.

His expression was pensive. "You know winning over the parents has never been my strong suit."

"They're the ones who should try to win you over."

He gave a half laugh. "Do you think your mom will like the flowers?"

Max had insisted on buying Mom the most gorgeous bouquet I'd ever seen. "She loves flowers."

He took a deep breath. "Okay, here goes nothing."

Initially, it was awkward. I could tell my parents were walking on eggshells, trying not to step on either of our toes. The four of us sat in the living room while a chef prepared dinner for us in the kitchen.

Dad cleared his throat. "We have something we'd like to say."

Mom reached over and took Dad's hand.

Max sat there, completely silent. Together we waited.

Dad took a deep breath. "I knew your father, Max. It was my first year as the owner of the Wolves and Garrett Walters was a phenomenal player, but he was out of control. Sharon, your mom, came and told me what Garrett had done to her. How he had attacked her. I'm ashamed of how I handled that situation. I should have called the police. Instead, I paid your mom money if she'd walk away and not report Garrett. The cup was more important than a young woman's life, and I've never forgiven myself."

I sucked in my breath. Max sat beside me, so still it scared me.

Dad continued. "When Garrett next attacked Rory's mom, the true magnitude of what I had done hit me. When Rory's mom found out what I had done to your mom, she threatened to leave me. We fired Garrett and worked to find your Mom to make amends, but it was too late. We couldn't locate her anywhere." He cleared his throat. "I did not know that she was pregnant."

Max blinked but didn't move a muscle.

Mom cut in. "I want to thank you for taking care of our daughter the way you have. She told me about how you took care of her on the plane crash, and it seems like when we misplaced our trust in someone dangerous, you protected her. We judged you and I hope you can forgive us."

Mom bowed her head, her shoulders shaking with tears.

Dad cleared his throat. "I know we've done nothing to warrant your forgiveness, but for the sake of our daughter, I was hoping we could still be part of your lives. I know you make Rory happy and that's more than I've done in the past few years."

"Dad," I whispered.

Max's eyes met mine and then he turned back to my parents. "I want Rory to be happy and I don't think having any hard feelings between us would make her happy."

Mom lifted her head. "I don't think so either."

Max stood up and so did Dad. They studied each other for an endless moment and then Max offered Dad his hand. Dad grabbed it and then pulled him into a hug. "Thank you, son. Thank you."

CHAPTER 61

THAT NIGHT I woke up alone in Max's bed. I walked into the living room. Max sat on the couch, watching TV.

I crawled into his warm lap and laid my head on his shoulder. On the TV, a film of an old hockey game played.

"What are you watching?"

"Your dad put all the footage he could find of my dad playing hockey onto a CD for me."

I lay back and watched Garrett play. "He reminds me of you."

"That's what everyone says."

I watched Garrett make an incredible goal that reminded me so much of Max. It felt like they were the same person.

"He's very good looking. He looks like you."

Max squeezed me.

Garrett hugged his teammates, a huge smile on his face. "He loved hockey."

"Yup."

I put my hand on Max's face. "How do you feel?"

"Confused."

I snuggled back on his shoulder. "I know."

He kissed my temple. "I think I need to go talk to my mom."

I nodded. "I think that's a good idea. Do you want me to come?"

He pulled his arms tighter around me. "I think this one I need to do on my own."

"I'll be here when you get back."

———

MAX LEFT for Ontario for a whirlwind trip to see his mom. He met up with the team on the road, so ten long days passed before he returned. We talked while he was away, but not about his mom. He seemed subdued on the phone, and I tried to quell the panic in my heart.

I waited with anxiety in his apartment, the night he was scheduled to come home.

When I heard the door open, I ran through his apartment. He swung me into his arms, burying his head into my neck.

"Oh, you feel good," I squeezed my body tighter against his.

He didn't speak, just carried me through the apartment and deposited me onto his bed. From my horizontal position, I watched him kick off his shoes and whip off his coat. Then he was crawling onto the bed towards me.

He pulled me against his chest, in the ultimate of cuddles. I burrowed my face against his neck, sniffing his gorgeous scent.

"You smell good."

I could hear the smile in his voice. "You feel better."

I lifted my head back so I could see his face. "Are you okay? I was so worried about you."

He kissed my forehead. "I'm okay."

"Do you want to talk about it?"

"I talked to my mom."

I held my breath.

"We had some tough talks." His eyes traced over my face. "She cried a lot."

"Max."

He sighed. "But you know, we talked, like two adults."

"And how did you leave things?"

He smiled. It was a sad smile, but a smile nonetheless. "I think we both want things to change between us, but it will not happen overnight."

"How do you feel about things?"

He rolled me over so I was on my back and his face hovered above mine. "I think I feel really happy to see you."

I smiled at him. "Dad's coming back to the helm soon."

He nibbled at the corner of my lip. "Does this mean you'll travel again with the team?"

"Thinking about it."

I could feel his smile against my lips. "Think harder."

And then his kiss stopped our conversation.

"Fuck," he groaned, lifting his head up to look at me. "I need you."

"I know," I sat up and ripped off my tank top. "I feel the same way."

He knelt in front of me and unbuttoned his dress shirt. I grabbed his belt and yanked his pants and underwear down. I moved my mouth towards his cock, but his hands caught me.

"No, fuck. I need to fuck you. Now."

"Not even a little nibble?"

"Why are your pants still on? Get naked."

I laughed as I lay back and kicked off my pajama bottoms. He stood up and dropped trou, and then he was crawling up the bed towards me with nothing but a hard cock and a smile. His hand slipped between my thighs.

"If I can't play, neither can you," I complained, eyeing the massive specimen that thrust proud and hard from between his legs.

"You ready for me?"

"I've been ready for you since the first time I laid eyes on you."

He grabbed my thighs and dragged me down the bed. "Slow or fast?"

I rolled over on my stomach and lifted myself onto all fours. "Fast and from behind."

He lined himself up behind my legs. I gasped when he dragged the head of his cock up my wet slit. "A woman who knows what she wants. I like that."

I gasped when he pushed the tip of himself in. "I'm thinking of a career change."

"Oh yeah," he hissed, as he pushed himself deeper inside. "To what?"

"Puck bunny," I glanced over my shoulder at him, and gave him a saucy look. "I want to be a puck bunny."

"You're too hot to be a puck bunny. And too smart," his lip curled as he pushed himself in deep.

I dropped my head, and took a deep breath, allowing my body to adjust around him. Fuck he felt good. "I'm trying to find a way to incorporate this into my day job."

He pulled his cock back and big fingers dug into my hips as he thrust into me. "I have a better idea."

My fingers curled around the sheet and I groaned. "Tell me."

Fingers grabbed my hair and pulled my head back. "Get a lock on your office door."

"Max!"

"I want to fuck you on that desk of yours and not worry someone is going to walk in."

"Isn't that half the fun? Risking my dad seeing you..."

He laughed and slapped my ass, hard. "You're forbidden from talking about your dad when I'm balls deep in your pussy."

"You brought him up."

He slapped my ass again. "Say something dirty."

"You say something dirty."

"I love it when your mouth is full of my cock."

I groaned. "More."

"I love the feeling when your pussy milks my hard dick when you come."

"Yes, oh yes. Tell me more."

"I want my hot seed to plant a baby inside of you."

I froze. He froze. Something delicious twisted in my gut. "Really?"

"Oh fuck," he groaned.

"You want to get me pregnant?" I panted.

"Talking time is over," he yanked my hair. "Time to get serious here."

CHAPTER 62
THREE MONTHS LATER...

THE PRE-GAME PLAYER MEETING ENDED. This was it. This was the last player meeting for the season. We were heading into game seven of the Stanley Cup finals. Tonight would decide whether the Vancouver Wolves celebrated its first Cup win in over ten years, or if we'd all be crying in our beer tonight.

Max's eyes found mine. I stood against the wall and he approached me.

"Are mom and Ronnie here?"

"Yup. They're in the box with my parents, Lolita, Katrina, Calder, Brian and his wife and Ola and her boyfriend."

"Did Mom tell you the news?" Those blue eyes I loved so much, dropped to my mouth.

"She said she wants to move here."

His smile was huge. "I told her we'd take her condo shopping in a couple days."

I gave a happy smile. Max and his mom's relationship had grown by leaps and bounds in the last few months. "My mom wants her to join her reading group."

"Oh, yeah?" His eyes stayed on my mouth.

I tilted my head and he came down for a hot kiss.

"You going to cheer for me?"

"Always."

"What if we win tonight?"

"Lots of hot sex."

"And if we lose?"

I pretended to ponder that. "I might be too depressed to have sex."

"Guess we better win then."

Our eyes met, and we shared a huge smile.

"Go have fun."

He stole another kiss. "See you after the game."

I watched as he moved with lithe grace away from me. He paused and turned back. "Almost forgot. Can you give this to your dad for me?"

He handed me an envelope.

"What is this?"

"See for yourself."

I watched him walk away before peeking into the envelope. I gasped. Max had signed an 8-year, multimillion-dollar contract with the Wolves.

———

I MOVED to the box in stunned shock. That was one contract Dad hadn't shared with me. Nor had Max. Max wanted to stay here. Max wanted to play in Vancouver.

I handed Dad the contract. He peeked inside and gave me a satisfied smile.

"It appears your boyfriend is going to stick around."

"Looks that way."

"What about you?"

"What about me?"

"Your year is almost up."

"It is."

"You've made me proud, Rory. This year I was more proud of you than I've been of anyone."

"Thanks, dad," I smiled up at him.

"So," he pushed his hands into his pockets and rocked back on his heels. "Do you know what you will do next year?"

I squinted up at him. "Well, I had a great internship, but..."

"But?" I could see him trying to hide his disappointment.

"But my boss hasn't offered me an extension."

He took a deep breath as emotion crossed his face. "Well, that was short-sighted of him."

"I'd stick around if he made the right offer."

"Oh yeah?" He swallowed hard. "Do you accept verbal offers?"

I nodded, pretending to consider that. "I do. But my demands will be high."

"I like a good negotiation. Let's hear what these demands are."

"I want to keep traveling with the team."

"Done."

"I want one Friday off a month, so I can volunteer with the skate-for-kids program we run."

"I think we could manage your absence one day a month."

"I'd like Mom and you to come over at least twice a month for a family dinner."

His eyes shone suspiciously. "I think we could fit that into our schedule."

"And I know my boss goes to the gym every morning from 11 to 12 PM. I'd like to work out with him, if he's willing."

He swallowed hard. "He'd like that, but on the condition we don't talk about work. We only talk about fun stuff."

I furrowed my brows. "Is there anything else fun besides the NHL?"

He put his arm around me. "Not that I've noticed, but maybe we can figure that out."

"Dad?"

"Yeah?"

"I'm really happy."

"Me too, kid. Me too."

                          ⌁

I STOOD IN SHOCK, staring down at the ice.

We won.

We did it.

We won the *freaking* Stanley Cup.

Around me, 20,000 fans were going berserk.

Everyone was screaming and hugging and cheering.

I stood watching as Max hugged his teammates. They ecstatically jumped up and down. Hugged each other. Screamed at each other. Mad joy between the team. They fought to get here, and this was their moment to share with no one else.

As if he could sense my gaze, his head lifted and his eyes scanned up. Our eyes met.

I blew him a kiss. His smile was perfect. Another teammate jumped on him and the craziness on the ice continued.

Dad touched my arm. "Let's go down to the ice."

Security guards led us to the ice. Dad stopped to shake the hands of his coaches. I stepped onto the ice, and stood off to the side, loving watching our team lose their minds over their win. They had fought long and hard this season for this win, and my eyes watered watching them celebrate with each other.

I watched Max as he hugged teammate after teammate. Then his eyes lifted to the box again, above me. When he didn't find what he was looking for, his eyes scanned the ice.

His face lit up when he saw me. He powered towards me and stopped short.

"You did it," I fought the tears in my eyes.

"We did it," he grabbed my hand and held it to his chest. "You and me. We did it."

"Nice winning goal."

His expression was serious. "Your sex talk motivated me."

"Oh yeah?"

He grinned. "I might be too tired to have sex."

"I'm confident I can keep you awake."

Max lifted me off my feet into his arms. When his lips found mine. I moaned as he kissed me like he had all the time in the world.

He started to skate, still holding me. "I want lots of dirty talk tonight."

I clung to him. "That's your department, you're the one with the dirty mouth."

"Yeah, but I want you to talk dirty."

"Not going to happen, 33. For one, I don't know how."

"It's easy. Just say something dirty."

"Like what?"

"Like whatever you want."

I thought about it for a second. "I want to go off the pill."

Max stumbled and his arms tightened around me. We both stared at each other.

"How was that?"

His mouth covered mine. "Yes."

"You sure?"

He groaned and pressed his lips to mine. "I want it all. You. A baby. Marriage. A lifelong commitment."

"Sounds pretty distracting."

"I've never felt more focused."

I looked over my shoulder. He was skating me towards the team. "Where are you taking me?"

"The guys want to congratulate you."

"What? No!"

"Rory," he looked me in the eyes. "Trust me."

He stopped and set me down where all the players still hugged and crowded around each other.

"Rory," a big player screamed, putting his face in mine. "We did it."

I laughed as he lifted me in his arms and spun me around. "We did."

The entire team crowded around me.

"Rory, you were with us every step of the way."

"Kid, you saved our team."

"You better sit in the back of the plane now. You're one of us."

"This cup has your name on it, you know that, right?"

I ended up back in Max's arms. I trembled like a leaf. He wrapped his arms around me and held me tight.

"You're shaking," he bent his head over me. "Why are you shaking?"

"They like me," I whispered in his ear.

"Are you just figuring that out right now?"

"I wasn't sure."

"You had them wrapped around your finger when you stood in front of the room in your pink little sweater and schooled us all with your ideas about offensive plays."

"Max," I stared up at him. "I'm so happy."

He lifted me into his arms again and spun us around in a circle. "That plane crash was the best thing that ever happened to me."

"Me too."

"I love you, Rory."

I put my hands on the sides of Max's face and we stared at each other for what felt like a million heart beats. "I love you, too."

EPILOGUE
SPORTS WORLD NEWS REPORT

"WELL, Dave, at the start of the season, Mark Ashford took a risk buying out Max Logan's contract, and that gamble paid off when Max Logan scored the winning overtime goal in game 7."

"Jim, this is the Vancouver Wolves' first Stanley Cup in over a decade, but I don't think it will be their last. That team is red hot, and we have heard that Rory and Mark Ashford are in contract discussions with three extremely talented players. They are remaining tight-lipped about it, but Mark promised that he's creating a team that every other NHL team in the league will fear."

"There is no doubt that Max Logan was the winning factor for that team. We have an unconfirmed report that Max has signed an eight-year, eighty-five-million-dollar contract to play as a Wolf."

"Jim, in an extremely ironic twist, it was reported that Joseph Flanynk, Max's old teammate, was sentenced today in Minnesota courts, to one count of rape. He brokered a different deal and was sentenced to twelve years in jail. It is reported that he will be eligible for parole in eight years."

"Baxter fared even worse when he admitted guilt to mischief, kidnapping, uttering death threats and domestic abuse. I know his defense team is hoping that his guilty plea will lighten his sentence, but rumor has it that he could face up to nine years in prison."

"It's been a crazy hockey year, one of the craziest years we've seen in a long time."

"I'm going to miss hockey."

"Don't worry Dave. In 3 short months, we get to start it all over again."

"Amen to that."

AFTERWORD

Hey,

Thank you so much for reading my book! Honestly, I can't believe I've written four full length books (and a novella)! Every time I start a book, I'm so excited about my characters and the story! And then halfway through, I think, will I make it to the end? <—#truth.

I never REALLY know what to say in these afterwards, so I'll keep it short.

THANK YOU to the awesome writers in my life who are basically my oxygen tank keeping me breathing and alive. You know who you are. You're worth your weight in gold.

THANK YOU to my fans. You are a small but mighty group and I write for you. ***Always for you***. My only goal is to write you a book that you can lose yourself in. I want to make you laugh, make you smile, make you feel.

If you enjoyed this story, can you do me a solid and post a quick review? The life blood of a book's success, is in part, due to having lots of (hopefully awesome) reviews.

And, if like hot alpha, strong-and-silent men, I also have three books in my Navy SEAL romance series. Okay, take care. Until next time! Stay cool.

Hugs,
Odette

ALSO BY ODETTE STONE

THE NAVY SEAL GUILTY SERIES

My Fiancé's Brother: Book 1 of duet

My Fiancé's Brother: Book 2 of duet

My Fake Fiancé: Stand alone

My Donut Princess: Free Novella

THE VANCOUVER WOLVES HOCKEY SERIES

Puck Me Secretly

Home Game

The Penalty Box

High Risk Rookie

Hook My Heart: Free Novella

VANCOUVER MAFIA ROMANCE

Dark Russian Angel

Beautiful Russian Monster

ABOUT ODETTE

Odette Stone lives in Vancouver, Canada. Writing is her passion but when you can pull her away from her stories she loves to read, drink coffee, go for long walks and is particularly fond of action or suspense movies.

Made in the USA
Las Vegas, NV
17 August 2022

53438902R00223